TERRI

Sharon Srock

Susan,
Enjoy Terri's story
Sharon

This is a work of fiction. Names, characters, places, and incidents either are the product of the author's imagination or are used fictitiously, and any resemblance to actual persons living or dead, business establishments, events, or locales, is entirely coincidental.

TERRI

COPYRIGHT 2012 by SHARON SROCK

Contact Information: titleadmin@pelicanbookgroup.com

Scripture quotations, unless otherwise indicated are taken from the King James translation, public domain.

Cover Art by *Nicola Martinez*

Harbourlight Books, a division of Pelican Ventures, LLC
www.pelicanbookgroup.com PO Box 1738 *Aztec, NM * 87410

Harbourlight Books sail and mast logo is a trademark of Pelican Ventures, LLC

Publishing History
First Harbourlight Edition, 2013
Print Edition ISBN 978-1-61116-237-0
Electronic Edition ISBN 978-1-61116-236-3
Published in the United States of America

Dedication

To my daughters, Amber and Tammi. You make me
proud every day. I love you.

Acknowledgments

I don't know a single author who will tell you that writing their book was a solitary endeavor. I won't be the first.

Thanks to God for giving me the desires of my heart by fulfilling a dream I had laid aside.

Thanks to my wonderful editor at Harbourlight, Barbara Early, for believing in a newbie. You have been a treasure to work with and I hope this is the beginning of a long friendship. Barbara is not the only person at Harbourlight who worked to bring Terri's story to print. I don't know all the names, so I'll just offer a blanket, heartfelt, "Thanks" for all of your hard work.

Robin Patchen, my critique partner, fellow writer, and friend, who never failed to give me an honest opinion even when she knew I wouldn't like it. I appreciate you more than I can say.

Fellow writers, Erin Young and Terri Weldon who read and advised. Each and every member of OCFW, for encouragement, advice, and for always being just an e-mail away.

My circle of readers and cheerleaders. It's been a long journey. Thanks so much for sticking with me. For reading, whether it was a paragraph, a chapter, or a whole story. For being able to bounce from one story to the next without losing your mind. For being patient when I left you hanging at a crucial point in one story when there were edits required on this one. Kaye Whiteman, Emily Whiteman, Anne Lee, Teresa Talbott, Michelle Smith, Barbara Ellis, Wanda Peters, Sandy Patten, Lynn Beck, Carol Vansickle.

Larry Srock Sr. I love you more than I can say. Thanks for believing.

1

Terri Hayes chewed her bottom lip and prayed. Outside her windows on this sunny Friday afternoon, the Oklahoma summer persisted in spite of the September date circled on her calendar. Her hands sweated, and she clasped them behind her back. She would have raked them through her hair, but she wanted to telegraph calm and collected, not the nervous anticipation churning like ocean waves in her stomach. The weeks of preparation, the evenings spent in class, the hours of prayer, all came down to this.

The curly black head of her visitor disappeared under the kitchen sink. Terri heard grunts and clanks as the woman shifted and examined the contents of the cabinet. Her visitor stood and yanked the top of her crisply tailored suit back into place, her stern face thoughtful as she scribbled notes on a clipboard.

Despite Terri's desire for calm, her lip chewing graduated to nail biting. Had she missed something? "Ms. Wilson, I…"

Cindy Wilson held up a hand. "Please, Ms. Hayes, I prefer to conduct my investigation uninterrupted. We'll discuss my findings when I'm done."

Terri swallowed her comments with a nod and trailed behind the imposing African-American woman whose job it was to poke and prod into every corner of Terri's home. She ran through her own mental checklist as they proceeded from room to room.

Outlets covered, medicines locked away, cleaning supplies stored out of reach, covers on all of her trash cans. A second perusal of Ms. Wilson's expression produced no further insight. *Pass or fail?* Terri shook her head. *I wonder if this woman plays poker.*

Terri opened the door to the larger of her two spare bedrooms. The odor of fresh paint drifted out to greet them. This was the pride of her summer. She motioned her guest inside, aching to point out the highlights of what she'd worked so hard to accomplish, but she held her peace in the face of Ms. Wilson's strident and silent inspection. More notes on the clipboard, murmurs, and hums. Approval or disapproval? *How can I tell?*

Inspection completed, Terri followed her visitor back to her sunken living room and made an effort to gain some control over the situation. "Have a seat, Ms. Wilson. I have iced tea or soda if you'd like something to drink."

"No, thank you." Ms. Wilson sat on the sofa and studied her notes. Her pen tapped an annoying beat as she read. Terri took a chair across from her and waited in helpless anticipation.

"It says here that your decision to apply to our program was motivated by a television show. Can you clarify that for me, please?"

Terri clasped white-knuckled hands in her lap. "It was a documentary. I cried for the whole hour. It broke my heart to see so much to be done and so few people willing to make a difference."

"So this is an emotional decision on your part?"

"Yes...I mean no. I—"

Ms. Wilson continued. "Ms. Hayes, you're a single young woman with a business to run. I'm told your day care center next door is a busy place. You spend every day in the company of other people's children. By all reports, you do an excellent job. You're already *making a difference*. I need you to tell me why you want to take it further."

"That's a difficult question to answer in a few words."

"You need to try. I take my job very seriously. If I approve you for our program, it's only going to be after I'm sure you're proceeding for legitimate reasons, not a passing emotional whim."

"Surely you've looked at all the paperwork I've already filled out."

"My decision will not be based on your answers to a standard questionnaire. Lives are at stake here. You need to convince me of your ability to handle this job."

Terri slumped back in her chair and exhaled a deep breath. *Jesus, I need wisdom*. With those four words she found peace. She pushed herself to the edge of her seat and leaned forward, elbows braced on her knees. "Are you a Christian, Ms. Wilson?"

"I like to think so, but I'm not the one being interviewed."

"But you understand the power of prayer, the direction of God in our lives?"

Ms. Wilson nodded.

"That television show moved me in ways I still don't understand. It *was* an emotional hour. Emotional because I desire God's will for my life, and I finally had direction. I prayed for days before I made the initial call to your office. I have experience and a heart full of love to share. If you're looking for a lifetime commitment to your program,"—Terri shook her head—"I can't promise that. But I know God has led me to this place and time. Somewhere there's a child, a family, who needs what I have to offer."

The two women studied each other for a few heartbeats. Terri's eyes held those of the social worker. *It's now or never, Father. This isn't what I've pictured for my future. I always saw myself with a husband before there were children, but if this is Your will for me…*

Cindy Wilson's eyes cut back to her notes, and Terri swallowed hard. *I blew it.* "Ms. Wilson…"

A smile transformed Ms. Wilson's forbidding countenance. She held out a hand. "Call me Cindy. You're going to make a wonderful foster parent."

****

Sean hurled the first thing he could lay his hand on.

From the corner of his eye he saw Ella flinch a split second before the vase shattered against the far wall.

"Get off my case!" Sean screamed. He ran an unsteady hand through his hair. "Nag, nag, nag. That's all you do anymore. It's Saturday…take the weekend off."

Ella crossed the room, stooped down, and began to gather the larger pieces of glass. She pricked the tip of her finger on a sharp edge and stared at the welling drop of blood. She looked up, her brown eyes moist with tears. "That vase belonged to my grandma."

Sean looked at the pieces of broken glass littering the apartment's threadbare carpet. Ella's tears made him pause. Tears of anger, sorrow, or fright at his show of temper? Hard to tell. He took a deep breath and tried to steady the trembling that racked his body. His heart raced out of control. He could almost hear the blood rushing through his veins. A headache pounded so hard behind his eyes he thought his head might explode like the vase had done. Why did he feel this way?

"Did you hear me, Sean? My grandmother gave us this vase when we got married. How could you—"

Sean held up a hand. "You need to be quiet."

Ella stood and closed the distance between them, facing him nose to nose, her brown eyes even with his blue ones. He saw the answer to his question in the hard line of her mouth. He'd never seen his wife so angry.

"I need to be quiet?" She met his temper with her own unaccustomed display of rage. "What's wrong with you lately? I'm not *nagging*. I just need to know if you got paid. The rent is past due. We need groceries, and Kelsey's shoes are falling apart. Did you get paid? It's a simple question."

Sean managed to take a step back, winning a hard-fought battle to keep his hands to himself. *I've never laid a hand on a woman in my life.* Why was the temptation so strong today? He frowned as his head continued to pound. "No."

"No what? No you didn't get paid, or no, you won't answer me?"

Sean struggled for control. Every word she spoke made his skin itch. What more did she expect him to do? Working fourteen and sixteen hours a day left him functioning on no sleep. Energy drinks and some pills he'd bought at the truck stop were all that kept him moving between long days on the construction site and moonlighting at McDonald's. He was so jittery right now he could hardly stand in one place. He made a conscious effort to calm down.

"McDonald's let me go."

"Sean." Panic and criticism laced his wife's voice.

"What do you want from me, Ella? The frame crew has work. They expect me to stay on the job until they're done for the day. I was late for my shift at McDonald's three times this week. I can't blame them for firing me. Construction jobs pay three times as much—"

"When they pay."

"You know we get paid when the job is done."

"And next week, when the crew is dead again? What are we supposed to do then?" Ella's voice rose with each word.

Sean's insides revved up once more. He turned away in an effort to prevent another outburst.

"Sean Michael Anderson, don't you dare turn your back on me. We're a week away from being evicted. What are we going to do?"

He lost the battle. With one swipe of his hand he cleared the top of a nearby bookcase. Picture frames and glass knickknacks crashed to the floor, joining the broken glass of the vase.

"Enough!" he yelled.

"Mommy?"

They both turned to the hallway where their three-year-old daughter stood, rubbing her afternoon nap from her eyes. Those eyes brightened at the sight of her father.

"Daddy!"

Sean held out his arms. A smile softened his features. "There's Daddy's baby girl. Come give me a kiss."

Ella put up a hand up to block her progress. "Go back to your room, baby. I'll be there in a few minutes."

Kelsey ignored the request and rushed forward.

Ella grabbed her daughter and swung her up off the floor.

"What?" Sean raised his voice again. "Now you're going to keep my daughter away from me?"

Ella raised her own voice to compete with his ranting. "Are you blind as well as stupid? There's broken glass all over the floor and she's barefoot."

"Hard to worry about a little glass when this place is such a pigsty. You're nagging me about *my* job. When was the last time your hands saw dishwater or touched a broom?" He held out his arms. "Now give me my daughter, and go fix me something to eat."

"You want dinner? So do we. We need groceries. Remember?"

Sean glared at his wife. He jammed his hand into his pocket and threw a single twenty-dollar bill at her feet. "There's your grocery money. Now get out of my face." He reached for his daughter again.

The toddler shrunk from his hands, buried her face in her mother's neck, and clung with both arms.

"You've turned her against me."

"Don't be ridiculous. She's scared by the yelling. When you calm down, she'll be fine."

His actions were deliberate. Sean reached back into his pocket and pulled out a baggie containing a single, half-smoked, crudely rolled cigarette. He lit it and took a deep breath, anxious for the calm he knew the drug would bring.

Ella's expression changed from confrontational to fearful. "What do you think you're doing?"

"Calming down."

"You brought drugs into our house—"

Sean cursed, his words hung in the air with the smoke. Where was the calm?

The child continued to wail, her sobbing a pathetic accent to the loud pounding on the front door of their apartment. Ella lifted a shaking hand to move the window shade aside. Her panicked gasp filled the room.

Sean joined her at the window and nudged her aside. He choked on his own smoke when he saw the black and white car parked at the curb four floors below.

****

Terri hummed, hands on the task in front of her, ears tuned to hear the timer in her kitchen, her heart filled with anticipation. Passing the home inspection yesterday had been the last hurdle. She tucked the corners of the freshly laundered sheets under the edge of the mattress on the toddler bed and smoothed the blanket. The room was ready, and so was she.

The oven timer dinged, prompting her return to the kitchen. Terri transferred the final pan of hot chocolate chip cookies to a wire rack to cool. Giving into temptation, she grabbed one of the gooey treats, blowing on it as she retreated to her bedroom to finish getting ready. Terri exchanged her flour-streaked T-shirt for a clean cotton blouse, brushed pale pink blush across her cheeks, and swiped on clear lip gloss. Blue eyes framed by a short, shaggy brown haircut gazed back at her from the vanity mirror. She finger combed her hair and gave her head a quick shake to settle the strays. *Looking good, girl.* The party at Steve's would last most of the afternoon. She wanted to look her best without the effort being too obvious. A spritz of her favorite perfume, and she was done.

She went to the closet to grab her new sandals. Her gaze fell on the zippered garment bag tucked into the back corner. The words stenciled on the plastic jumped out at her. *Princess for a Day Bridal Shoppe.*

Terri pulled the bag from the rack and hugged it to her chest. Time ticked away, but there was always time to dream. She lowered the zipper slowly, almost reverently, brushing the shimmering white satin it protected with gentle fingers. "I remember you." The perfect wedding dress came along only once in a lifetime. The fact this one had been hidden in her closet for three years, without a single proposal, made Terri either optimistic or pathetic. Since her own feelings on the subject vacillated with her mood, she tried to ignore the gown's presence as much as possible. But a girl was allowed to enjoy a fantasy here and there, wasn't she?

So many faces flooded her memory. Kyle, her first love from junior high. Aaron's innocent blue eyes as he stole that first high school kiss. Cris and Duke from her college years. Ino, dark and handsome. Darrick's brown eyes, Mike's sweet smile. Gary…Gary. She'd been so sure that each was the one God picked for her. Each had retreated from her life with hardly a ripple. What would Steve say if he knew he held the starring role in those dreams now?

Terri lifted the dress from its bag and held it against her while she studied her reflection in the full-length mirror. She knew just how she'd look on her special day. Today Steve's face occupied the space beside her, with his piercing blue eyes, collar-length black hair, and swashbuckler good looks. Terri shook the image from her mind.

Samantha's party took center stage in her attention today. Terri smiled at the thought of Steve's daughters. Sam and Iris had come so far over the summer, their lives changed by salvation and Steve's return. This was Sam's special day. Terri's future with Steve, if there ever was one, would work itself out in due time.

Terri replaced the dress and hurried from the room. She stopped on her way down the hall and opened the door that led to the most immediate step in her future. Her birthday was less than a month away. *My big three-oh.* The things she wanted hadn't changed: a husband, children of her own, the fairytale wedding she'd dreamed about all her life. This room represented a new layer, a new direction. The Mickey Mouse clock on the night stand chimed softly, interrupting her musings. *Two o'clock. Better get a move on.* She closed the door. She hadn't shared her decision to become a foster parent with anyone. She couldn't wait to see Steve's reaction to her news.

2

The baby's hands and knees hit the grassy ground, eliciting a howl, more frustration than pain. Steve Evans scooped up his ten-month-old granddaughter. He brushed at the exposed skin, checking for scrapes and bruises. Unable to find a boo-boo to kiss better, he tilted Bobbie in his arms and blew raspberries on her bare tummy. The baby's cries changed to gurgled laughter.

Terri shook her head, hands on her hips. "I'm telling you. She took two steps yesterday."

"I believe you. Just don't tell Samantha. She'll be heartbroken if she thinks she missed her daughter's first steps."

"Ah dab cho bob," Bobbie said, stretching out her little hands to Terri.

Terri took the baby. "She wants her bottle."

"You understood that?"

"You own a day care center. You better learn to speak the language." She settled his granddaughter on a slender hip. "Come on, sweetheart. Let's go get you something to drink. Then I think it's nap time."

Steve watched Terri and his granddaughter disappear into the house. Terri had such a natural way with kids. It seemed a shame she didn't have a family of her own to dote over. *Someday God will send the right guy her way.* A frown formed on his face, and a small cloud of anxiety shadowed his heart at the thought of that happening. He brushed it aside as selfishness. Everyone deserved a shot at happiness. He'd had his, wasted or not.

He turned to survey the rest of the party preparations. Mitch and Benton manned the charcoal grill at the far end of the patio. A thick cloud of smoke billowed up from the brick structure. Mitch, his thinning gray hair looking even thinner in the late summer sunshine, stooped to look inside the grill and pointed at something Steve couldn't see. Benton's response was a sage, bald-headed nod while he stroked his short beard. Steve decided to leave whatever problem they might have encountered to their expert ministrations.

Karla and Pam arranged plates of food on a long table set up next to the back door. Pam's husband, Harrison, occupied himself with pounding horseshoe stakes into the ground at the back edge of the yard.

Things were coming together with incredible ease. He owed most of that to Terri Hayes and her three friends. He'd mentioned the desire to throw a party for his eldest daughter, Samantha, something to celebrate both her eighteenth birthday and her graduation from high school. The women had taken the planning of today's event out of his hands almost before the words left his mouth.

A muffled grunt drew Steve's attention back to Harrison. The rubber mallet lay at the lawyer's feet. His curly dark head tilted heavenward as he shook his hand and danced in place.

Steve turned his back and hid a sly smile. He'd heard snippets of conversation between the three other men about "teaching the city boy a lesson" and "drawing the short straw" to be his partner this afternoon. *Let 'em talk*. Just because Steve had been living in Chicago when they'd found him five months ago didn't mean he'd always been a city boy. He'd grown up in the Illinois countryside. Long before his career as an author brought him success, there'd been many afternoon horseshoe games—a fact he planned to keep to himself until he could wipe some grins from those country-boy faces.

Under the shade of the huge oak in the center of the yard, David and Lisa Sisko worked to establish their campsite for the day. The Siskos led the youth program at Valley View church. Today they played the role of busy young parents, spreading quilts, setting up playpens, and organizing strollers and diaper bags. Their two-year-old daughter was *helping*. Mainly she was playing with Bobbie's Labrador puppy. Together dog and toddler disrupted the camp's progress with a noisy game of tug-of-war with the corner of one quilt while trampling fresh cut grass across the top of the other.

Dave swung his daughter away from the excited puppy, distracting her with a new task. Lisa retrieved the quilts, shook them free of grass, and started over. Their brand new twin sons slept through it all. Steve marveled at the amount of work required just to enjoy a simple barbeque. If he had three little ones like that, he'd be tempted to stay home until they were in college.

Terri came out with a platter of sliced vegetables and caught him staring. "Something wrong?"

"No, just watching Lisa and Dave settle in. That's an awful lot of work for an afternoon in the sun. Makes me tired just thinking about it. I guess that's why God gives babies to young people."

Terri glanced over to where the young family worked and laughed together. Her expression shifted from curious to wistful. Her blue eyes clouded with a combination of emotions he couldn't identify.

The platter in her hands landed on the table with a little more force than necessary. "It's probably not as bad as it seems." She rushed back into the kitchen on the tail of her whispered comment. The door slammed behind her with loud bang.

Steve stared after her, puzzled by her tone, and not sure what he'd done or said to cause it.

****

Terri winced at the sharp noise the door made when it closed behind her.

"*Young people*?" she muttered. Was he implying that they were old? Too old? She assembled another platter, her movements jerky, her irritation bubbling to the surface. Well, maybe at thirty-nine he was too old, but she still had dreams—dreams she'd foolishly woven around him.

Moving to the fridge to get a platter of hamburger patties, she took a second to lean her flushed cheek against the cool stainless steel surface. When would she learn to leave her future in God's hands? She'd enjoyed some pretty summer fantasies with Steve as the centerpiece, but it was obvious those thoughts were one-sided. Terri closed her eyes. Better to know now. At least she'd kept her budding feelings to herself.

Pressure built against the backs of her eyes, but she refused to let the tears fall. God had given her a new direction for her life. She'd hoped Steve would share that with her at some point in the future.

"Terri?"

Terri's heart dropped to her stomach at the sound of Karla's voice. *Great, just great.* She straightened and retrieved the meat from the refrigerator. When she turned she made certain she had a carefully constructed smile on her face. "Is the grill ready?"

"Just about." Karla tilted her head. "What's wrong?"

Terri shook her head. "Nothing."

Karla pulled out a chair. "Not buying it. You don't slam doors for *nothing*."

Terri allowed herself a small defeated sigh. Very few secrets escaped her three friends. But Terri had hoped to keep her attraction to Steve to herself. With Callie busy distracting Samantha and no sign of Pam, maybe she could limit the damage control to Karla.

"Where's Pam?"

"Tending to Harrison's smashed thumb. Don't try to change the subject." Karla crossed her arms and settled her plump frame into a chair. "What's got you slamming doors?"

Terri felt renewed frustration wash over her. *Damage control be hanged.* She waved in the direction of the backyard. "Why are men so...so...pigheaded?"

Karla's green eyes widened, brows arching beneath her permed, silver hair. "Are you asking about the species in general, or is there a particular specimen giving you grief?"

"Steve."

"Steve?" Karla looked out the storm door. "You want me to beat him up for you?"

Terri smiled at the picture Karla's offer painted, almost able to see the sixty-year-old woman taking down the much younger man. Terri pulled out a chair for herself. "I need a vow of silence from you, Karla. I won't mess up Sam's day with my foolishness."

"OK." Karla's agreement was immediate.

"Short version. I thought Steve might be *the one*. I allowed myself to indulge in some pretty daydreams over the last few months." Terri shrugged. "I was wrong. It stings a little, but I'll get over it." She scooted the platter of hamburger patties across the table to her friend. "It's all good. God has a plan. I'm content to wait for it." *What choice do I have?*

Karla opened her mouth, and Terri shook her head, her implication plain. Subject closed. Karla let it drop and took the patties outside.

Terri lowered her head to the table and took a deep breath. She promised herself that Steve Evans would be relegated to the very crowded friendship column of her life. The side of that page listing possible husbands and future fathers for the babies she craved remained conspicuously empty.

****

The door to the stockade fence banged open and Steve's younger daughter Iris and her best friend, April, burst into the backyard. The twelve-year-old girls raced each other to a small table decorated in lavender and white and stacked high with gifts. They examined a few of the brightly wrapped packages before adding April's to the pile.

Steve's heart hammered at the sight of his baby. *Baby?* With her straight brown hair cut fashionably short, new curves in her figure where parallel lines had existed only months before, and subtle experiments with Sam's makeup, Iris couldn't be mistaken for anyone's baby.

Some days he still couldn't believe they were all back together again. The drug addiction that pulled him out of their lives when Iris was just a year old had destroyed his young family and nearly killed him. God's grace turned his life around, but it took years to locate his daughters and begin the task of rebuilding his relationship with them.

The death of the girls' mother two years ago forced his daughters into the care of abusive foster parents. The girls fled that arrangement only to end up in the clutches of the con man who'd fathered Samantha's daughter. Running from that situation, they'd landed in Garfield, struggling to make it on their own with seventeen-year-old Samantha in the role of mother, father, and breadwinner. That's how Terri and her friends found them last spring. From there they'd worked to locate Steve and bring him back into the lives of his daughters.

Joined at the hip, Iris and April grabbed a bag of chips from the food table and continued in his direction. Iris swept her arm in a motion that encompassed the entire yard. "This is so completely *awesome*. How much longer 'til Sam gets home?"

"Callie took her shopping. She knew we'd need a couple of hours to put this together, but I don't imagine they'll be gone too much longer." His gaze shifted to April. "How are you this afternoon?"

"I'm fine," April answered, "but if Grandma took Sam shopping, we could be waiting a long time."

"If they aren't back soon," Steve teased, "we'll send out a search party."

April laughed in response. "Mom wanted me to thank you for letting me spend the night tonight and to apologize, again, for them not being here this afternoon."

"Not a problem," Steve told the youngster. "Their anniversary trip trumps my party."

"Mom's really been looking forward to this trip," April agreed. "Oh, and I'm also supposed to tell you that my dad's parents will be here bright and early in the morning to pick me up."

"Camping trip with the grandparents, huh?"

"Yeah, with Mom and Dad gone and school out for state teachers' meetings, it was the perfect time."

Terri came out of the house, waving her cell phone. "Callie just sent the signal. They're on their way."

Nervous sweat prickled the back of Steve's neck. He grabbed a napkin from the table and blotted at the beads of moisture. "OK, everyone, we're out of time."

Terri laughed at him. "Calm down. Take a deep breath. It's going to be fine."

"I hope God is paying attention," Steve said. He leaned forward and lowered his voice. "Sam still gets a little touchy about things sometimes."

"It's a party, with presents. There isn't a red-blooded girl in America who wouldn't be pleased with that."

Steve grabbed Terri's hand and pulled her back into the house. "It's not the party I'm worried about. It's my *graduation* gift she might object to."

"What?"

Steve opened a drawer and pulled out a small wrapped box. He lifted the lid and dumped the contents into his hand.

Terri gasped. "Those are car keys."

He nodded. "Yep. In the garage. Brand new

Mustang convertible."

She took a step away. "Will you adopt me? Better yet, I have a birthday coming up in a few weeks."

The tension between Steve's shoulder blades dissolved a bit. "Seriously? This wasn't part of the original plan, but I got a nice advance on my new book last week, and I figured why not? Sam's going to be driving back and forth to the university every day. She needs something dependable. There's no law that says it can't be *cool* as well as functional." Steve closed the box and shoved it back in the drawer. He pinched the bridge of his nose. "Why don't I think through these things before I do them?"

Terri stepped around him and opened the door to the garage. The naked overhead bulb cast a puddle of light around the black Mustang. The huge silver bow perched on the hood perfectly matched the pin striping and chrome accents of the car. "Steve, she's going to love it."

"You don't think it's too much, too soon?"

"I think it's perfect. I'll bet you a pepperoni pizza she'll feel the same way."·

Steve looked up at the sound of car doors slamming in the driveway. "We're about to find out." He pulled Terri back outside. "Come on. She's going to know something's up when she sees all the cars parked out front. She'll be less inclined to kill me if there are plenty of witnesses present." He motioned for everyone to join him by the door. "They're coming."

The party guests crowded around Steve as Callie's voice filtered through the back door.

"I've been with you all day. Why would you think I'd know what was going on?"

The back door opened and Sam stepped through.

"Surprise!"

Sam took a startled step back, but Callie kept a hand on her shoulder and forced her out into the yard. "What...?" She stopped and looked around, taking in the friends, the food, and the small mountain of gifts. Her blue eyes found her father, and her face lit up with a smile. "Wow!"

Steve put his arms around his daughter. "I know it's a little late, Sam, but happy graduation." His muscles relaxed when Samantha returned his embrace. He let her go and searched her face. "Surprised?"

"Oh yeah."

Steve waved at the tables. "Do you want food or presents first?"

"Are you kidding me? Presents."

Samantha's long dark hair bounced around her slender shoulders as she moved towards the gift table. Terri stepped back to Steve's side. "I told you so."

"One hurdle down, one to go." His nerves returned full force when he thought about his gift.

"Oh good grief. Where are the keys?"

"Still in the drawer," Steve said.

"Go get them." Terri pushed him.

"Now?"

"Yes now. She's opening gifts. She's in a good mood. I don't think you have anything to worry about, but if she's going to be upset, you might as well get it over with." Terri gave him another shove in the direction of the house. "There's no need to fret over it for the rest of the afternoon."

Steve let himself back into the kitchen and retrieved his gift. The small bow on the box shook in his nervous hand. *Man up, Evans*. He returned to the yard and joined the group of people at the gift table. A pile of discarded wrapping paper and ribbon lay in a heap at his daughter's feet.

Sam held up a vivid blue sweater and turned to face Mitch and Karla. "Oh, guys, it's beautiful." She kicked the trash aside and pulled them both into a hug. "Thanks!"

"Mitch picked it out," Karla said. "He thought it matched your eyes."

Mitch's face glowed red at his wife's words. He shrugged, his embarrassed expression turning to a pleased smile when Sam kissed his cheek.

Steve cleared his throat and waited for Sam's eyes to meet his. He held out his gift. "Open mine next."

Sam placed the sweater aside and took the small box. She weighed it from hand to hand. "It's not very big."

Terri smiled. "You know what they say about small packages."

She held it up, and shook it, greeted with a muffled rattle. "Jewelry?"

"Sam…" Steve pleaded.

Sam grinned at her father's impatience and slowly lifted the lid. She sucked in a breath and raised her eyes to his face. He jerked his head towards the house. "Garage."

Sam dumped the keys into her hand and ran back into the house.

Terri clutched Steve's arm before he could follow his daughter. "Wait for it."

Thirty seconds later the back yard echoed with Samantha's excited screams.

3

Sean watched, helpless, as they pried Kelsey out of Ella's arms. He cringed as his daughter cried out in fear.

"Mama!"

He heard the telltale hiccup in her breathing. *Her asthma. They need to know.* The car started, tires crunching on the gravel-littered street as it pulled away with their baby. Ella started forward, and Sean placed a hand on her shoulder. She shook it off and turned to glare at him, tears running down her cheeks like twin rivers.

"Ella, I…"

Ella shouldered past him without a word.

"Ella…" He trailed behind her. "Ellie."

She climbed four flights of stairs without acknowledging his presence. His wife clearly did not want his explanations, or his comfort. *Can't really blame her.* He followed her, stopping in the doorway as she bent and began to pick up the larger pieces of glass that lay shattered on the floor of their apartment. Her lips moved as she worked, and Sean had to strain to hear what she was saying. Her defeated whisper almost broke his heart.

"Broken, just like my life."

****

Terri relaxed under a shade tree, shifting the infant she cradled to her shoulder. Contentment flooded her as she rubbed the little back while his baby breath tickled the tiny hairs at the nape of her neck. She wasn't sure which twin she held. It didn't really matter.

The party had been a great success. Her earlier frustration with Steve melted away as the afternoon wore on. It wasn't fair to blame him for not sharing her feelings. He hadn't done anything to encourage the way she felt. She could hardly remain insulted at a rebuff he probably didn't even know he'd delivered. As for the rest, he had a family. Thinking that he might consider starting over was sheer folly on her part.

Samantha had taken Iris and April for a test drive. The toddlers were down for the count, and the puppy lay next to the doghouse, exhausted by an afternoon of uninterrupted play, her belly rounded from all the tidbits she'd nibbled throughout the picnic. The aroma of charcoaled burgers lingered in the air, mixing pleasantly with the smell of new baby. A breeze stirred the tree above her head, and she lifted her face to watch as two or three leaves dislodged and floated to the lawn. *Fall's coming.*

The temperature had gone from warm to mild as the sun inched its way to the western horizon. She figured they had an hour before the twilight mosquitoes donned their vampire cloaks and drove them all indoors. Surrounded by her friends, a borrowed baby wrapped in her arms, Terri took a deep breath of satisfaction. *How did I ever earn such blessings?*

Terri's attention returned to the horseshoe game. She leaned forward as Steve gauged the distance before taking his turn. The horseshoe sailed in a perfect arc, clanking loudly as it spun around the stake. Another five points scored by the city boy. Laughter bubbled in her throat when Mitch and Benton groaned, again.

Harrison had drawn the short straw to partner with Steve. Mitch and Benton smugly offered to handicap them ten points on the first game. After all, poor city boy paired with a lawyer nursing a smashed thumb…They'd need all the help they could get. So far, the older men were down four straight matches and smugness had turned to aggravation.

Terri cheered the underdogs. "Way to go, Steve."

"That's just sad." Callie sat down next to Terri and held out her arms.

Terri kissed the baby's head and passed him to her friend. "They're only getting what they deserve."

"I know." Callie's blue eyes sparkled with mischief when she raised her voice to encourage her husband. "Benton, are you and Mitch going to let that city boy beat up on you all night?"

"One more game," Benton answered as Mitch stepped away to get a cold soda from the ice chest next to the back door. Benton looked at Harrison. "Want to trade partners?"

"Not on your life." Harrison gave Steve a left-handed high five as they switched ends to start a new game. "Me and my bud got it goin' on."

"Bud?" Benton asked. "He was a rookie two hours ago."

"Ancient history. You and Mitch are stuck with each other."

Mitch came back to the game, a soda can in one hand, the other hand wedged into the back pocket of his jeans. "Stuck?"

Harrison smirked. "He tried to trade you while you were gone."

Benton rested a hand on Mitch's shoulder and hurried to reassure his friend. "That's just an ugly rumor."

Mitch looked across the yard at his wife. "Honey, they're being mean to me."

Karla shook her head at the men while she and Pam joined the other women. "You guys play nice, or I'll have to take Mitchell home."

Lisa and Dave came out of the house together. Lisa, baby on her shoulder, joined the women while Dave wandered over to watch the final game.

Pam held out her arms and took the newborn. "Which one is this?"

Lisa handed the infant to Pam. "Jared."

Pam shoved shoulder length brown hair away from her face and studied the baby resting in her arms. Her chocolate brown eyes were puzzled. She looked from the baby she held to the one nestled against Callie's chest. "How can you tell?"

Lisa laughed as she worked her long black hair into a thick braid. She tugged an elastic band from her wrist to secure the end and tossed the heavy rope of hair over her shoulder. "A mother just knows." She shrugged under the dubious looks of the older women. "Jordan has a small birthmark on his hip, Jared doesn't."

"So you have to change their diapers to know who's who?" Pam asked.

"Pretty much."

Callie laughed. "Won't that be fun when they start school?"

"Tell me about it."

The final horseshoe game broke up, and the men joined the circle of women.

Callie looked at Benton. "Five to zip?"

"Yep."

"Poor baby," she teased.

Benton grinned down at his wife and pulled her close for a quick kiss. "Careful, woman. My ego is bruised enough without any help from you."

Terri smiled at the easy affection of the older couple. *That's what I want someday, Jesus.*

With the sunlight finally fading, the men all lounged in the thick green grass next to their wives. Steve snagged a handful of cookies from the leftover desserts and fell into the vacant spot next to Terri. When her hand came out, he dropped one of the cookies into it.

"Thanks." She broke off a small piece and threw it at Benton to get his attention. "I got the plans for the expansion the other day. Will you have time to stop by on Tuesday to take a look?"

"I'll make time," Benton said. "I'm anxious to see what you have in mind."

Steve looked up. "Expanding?"

"Thinking about it. Business is good, and we're bursting at the seams. If I added a couple of rooms, we could accommodate a dozen new kids, and I could afford to hire more full-time employees. What I really want is a second building with a designated area for infants." She shrugged as she explained. "They need more space than the older ones, but I have to work with what I've got. Some centers are experimenting with 24/7 child care. I'd love to give that a try as well, but again, space is a problem."

"Twenty-four hour care? Isn't that a little

extreme?" Steve asked.

Terri laughed. "Not the way you mean it. There are a lot of legitimate reasons why a parent might need expanded child care hours. Parents who are moving and need a couple of days to pack or un-pack." Her fingers came up as she ticked off examples. "A sibling with a contagious illness they don't want another child exposed to. A single working parent with an unexpected business trip. Sometimes you just need a safe place to leave your child for more than the standard eight hours." Terri finished her explanation with a hastily covered yawn and stood to stretch. "I hate to be the first to leave, but I need to go." She smiled down at Steve. "You threw a wonderful party."

"I had lots of help." Steve got to his feet. "I'll walk you out."

They walked side by side to the front yard. Steve stood in silence as Terri dug her keys out of her pocket and pushed the button on the remote to unlock the door. They both reached for the handle at the same time, laughing when their heads and hands collided. Steve hung onto her hand as she took a step back.

"Thanks for everything you did today," he said.

"I enjoyed it." She looked from Steve to the house. The mumble of voices and laughter filtered from the backyard. "You're building something very special here."

"Yeah, I know. Some days I feel like I must be God's favorite, the way He blesses me." He rubbed a thumb across her knuckles. The motion sent a shiver up Terri's spine. "I owe you a pizza."

Terri pulled her hand back slowly. "Yes, you do."

"I'll call you next week."

"Works for me." She pulled away from the curb,

her fingers warm where he'd held them. Terri shook her hand in the dark, trying to rid herself of the lingering effect of Steve's touch. "Friends," she mumbled to herself. "Just friends."

Terri found a comfortable escape from her troubled thoughts in the sanctuary of her home. She liked light and noise, and since this was her space, she indulged in both, striding up and down the hall switching on lights before loading her CD player with a stack of her favorite music.

She showered and changed into her standard sleeping attire of baggy flannel pants with a matching oversized T-shirt. Tonight's selection featured Eeyore the donkey.

Her cluttered kitchen beckoned for attention. Hair wrapped in a towel, Terri stacked the last of the morning mess into the dishwasher. She gave the countertops a final swipe before draping the damp dishtowel over the faucet. The dishwasher hummed into its first cycle as she took the step down into the sunken living area to enjoy some private time.

The soft glow of carefully placed lamps threw cozy shadows onto the earth-tone colors of her living area. The day care center next door was bold in bright primary colors. She lived with those ten hours a day and preferred something a little more peaceful for her personal space. Her home might not be new, but it was big and sturdy. She called it her *tri-level mansion* and she was proud of every square inch of it. It seemed a little empty sometimes, but she hoped to remedy that soon.

She'd purchased the two houses six years ago with visions of filling them both with children, the day care center with everyone else's, this one with her own. At twenty-nine she still had strong dreams for a husband and children. But her internal clock ticked louder every day, and she couldn't keep hitting the snooze button indefinitely. The extended wait made her antsy.

Terri was thankful for the time spent with friends who loved her and for being a part of a church family she couldn't live without. She knew they cared about her, but she didn't think they could really understand how lonely she felt at times.

Karla and Mitch had been married for almost forty years. Their relationship seemed to be evolving in new directions since they'd both retired. Just the next phase in a lifetime of being together. Callie had Benton. A smile lifted the corners of her mouth. If Benton were single and thirty years younger... Terri shook her head. They were both happy with the surrogate father role he'd adopted. She loved him almost as much as the real thing.

At forty, Pam was closest to Terri's age. Married to her high school sweetheart, divorced, and married again to Harrison, they had something very special—with Pam's two children to make their home complete.

Terri had an empty house, and a lot of love going to waste. But not for long. The classes were over, the small renovations to her home complete, and the dreaded house inspection behind her. Now she waited.

She considered her friends and how surprised they'd be by her decision. Terri hadn't kept the foster parent thing a secret on purpose. Every week this summer she'd attended their Monday night Bible study with the intention of sharing, and every week something stopped her. First her own indecision, then the business of preparing. By then she was embarrassed that she hadn't told them and determined to make it a surprise.

In addition to a new coat of paint, the larger of her spare bedrooms boasted a second-hand crib and a toddler bed along with a supply of diapers, clothing in several sizes, and some simple toys. Garage and yard sales became her favorite weekend entertainment, aiding her search for bargains to furnish the renovated space.

It sounded cliché to say a television show had changed her life, but it was true. Terri drew up her feet onto the couch and lowered her forehead to her knees. "Father, thank You for a wonderful day with my friends. I'm so grateful that You've filled my life with people who love me. Bless each of them with rest this evening and a good week.

"Father, Psalm 5:3 instructs us to look up once we've prayed. I'm putting it in Your hands now. I've done everything I can think of to prepare. Please grant me patience while You find the right child for me."

Terri picked up her Bible and found her place, still in Psalms. She read quietly for a few minutes, setting it aside when her phone rang. She padded barefoot to the desk in her study and peeked at the caller ID before picking up the receiver. Her heart skipped a beat when she recognized the number. *Cindy Wilson.*

"Hello."

"Terri? It's Cindy. Are you ready to be a mommy?"

Terri nodded in response then laughed at her own foolishness. "Right now?"

"Yep, I need you to put the car seat in your car and come to the hospital. I have a three-year-old little girl who needs some serious TLC."

"Right now?" Terri repeated. "I mean, right now.

I'm headed your way right now. I just need to get dressed." *Did she say...*"Wait a second. Why the hospital?"

"We're treating her for asthma, nothing serious," Cindy assured her. "I'll tell you all about it when I see you. You can take her home from here."

Terri looked at the clock. It was just approaching nine. "I can be there in about an hour. Is that good enough?"

"Sure thing. Just come around to the emergency room entrance. I've got all the paperwork with me."

"OK, I'll be there just as soon as I can. Bye." Terri didn't wait for a response. She dropped the phone in its charger then immediately grabbed it back up. "Cindy, what's her name? Cindy?" She hung up the phone a second time.

"Girlfriend, you need to get a grip," she admonished herself in a whisper. "A little girl!" She squealed and danced a little jig in front of her desk before sprinting down the hall. Once in her room, she yanked on a pair of jeans and slid bare feet into tennis shoes. Terri turned for the door and caught her reflection in the hall mirror. The towel remained wrapped around her head. "Good grief." *Slow down.* She pulled off the towel and ran a brush through her hair. Keys in hand, she grabbed the car seat from the spare bedroom and hurried out the front door.

She never looked into the kitchen, never saw the puddle of water forming on the floor in front of the dishwasher.

4

Terri parked in the emergency lot at the hospital and stared at the brightly lit entry. How was it possible to be so excited and so terrified at the same time? She rested her head on the steering wheel and waited for her heartbeat to slow to a more normal level. "This is it, Father. I've trained, I've prayed, and I've prepared. There's a little girl in there waiting on me. She must be frightened and unable to understand what's happening to her. Help me be what she needs. Please give me the wisdom I need to be part of the healing process for her family."

The hospital door swished open at her approach, and she walked straight through to the admissions desk. The nurse on duty looked up with a cheerful smile.

"May I help you?"

"Hi, I'm looking for Cindy Wilson."

"She's in a treatment room with one of her little patients. If you'll have a seat in the waiting area, I'll send her out."

Terri thanked the nurse and found a seat. Several people awaited their turn to see a doctor. They conducted muted conversations with companions or thumbed through aging magazines with undisguised irritation. Terri joined their number, taking a chair that allowed her to watch the hallway.

A child cried from behind one of the closed doors.

Is that mine? Terri chewed a hangnail while she waited and battled emotions that seesawed from one extreme to another. She knotted the shoulder strap of her bag in her hands, realized what she'd done, and forced herself to smooth it out across her knees. Her impatient toes tapped a nervous beat on the tile floor. *What's taking so long? Stop it!* She picked up a dog-eared magazine and forced her eyes to focus on the cover story. The sound of soft footsteps drew her attention back to the hall.

Cindy slid into the empty seat beside her. "I hate hospitals, don't you?"

"Most of the time," Terri agreed. "This could be the exception. Tell me about her."

Cindy pulled some papers out of a manila folder and ticked off the relevant facts. "Kelsey Brianne Anderson. Age three. We took her into protective custody this afternoon after the police responded to a domestic dispute call. Her very young parents were involved in a healthy argument when the police arrived.

"Responding officer's report states they suspect, but found no physical evidence of, marijuana use in the home. The police called us in, mostly due to the condition of the home and the violence of the argument. Mom was almost hysterical when I got there, and Kelsey was struggling through the beginnings of what turned into a nasty asthma attack— probably stress induced."

Terri's eyes darted towards the treatment rooms. "Oh, poor baby."

Cindy shook her head and replaced the papers in the folder. "That's the official version. I can tell you Dad *reeked* of marijuana smoke. He either smoked it all or managed to dispose of it because the police didn't find anything. The apartment was a mess. Broken glass, unwashed clothes, and dishes everywhere. Cabinets almost bare. I've seen worse, but this was bad enough for me to recommend Kelsey's removal until we can get those parents enrolled in some parenting courses and get some aid flowing into the home. Mom said she didn't know anything about the WIC program. They should certainly qualify for that and some health benefits for Kelsey. The girl has serious asthma and needs continuous access to breathing treatments. We'll be sending you home with a nebulizer and all the medications you'll need." Cindy looked into Terri's face. "Are you ready to meet her?"

Terri nodded, eyes straying again to the line of closed treatment rooms.

"Follow me."

They paused outside a heavy wooden door with no markings other than a large tarnished number five. Cindy laid a hand on Terri's arm. "Remember to take things slow. It's been a hard day for her, and she probably won't be real receptive to you at first. Don't let her physical appearance upset you. She's filthy and scared. She needs a warm bubble bath, clean clothes, and lots of love."

"I just happen to have an abundance of all three."

"Good girl." Cindy pushed the door open.

The toddler sat on a narrow bed in a tangle of white sheets. A nurse stood nearby, making notes on a clipboard. Someone had given the child a stuffed bear. Fresh tears tracked down her dirty cheeks, and oily blonde hair framed a face that held suspicious blue eyes and a pouty mouth.

Cindy nodded in the child's direction, hanging back a few steps.

Terri moved forward to get acquainted with her new foster daughter.

This is the easy part. If there was one thing she'd learned after all the years spent running a day care center, it was how to deal with a child suffering from separation anxiety. Terri approached the bed and spoke to the stuffed animal instead of the child. She tweaked the bear's ear. "Hey there, Fuzzy Wuzzy. Who's your pretty friend?"

Blue eyes studied Terri above the bear's head. Kelsey wrapped her arms around the toy and held on like a drowning man clutching a life preserver in a rough ocean. She buried her small face in the fur.

Terri sat down on the edge of the bed and picked up the discarded nebulizer mask. She disconnected the plastic tubing before handing the mask to Kelsey. "You're loving him real good, sweetheart, but I don't think he can breathe. Maybe this will help."

The child took the mask and held it to the bear's face.

"Wow, you're a good nurse. Can I have some of that?"

Kelsey hesitated for a few moments before moving the mask to Terri's nose.

Terri took a deep breath. "That makes me feel so much better. Does it make you feel better?"

Kelsey's nod was almost imperceptible. She kept her attention focused on the bear.

"Makes me hungry for ice cream, though."

Kelsey glanced up, speculation replacing some of the fear in her blue eyes. Terri looked at the nurse. "Do they have ice cream in the cafeteria?"

"Probably so."

The speculation made a quick transition to

anticipation. "What kind of ice cream do you like, Kelsey?"

"Nilla."

"Do you think we could get some 'nilla' ice cream?" Terri asked the nurse.

"Let me see what I can do." The nurse left the room, returning a few minutes later with two small cups of vanilla ice cream and little wooden spoons to scoop it with.

"Mmm, that looks good," Cindy said. "Makes me want to break my diet, though. I'm going out to the nurse's station to finish our paperwork. You two enjoy your snack."

Terri and Kelsey sat on the hospital bed in quiet companionship while they ate their ice cream. Kelsey managed to get half of hers down before her eyelids began to droop. Terri laid their snack aside. "Are you sleepy, baby?"

Kelsey rubbed her tear-streaked face with ice cream smudged fists. A fresh tear slipped free when she nodded.

Terri held out her arms. "Want me to rock you?"

The child didn't answer. She simply climbed into Terri's lap, snuggled up with the bear, stuck a thumb in her mouth, and fell asleep.

Terri scooted up in the bed and leaned back against the headboard. She lowered her cheek to Kelsey's dirty blonde curls. *Father, thank you. Please show me what she needs.* Terri's own eyes drifted closed.

****

Sean opened the door to the small bedroom he shared with his wife. Ella lay in the middle of their full-sized bed surrounded by toys, her arm thrown over a large purple monkey. From what Sean could see, she'd taken every stuffed animal Kelsey owned to bed with her.

He walked to the edge of the bed and stopped to study his wife's face in the semi darkness. Her lashes lay against her cheeks, spiky and wet with tears. Her eyes were puffy from hours spent crying while she paced and cleaned, ignoring his efforts at apology and re-assurance. He reached out to remove some of the toys to make room for himself.

Ella turned her back to him, taking the monkey with her, her whisper in the darkness barely audible. "Don't."

"But…"

"Get out." This instruction was delivered with a little more force.

"I want to come to bed."

"And I want my baby. I guess we'll both do without what we want tonight. Now leave me alone."

Sean tried to stand his ground. "They can't keep her. I'll call that caseworker person first thing Monday morning. We'll get her back."

Ella turned over to face him with a jerk, spilling animals and dolls off both sides of the bed. "Monday?"

"Yeah, I'll…"

"Monday?" Ella sat up, her voice shrill. She stopped to suck in a couple of ragged breaths. "You do that. But don't speak to me in the meantime." She threw herself back down, gathered several more of Kelsey's animals close, and turned away from him again.

Sean waited a few seconds to see if she had any space for him, either in her heart or in their bed. Her stiff back spoke loud and clear. No vacancies here. He bent to pick up a toy for himself, carried the orange zebra to the smaller bedroom, and crawled into his daughter's empty twin bed. *What's wrong with me?* The headache still pounded, but he didn't feel so jittery anymore. His face grew warm in the dark. He'd never lost his temper like that in his whole life. Sure, he worked long hours when he was fortunate enough to get them, but he loved his family. They were more than worth the sacrifice. Sean cringed when he remembered Kelsey's screams as they took her away. Ella would get over his temper and the broken glass, but losing Kelsey? He would never forgive himself, so how could he expect Ella to forgive him?

What if they kept her? *Can they do that?* He'd heard horror stories of families ripped apart by interfering social agencies. They had no right…

Ella's horrified words replayed in his head. "You brought drugs into our house." Feeling more helpless than he'd ever imagined possible, he buried his face in the zebra's yellow mane and searched for sleep.

****

A wide yawn scrunched Terri's eyes closed as she parked in her driveway. The clock on the dash read just after one in the morning. Way past bedtime for both of them. Kelsey slept in the car seat, her head tilted at an angle that would have broken an adult neck. Terri picked up her copy of all the paperwork. Clothing vouchers, WIC vouchers, instructions for this and that. She had the nebulizer, a bag of medications, her purse, a child, and a bear. No way to get everything into the house in one trip. The child slept while she carried everything else to her front door. After piling it all on a small table in her entryway, she went back out to the car and unbuckled Kelsey as gently as she could, holding her close as she carried her up the steps. Debating between the necessity of a bath and clean clothes for the child versus the luxury of just falling into bed, she bypassed the entry to her living room and walked straight back to the newly painted bedroom. Terri laid Kelsey on the toddler bed and studied the child's dirty face and hands. The bath couldn't wait. After selecting a clean T-shirt and panties from her limited collection, she went to turn on the water.

Terri considered her options while she waited for the water to heat. Kelsey should probably sleep with her tonight. That way if she woke up before morning, she wouldn't be alone and frightened in a dark, strange place. Tomorrow they'd spend some time exploring the house together. They could take the whole day to get her comfortable in her new surroundings.

Pleased with her plan, Terri crouched beside the tub and held her fingers under the faucet, growing more puzzled by the second when the water failed to warm. "Maybe the pilot light on the hot water heater went out." There was a muffled cry from the bedroom. Terri turned off the water and hurried back to Kelsey. The child sat in the middle of the bed, rubbing her eyes against the light, staring from one unfamiliar object to another.

Terri sat down in the floor next to the bed. "Hey, sweetheart, remember me?" Bright blue eyes locked onto Terri and the grimy thumb went back into the child's mouth.

"Mama?"

"Mama's not here, baby."

The lips puckered around the thumb and the small eyes grew bright with new tears. Kelsey looked around the strange room. "Mama…"

"Oh, sweetheart." Terri stood and lifted the child into her arms. She carried Kelsey to the rocking chair in the master bedroom. "Mama's not here, but I'm gonna take such good care of you." It wasn't long before the motion of the rocker had Kelsey's eyes drifting closed again. At 2:00 AM, Terri laid Kelsey in the queen sized bed and eased in next to her.

As tired as she was, Terri's mind refused to shut down. The box of night-time tea bags in her pantry whispered her name. Maybe that's what she needed, something soothing and warm to ease her into relaxation mode.

Terri shifted under the covers. Just five minutes to sneak into the kitchen, boil some water, and relight the hot water heater for morning. Surely Kelsey would be fine for just that little bit. Terri started to roll out of the bed but stopped at the muffled whimper beside her.

No tea tonight.

She pulled the fretful child into her arms and found all the soothing and warm she needed in that small body. Terri too was asleep in seconds.

5

"Tinkle."

Terri felt something flutter against her ear and waved an impatient hand to brush it away. Still half asleep, she turned to her other side, burrowed under the blanket, and waited for the alarm.

The whisper came again, louder this time and more insistent. "Tinkle."

This time when her hand moved to brush the disturbance aside, she connected with something solid. Startled, her eyes jerked open and she sat up.

Kelsey sat beside her in the dim morning light, head cocked to one side, thumb in her mouth, lines of concentration imbedded between her little eyes.

Memories of the previous night flooded back in force. *I'm a mommy, sort of.* Joy warmed Terri's heart as sleepiness fled. "Good morning, Kelsey."

The toddler removed the thumb from her mouth and the concentration lines grew deeper. "Tinkle."

Terri's brows lifted as she came fully awake. "Of course you do. What a big girl you are to tell me." Getting out of bed, she swung Kelsey to the floor, and led the way to the bathroom. Morning necessities accomplished, Terri washed her hands and boosted Kelsey up onto the counter next to the sink. She retrieved a washcloth from the cupboard and wet it for Kelsey's face.

"Are you hungry, baby?"

Kelsey nodded as Terri squeezed out the cold cloth. "Well, let's get you cleaned up a little bit. Then we'll have some breakfast and get ready for church."

Kelsey batted the cloth away from her face. "Cold."

Terri laughed. "Hold still, sweetheart. We just need to get the worst off so we can eat. By the time we're finished with breakfast the water should be hot enough for us both to have a nice warm bath before church. I just hope I have something for you to wear." She studied the child's face and hands. Satisfied the worst of the grime was gone, she tossed the cloth into the sink, and bent down eye to eye with Kelsey. "Do you like eggs?"

Kelsey shook her head no.

"Pancakes?"

"Cwispies," the toddler answered.

"Cwispies…crispies…Cereal?"

"Yes…cwispies!"

"Let's go see what we can find." Child perched on her hip, she took the step down into the kitchen and froze in place when her foot hit water. "What?" She jerked back and fumbled for the light switch. Terri stared in disbelief. Her kitchen was a lake. Across the room water poured over the step down into the living room. She backtracked to the living room doorway. When that light came on she caught her breath. The water was almost even with the lower of the two steps.

"Oh my…" Terri hurried back to her bedroom and grabbed her phone. She sat Kelsey back on the bed and scrolled through the preprogrammed numbers.

"Cwispies?"

"Oh, baby, I know. Give me a second." She selected a number, her eyes focused down the hall, her foot tapping as she waited for someone to pick up the phone.

"Hello."

"Benton, it's Terri. Are you guys up?"

"Just barely. What's wrong?"

"I have a lake in my living room."

"Excuse me?"

"A lake, Benton. My living room is flooded. So is the kitchen. I haven't gone in there to see where the water's coming from, but there's at least three inches of water standing in my living room and it's getting deeper by the minute."

"Ah, hon…"

"Can you come?"

"Of course. Give me thirty minutes—"

Terri interrupted him. "I need you to bring Callie with you. I know this is going to sound weird, but could you stop by McDonald's? I need chocolate milk, orange juice, and a sausage biscuit. I'll explain when you get here."

"Tool belt, Callie, and breakfast. Check. Make that forty-five minutes, and I can't wait to see what this is all about."

Terri pushed the disconnect button and sat on the edge of her bed.

Kelsey tugged on her shirtsleeve. "Cwispies?"

Terri threaded her fingers through her hair. "Crispies. Why not?" She reached down to roll her pant legs up and turned to face Kelsey. "Sweetheart, I need you to sit here for a minute. I'll be right back."

Kelsey shook her head no, her eyes growing bright with fresh tears. She held her arms out to Terri.

"Kelsey, I'll be right back."

Silent tears tracked down Kelsey's cheeks, and

Terri gave in. "Come on."

At the kitchen door she stood Kelsey on the step where the child could see her. "Stand right here. Let me see what I can find in the pantry." Kelsey nodded her agreement, and Terri stepped down into the kitchen. The water was frigid enough to raise goose bumps on her arms. From where she stood, Terri could see water pouring out from under the dishwasher. It wasn't deep here since it was running down the step into the living room. She tiptoed through the icy water to the pantry, yanked the door open, and took a quick inventory. No cereal. She snatched a bag of cookies, grabbed a dishtowel for her feet, and stepped back up into the hall. Her first day as a mommy and her foster child would have cookies for breakfast. Not the beginning she'd envisioned.

Thirty minutes later Terri answered the door with Kelsey in her arms. Benton and Callie stepped through, handing her a fast food bag as they moved past.

Benton stopped first at the door to the living room and whistled. "I should'a brought the boat." He continued down the hall to the kitchen door. "Not as bad here as I expected. Where's your breaker box?"

Terri motioned to the door on the other side of the kitchen. "In the utility room, above the dryer. Why?"

"I'll need to shut off the electricity 'til we see what we're dealing with. It's a shock hazard." He hitched up his tool belt. "After I get the power off, I'll go back out to the water main to turn off the water.

"It's coming from under the dishwasher."

"Roger that. Be right back."

Terri watched him leave and motioned for Callie to follow her back to the bedroom. She sat Kelsey in the rocker and opened the biscuit for her. She held up the drinks. "Juice or milk?"

Kelsey pointed. "Milk."

She opened the milk and put the carton on a small table next to the chair. A snap echoed through the house as Benton shut off the power. Terri reached behind the rocker and opened the blinds. "Eat your breakfast, OK? I need to talk to my friend."

Kelsey reached for her milk and took a loud, happy slurp. "K."

Terri smiled and ruffled the toddler's Shirley Temple curls before joining Callie on the side of the bed.

"She's a cutie. Where'd you find her?" Callie asked.

Terri made a sound, part laugh, part groan. "I was going to surprise everyone today... Her name is Kelsey. She's my foster child. Surprise."

Callie looked from Terri to Kelsey and back to Terri. "Foster? When...You never told us."

"Last night." Terri stopped to smother a yawn, pinching the bridge of her nose between her fingers. "Late, last night. Like I said, I wanted it to be a surprise. I didn't have anything quite this dramatic in mind."

Callie looked at the child rocking happily while she ate her breakfast. "I'm definitely surprised. But foster care? What pushed you in that direction?"

"God, I think," Terri answered. "Once Sam quit her job and I didn't have Bobbie here in the evenings, the house was too quiet. One night I was flipping through the channels and I watched a show about foster care. It felt like my wake-up moment from God. I tried to ignore what I was feeling, prayed for God to take it out of my heart if I was just acting like a desperate old maid—"

"Terri—"

"I didn't sleep for a week. The afternoon I went and signed up for the courses, I came home and slept like a baby. I know I should have told you guys. I meant to. But I needed to get used to the idea myself. I had classes to go to, and stuff that needed to be done around the house. Then we had Samantha's party to organize. It just never felt like the right time. My caseworker called last night after I got home and, well, here we are." She lifted her hands in frustration.

"Her first morning here and I couldn't even fix her a decent breakfast. She hasn't had a bath, and,"—Terri fell backwards on the bed—"we got up to this mess and I forgot her nebulizer treatment."

"Nebulizer?"

"She has asthma. She's *supposed* to get a breathing treatment every six hours for the next few days."

"Wow," Callie said, "you've been busy."

Terri crossed her arms over her head and groaned. She sat up when she felt a tug on her pants leg. Kelsey stood next to her with the unopened cup of juice.

"Juice."

Terri took the cup, punctured the seal with a fingernail, and stuck in the straw. Kelsey pushed it away when Terri handed it to her. "Fow you."

"Awww," Callie said as the child's intent registered.

Terri pulled the toddler up into her lap and snuggled her close. "Thanks, baby."

"Terri." Benton's voice echoed up the hall. "Can you come down here for a few minutes?"

Terri handed the juice and the child to Callie. "Can you watch her for me while I see what's going on?"

"Sure."

Terri made it to the door before Kelsey stopped her.

"No!" She struggled out of Callie's lap, ran to the bedroom door, and held up her arms. "I go, too."

Terri stooped down. "I need to go to the kitchen for a few minutes. It's just down the hall, remember? I'll be right back."

Kelsey's answer came without words. She threw her arms around Terri's neck and refused to let go.

Callie joined them at the door and nudged Terri through it. "Why don't we all go to the kitchen?"

Benton waited at the end of the hall on the kitchen side of the doorway. He wore knee high rubber boots, a large wrench rested on his shoulder. "I got the water off. I have good news and bad news."

"Just tell me what happened."

"You have a broken pipe behind the dishwasher. When's the last time you were in here?"

Terri replayed the events of the previous evening in her mind. "About eight, eight thirty last night, I guess. I took a shower when I got home from the party and decided to finish cleaning up the kitchen. I reloaded the dishwasher and everything sort of bloomed out of control after that. I tried to give Kelsey a bath around 1:00 AM and couldn't get any hot water. She woke up crying before I got down here to check things out. I didn't get back in here 'til this morning."

"That pretty much explains it. I'd bet you've had water running in here for almost twelve hours," Benton said.

Terri leaned her head back against the wall. "You said you had good news?"

"Good news is that with the way this place is laid

out, most of the water damage is confined to your living room and study. That's extensive, but not nearly as bad as it would have been if it had gotten over the steps and into the bedrooms. The water flowed to the lowest point, so even the damage to your kitchen is going to be minimal. You're insured, right?"

Terri nodded, dazed by Benton's assessment.

"You need to call them and arrange to get an adjuster out here. I'll work you up an estimate, but I can tell you, based on what I can see, the carpet and pad will need to be replaced. You have baseboard and sheet rock damage. The insulation in the walls is going to soak the water up like a sponge, so some of that will need to be torn out and replaced. The jury's still out on your furniture. I'll leave that to you and the adjuster. There's another piece of good news. The water didn't reach your electrical outlets. You've got all your wiring for the TV and stuff tied up and off the floor, so none of your appliances, or electronics should be affected."

Terri breathed a prayer. "Dear Lord…"

"Yeah, it's going to be a mess for a few weeks, but it's nothing I can't fix. We're going to have to pump out the water before we can see the full extent of the damage. I don't have a pump, but I can borrow one from a friend." He glanced at his watch, "I'll call him right after church and get that going for you."

Terri buried her face in Kelsey's neck, took a deep breath, and searched for the next step. "Do I still have water and power next door?"

"Yep, separate shut off valves. Remind me to show you how those work just in case something like this ever happens again."

Terri straightened up, making an effort to gather her scattered wits and prioritize the things she needed to do. "OK. Thanks, Benton. I'll get a call in to the insurance company. Then I'm going to take Kelsey next door for a bath—"

Callie interrupted her. "There's not a single thing you can do here. Why don't you pack a few things and go on over to the house? You can give Kelsey her bath and wait for us to get home from church. We'll bring Mitch and Steve home with us. They can help get the water pumped out and the carpet up."

"The bedrooms are fine. Even without power, we're good 'til this evening," Terri countered. "I have kitchen and bath facilities next door, there's no reason for me to impose on you guys any more than I already have."

Callie crossed her arms, tapped her foot, and narrowed her blue eyes at her friend.

Terri relented under the frosty stare. "I didn't mean it that way. I know it wouldn't be an imposition, but it's not just me, it's a three-year-old, too."

"Speaking of…" Benton winked at the child in Terri's arms. "Is there an explanation or, at least, an introduction anywhere in my future?"

Callie shushed her husband. "I'll explain everything on the way to church." She took a key from her key ring and passed it to Terri. "We won't take no for an answer. You know where everything is at the house. Go make yourself at home, and we'll see you in a couple of hours."

"All right, thanks," Terri said. The extent of the damage finally began to register. *My house.* The tears she'd held back all morning stung her eyes.

Benton took her hand. "I know how much you love this place. I promise we'll put it back together for you, good as new." Terri bit her lip and nodded.

"Callie, I'm going to hug your husband."

"I think I can live with that," Callie answered.

Terri joined Benton on the kitchen step. She wrapped her free arm around his shoulders. Kelsey reached out to make it a three-way hug.

"Thanks. You're the best."

Secure in Terri's arms, Kelsey laid her head on Benton's shoulder and patted his back. "Tanks."

Benton's sharp bark of laughter undermined the toddler's courage. Kelsey pulled out of the hug and buried her head in Terri's shoulder. Terri tightened her arms and gave the youngster's back a few reassuring pats as the group headed to the front door. She could hear them laughing all the way to Benton's truck.

6

Sean watched from the landing as Ella hauled an over-loaded laundry basket up four flights of stairs. He swallowed back the automatic urge to help. He'd learned his lesson earlier in the day when his normally mild-mannered wife refused his offer in words he hadn't known she knew. Well, maybe knew, but never used.

He trailed her to Kelsey's empty room, leaning in the doorway. Was there anything he could say that he hadn't already said? *Nope.*

Ella sorted out the neatly folded clothes. Her hands hesitated over a pink top with a purple princess silk screened on the front. *Kelsey's favorite shirt.* Ella picked it up and sank to the side of the bed, clutching the shirt to her heart. She began to rock as fresh tears streaked her cheeks, tears he would have sworn were all cried out.

Her voice was a broken whisper. "Oh, baby. What have we done?"

"Ellie, please don't cry anymore."

Ella met his gaze from across the room. Wet, narrowed eyes and continued silence were the only acknowledgement she offered. She used the shirt to dry her face then slipped it over the head of her daughter's favorite stuffed bear. She propped the bear on Kelsey's pillows and walked from the room with no further recognition of her husband's presence.

Sean's shoulders sagged under the burden of her unspoken blame. Yes, the house had been a mess yesterday. Dishes and laundry piled up, pantry almost empty, and bags of garbage waiting to be taken down to the dumpster. Ella had been in bed with a migraine for days. Stack those days on top of weeks of depression and worry over unpaid bills. Kelsey pretty much had free rein in the tiny apartment with Ella sick and him working two jobs.

When was the last time your hands touched a broom? He cringed at the memory of those unjustified words, still unable to figure out what had gotten into him. Ella was a good wife and a great mother. She didn't deserve separation from their child. But he'd brought drugs into their home and used them in front of his daughter. Only his mad dash to the bathroom to flush away the physical evidence of his stupidity—while the police pounded on the door—had kept him from being hauled away with Kelsey.

He sank to the floor in the hall, haunted by Kelsey's screams, condemned by the silence of his wife, defeated by his own guilt. *God…*Sean pushed the beginnings of the prayer aside. God had abandoned him and his family a long time ago.

****

Terri parked in front of Benton and Callie's house. She turned in her seat to look back at Kelsey. The toddler sat in the car seat, bear in her arms, thumb in her mouth. She grinned when Terri caught her eye. "Ready for that bath I promised you?"

Kelsey shrugged.

"You don't say much, do you?"

52

Kelsey answered with a second shrug.

Terri stepped out of her car to the noise of loud, happy barks. Opie, a leggy Irish setter, and Sara, a full-grown blonde Lab, rushed around the corner of the house, skidded to a stop next to her car, and jostled for position around her legs, each trying to be the first to win Terri's attention and a coveted belly rub. "Down," she told them in a firm voice.

She opened the back door to unbuckle Kelsey. The rowdy dogs, excited at the prospect of a new playmate crowded through the opening to investigate the newcomer. The car echoed with the toddler's terrified screams. Kelsey closed her eyes and strained against the confinement of the car seat straps.

Terri pushed the determined dogs aside, struggling with the buckle of the harness pulled tight by Kelsey's efforts to get away from the nosy canines. She did her best to calm the frightened child. "Kelsey, it's OK. They just want to play." Her assurances were wasted breath. Freed from the seat, Kelsey wrapped her arms firmly around Terri's neck, her feet scrabbling as she tried to climb out of reach of the dogs.

"Sara, Opie, sit. Kelsey, baby, stop. It's OK." Sara and Opie finally sat. Kelsey continued to scream.

Terri hurried up the steps to Callie's front door. Her efforts to fit the unfamiliar key into the lock were hampered by the child Velcroed around her neck. She took a deep breath of relief when Kelsey's screams stopped abruptly. Relief nosedived into panic when the silence filled with Kelsey's ragged attempts to breathe.

A cold sweat broke out on the back of Terri's neck as Kelsey went limp in her arms.

"Oh, baby." Terri rushed down the short hall to

Callie's living room and laid the child on the couch. "Sweetheart, calm down. I've got to go get your medicine. I'll be right back."

Terri sprinted back to her car and grabbed the small bag containing the nebulizer and Kelsey's medicine. She tore the bag open as she raced back into the house and fumbled with the emergency inhaler and the air chamber. When she couldn't get the pieces to fit together properly she discarded the chamber, lifted Kelsey to a sitting position, and administered two puffs of the medicine straight into her mouth. Thirty anxious seconds passed as she watched for a sign that the medicine was working.

Kelsey's labored breathing began to even out. Terri laid the child back down on the couch then sat on the floor and pulled up her knees. Terri buried her face in her arms. She shivered as adrenalin seeped out of her body. "God, this is *not* what I signed up for. I can handle a flooded house. I can handle a sick child, but I'm not sure I can handle both. I know this is where You've led me. Now please give me the strength and wisdom I need to see things through."

She lifted her head and studied the child. Kelsey's color was coming back, and her breathing had almost returned to normal. Terri took a deep breath of her own and assembled the nebulizer with hands that still shook. "I don't know if missing your treatment this morning had anything to do with what just happened, but we won't miss another one." She sat down and shifted Kelsey into her lap. They rocked together as the vapor from the nebulizer formed a small cloud around them.

Kelsey sat up, removed the mask from her face, and passed it to Terri. "Feel bettew?"

Terri laughed and inhaled the cool mist. "Sweetheart, it certainly can't hurt."

****

Driven from the apartment by self-condemnation and Ella's continued sniffles and scathing glares, Sean loped down four flights of stairs, looking for a neutral place to think. He leaned against his old truck and pulled loose change from his pockets. His mouth puckered in a frustrated sneer at the few coins and lint that lay in his hand. This is what he had to show for weeks and months of struggling to support his family. It might buy a soda if he was lucky enough to find a few more cents discarded in the console. A quick search of the truck netted him an extra two bucks and forty-three cents. A grand total of three dollars and twenty-eight cents.

His shoulders lifted in a disconsolate shrug. He'd run to the Sonic and get Ella a cherry limeade. The offering would be pretty lousy, but it was the best he had right now. Cars crowded the parking lot, and Sean made the circuit twice before one of the stalls opened up. He pulled his battered truck into the empty space and cranked the window down with a protesting squeal. Sean reached out to press the order button, his movement arrested by voices from the shiny black double cab in the spot beside him.

"What do you think we should order for Kelsey?"

"I don't know, Callie. She's three; I guess get her what you'd get Trent."

His heart thudded in his chest. *What?* He slumped down in his seat, grabbed for his sunglasses, and pretended to read the menu. Instead of studying the board, he studied the people in the vehicle beside him. A blonde woman leaned on the sill of the open passenger window and frowned at the menu. A bald, bearded man sat behind the wheel. Sean averted his gaze and slid further down, ears straining to hear the rest of the couple's conversation.

"I guess the corndog kid's meal," the woman said. She sat back and the window came up between them, cutting off any further chance to eavesdrop on their conversation. Sean mulled over what he'd heard. *What were the odds?* He watched as the carhop delivered two large bags and several drinks to the black truck. When the engine next door roared to life, Sean's decision to follow them was made without hesitation. His original errand forgotten, he eased the truck out of the stall and fell in behind his prey.

He'd get Kelsey back. He'd clean up his act. He'd make things up to Ella. He'd do these things on his own. *I'm a man, after all.*

****

Terri positioned a child-sized rocking chair in front of Callie's television and plugged in a Veggie Tales video. She settled Kelsey, fresh from her bath and dressed in an oversized T-shirt, in the chair and bent to kiss the quickly drying blonde curls. The fragrance of soap and shampoo filled her nostrils. "You smell good, sweetheart."

"Telwy, whele's Mama and Daddy?"

Stunned by the use of her name and the unexpected question, Terri crouched next to Kelsey. "Mama and Daddy can't be here right now, baby." How can I explain foster care to a three-year-old? *Jesus, give me the right words.* "They have to go to school. Do you know what school is?"

Kelsey shook her head, her earnest blue eyes locked on Terri's face.

"It's where you go to learn things," she explained. "They have to learn how to take real good care of you. While they're doing that, you get to live with me."

"Fowevew?"

"Oh, baby, no. Just for a little while. I'll take you to see them in a few days."

"Is a few days vewy long?"

"Not really, and we have lots to do between now and then. We have to go shopping for some new clothes, and you can help me work on the house. On Tuesday you get to go to school too."

Kelsey's face lit with anticipation. "With Mama and Daddy?"

Terri laid her cheek on Kelsey's head. "No baby, not with Mama and Daddy. They have to go to school with big people and work really hard. You get to go to school with kids and play all day. Do you like to play?"

"I like to dwaw and colow."

It took Terri a few seconds to translate. "Dwaw, you like to draw and color. So do I. When we go shopping tomorrow, we'll buy some new coloring books and a big box of crayons so we can color together. Would you like that?"

Kelsey nodded, but her chin quivered.

"Oh, sweetheart, I know you don't understand. We both have a lot of adjustments to make right now." Terri searched for a happy way to change the subject. She was saved from that necessity when the front door opened.

Benton and Callie came through the door, Karla

and Mitch on their heels. They were loaded down with carry-out bags and drink holders from Sonic.

"We brought lunch," Callie said. "Give us a couple of minutes to get everything plated up then come on back to the dining room." Callie and Karla took everything from their husbands and continued to the kitchen. In a synchronized effort to avoid KP, the men ducked into the living room.

Benton steered towards his recliner, winking at Kelsey on his way across the room. He kicked the footrest up and glanced at the television. "Oh goodie. Jonah. That's my favorite Veggie video."

Mitch sprawled on the sofa. "You are *so* behind the Veggie power curve. The new pirate one is too funny. Karla bought it for the grandkids last weekend. They haven't seen it yet, but I've already done the necessary grandpa prescreening."

Benton looked at his best friend. "This is what you're doing with your retirement? Watching children's movies?"

"Hey, you're the one who said you had a favorite."

"It's a talking cucumber, Mitch. I don't have a favorite. I was playing with the child. Are you that bored?"

Mitch shrugged. "It's only been a month since I retired. I'm still in transition." His shoulders slumped. "Who am I trying to kid? I'm going out of my mind."

"Hold that thought." Benton turned to Terri. "Do you trust him?"

"Him? Mitch? To do what?"

"To start the work on your house. My guys and I are about a week away from completing our current job. If I put Mitch to work, pair him up with one of my guys, they can start on the initial grunt work at your place while I finish the Thompson job. Then we can focus on getting you done."

"Is he any good?" Terri asked.

"He'll be fine with some supervision."

"Sitting right here," Mitch reminded them. "Actually, that's the strangest job offer I might ever seriously consider. Karla told me last week that if I didn't get out from under her feet, our children were going to be fatherless. I expected a little more compassion from the woman I've been married to for thirty-nine years."

Karla stepped into the room. "I heard that. In my own defense, I need to remind you that in the last four weeks, you've turned all the whites pink, sharpened the serrations off our steak knives, and let's not forget the comprehensive and *alphabetized* list you typed up to help me organize my pantry."

Terri laid a sympathetic hand on Mitch's shoulder. "You're lucky to be alive."

"He needs to find something *constructive* to do with his time." Karla emphasized *constructive* and sent a pointed look towards Benton. "Or he won't be much longer."

Terri laughed. "Benton, you're the expert. Whatever works for you, works for me, but please," she patted Mitch's back, "keep him out of my kitchen as much as possible." She leaned down to pick up Kelsey. "Come on, baby girl. Do you like Sonic?"

"Fwies?"

"No doubt," Terri promised her.

7

Dinner was laid out, complete with a booster seat for Kelsey. Terri scooted her up to the table, and Kelsey reached for her fries.

"Just a minute, baby." Terri gently retrieved the fry and laid it back on the plate. "We need to bless it first." The adults took their places with Kelsey seated between Terri and Callie. They all joined hands as Benton said the blessing.

"Father, we give You thanks for the day and for this food. Please bless this to our bodies and our bodies to Your service. Amen."

As amen's echoed around the table, Terri returned the fry to Kelsey and looked at her friends. "I apologize for being negligent this morning, Benton. I'd like to introduce everyone to my new foster daughter, Kelsey Brianne Anderson. Kelsey, can you say hi?"

Kelsey looked up from her plate, mouth already smudged with ketchup, a french fry clutched in one hand, a corndog in the other. She grinned at Terri and continued to eat.

Terri shrugged. "Kelsey says hi." She focused her attention on Karla. "I explained everything to Callie earlier, and I know everyone's going to be surprised, but—"

Karla interrupted her. "Callie told us all about it. I—"

Mitch broke in on his wife. "Your surprise isn't a

secret anymore, hon." He motioned to Callie and Karla. "I saw these two in a deep huddle with Pam and Samantha after church this morning. I'd say it's only a matter of time before every lady in the church knows about Kelsey."

Karla pointed a french fry at her husband. "You need to remember that you're already on thin ice with me and focus your attention on your hamburger." She turned back to Terri. "As I was saying, I think it's terrific. How do you like it so far?"

Terri laughed at her friend's enthusiasm. "I'm less than twenty-four hours into my first foster parenting experience. I spent a large majority of last evening at the hospital, part of my house has been transformed into a lake, and I dealt with the mother of all asthma attacks this morning. I just hope the next twenty-four hours are calmer than the last."

"You mentioned the asthma earlier," Callie said. "What happened this morning?"

Terri shuddered at the memory but recounted the story for her friends. "I've never been so scared in my life."

"Honey, I'm so sorry," Callie began to apologize. "Sara and Opie are used to the grandkids. Trent would ride one of them if they'd hold still long enough."

Terri waved away her friend's apology. "Hey, it's their yard. They weren't doing anything wrong. I'm not sure what had her so jacked up, but I think it took five years off my life."

"Probably just the confusion of being in a strange place with strange people," Karla offered. "If the last twenty-four hours have been stressful for you, we can only imagine what it must be like for a three-year-old."

"Agreed," Callie said. "But the bad news is, you're

going to have to go back out there at some point." She smiled at Kelsey. "Let's try a little experiment."

Callie excused herself from the table. When she came back she stopped just outside the dining room door. "Kelsey, do you want to see a funny trick?"

Kelsey looked up from her plate.

Callie came around the table with a very subdued Sara on a leash. Kelsey looked at the dog with a wary expression and scrambled into Terri's lap.

Callie unclipped the leash. "Sara, sit. Stay." The dog sank down and stayed put, even though her hind legs quivered with pent-up excitement. Callie walked around to her plate and picked up a french fry. "Kelsey, are you watching?" She tossed the fry to Sara. The dog caught it in midair. "Good girl," Callie told the dog. "Sit." Callie tossed a second fry, and when Sara caught it, Kelsey clapped her hands.

Callie handed Kelsey a fry. "Do you want to try?"

Kelsey looked from the fry to the dog and threw it. The french fry landed at Sara's feet and the dog quickly snapped it up.

"Good doggie," Kelsey mimicked.

"Well, that works, too," Callie said. She came around and clipped the leash back onto Sara's collar. "Sara needs to go back outside. Do you want to tell her bye?"

Kelsey nodded, and Callie led the dog over to Terri's chair. Kelsey reached out a tentative hand while Sara sniffed at the toddler's feet. "Bye, Sawa."

Callie led Sara away and returned with Opie. The exercise was repeated with similar results. When it came time to tell Opie good-bye, Callie led him over. Kelsey reached out a hand to pat his nose. The big red Irish setter dodged the hand and angled in to lick ketchup from the child's face. Kelsey drew back with a startled expression. The adults held their breath while the toddler decided whether to laugh or cry. Laughter won.

Kelsey swiped at her mouth. "Silly doggie." She reached for another fry, bit it in half, and shared the rest with her new friend.

"All right," Terri said with obvious relief, giving Kelsey a quick squeeze.

Callie led the dog away with a smile. "It's all in the introduction."

Karla and Callie cleaned up the dinner mess while Terri took Kelsey to the spare bedroom in hope of convincing her to take a nap. Braced for an argument, she was pleasantly surprised when the child snuggled up with her bear and was asleep in a matter of minutes. *Poor worn-out baby.* Terri bent to tuck the throw securely around the little bare legs and brushed a kiss across the plump cheek.

"God, thank You for bringing Kelsey into my life. I know I panicked earlier. Sorry about that, but I think I'm getting the hang of things. She has so many questions in her little mind. Help me find the right answers for her. I need You to give me wisdom. I'm asking You to do a special work in the lives of her parents. They must miss her. Help them see what a precious gift they've been given. Help them do whatever's necessary to bring their family back together."

She sat with the child for a little longer then joined her friends in the living room to discuss repairs to her house.

****

Sean shifted in the seat of his truck as it idled just up the road from where the double cab sat parked. The road only had a half dozen widely spaced houses, complicating his efforts to remain inconspicuous. His fingers tapped the steering wheel while he watched the front door. Nothing moved except for two dogs patrolling the yard. The truck had been dutifully sniffed and obviously deemed non-threatening.

Sean pounded his fist against the wheel. Kelsey had to be in that house. How many three-year-old Kelseys could there be in this stinking town? He needed a plan. Part of him wanted to just go up to the door and demand they hand over what was his. Probably not the best plan. *Think, Anderson!*

Like a cartoon from his childhood, Sean felt two little figures settle on his shoulders.

The red-suited one whispered in his left ear. "Go get her. What can they do to you?"

The white figure tugged on his right ear lobe. "That's bad advice, Sean. What good will you be to your family sitting in a cell?"

The voice in his left ear spat, "You'll be long gone before they can get a cop way out here."

"The word *kidnapper* on your record will not help you get your daughter back."

Sean rolled the word around on his tongue, surprised at the bitter taste it left in his mouth. "*Kidnapper*? She's my own flesh and blood."

"Exactly," the voice on the left encouraged him. "They took her from you without permission. If they can, you can. Don't be a wimp."

All that remained on his right was a loudly whispered scream. "Kidnapper!"

Sean blinked and found himself alone in the cab of his vehicle, his hands clenched on the wheel so tightly his knuckles were white. He studied the truck he'd followed from the Sonic and the business advertisement painted on the door. STILLMAN HOME REMODELING. The idea of leaving here without Kelsey broke his heart, but at least he knew where she was and who had her. He pulled an envelope out of a pile of unpaid bills stacked in the glove box. A stubby piece of an orange carpenter's pencil followed. Sean noted the information from the sign. He'd ask around at work and see if anyone knew these people. If his trip to see the social worker in the morning failed to get Kelsey returned, he'd be back.

****

Terri stopped by the kitchen to see if there was anything she could do to help Callie and Karla with the lunch cleanup.

Callie waved her toward the living room. "We've got this. I heard Benton on the phone earlier. He mentioned your house. Why don't you go see what's up? We'll join you in a bit."

Benton glanced at his watch when she came in. "Terri, my friend with the pump is going to meet us at your house at five. We'll get everything set up and let it run while we're at church tonight so we can get as much of the water pumped out as we can. What time are you expecting your insurance adjuster?"

"Around ten in the morning."

Benton nodded. "Mitch, Tom Stanton, and I will meet you at the house first thing in the morning. We can go over a work plan with the adjuster. After you guys decide what can be salvaged and what needs to be replaced, we can help you make a couple of trips to the storage place. Once we get everything cleared out, we can start ripping up the carpet.

"Harrison and Steve have both volunteered to help. It won't take that long. After tomorrow, I'll stop by every morning to get Mitch and Tom started. It'll be slow going until I finish up the job at the Thompson place, but we'll get there." He turned to Mitch. "You know Tom, don't you?"

Mitch nodded. "Young guy, sandy hair?"

"That's him. He's a jack-of-all-trades. I think you guys will work well together."

Mitch laughed. "I'm not complaining. Your job offer is saving my life as well as my marriage."

Terri sighed. "At least we have a plan. I can work with a plan. I'll call my girls and let them know I'm gonna miss the next couple of days. On top of what we have to do at the house, I need to take Kelsey shopping for clothes, and I'm going to buy a couple of those toddler gates to keep her out of the work areas when we're home in the evenings. I'm just glad we have a full kitchen and bath right next door."

The doorbell rang. Callie got up to answer it while Benton looked at Terri. He shook his head. "You're not going to be able to live in the house while we work."

Samantha rushed in on the heels of Benton's comment. "Sorry," she told the adults. "I don't mean to interrupt, but this is the reason I came over with Dad." She sat and tucked her arm through Terri's. "We want you to come stay with us 'til your house is fixed."

Terri pulled back a bit so she could look into Sam's face. "Do what?"

Samantha's sigh carried a clear comment on

grownups. "I talked it over with Dad. We want you and the baby to come stay at our house. I'm moving into the spare room upstairs. We've already moved Bobbie's stuff upstairs to her playroom. You and Kelsey can have the whole basement apartment to yourselves until your repairs are complete. Two bedrooms, full bath, a kitchenette, and living area." Sam ran out of breath and sat back, obviously pleased with her solution to Terri's problems.

"That's a generous offer, sweetheart, but I can't move you two out of your apartment." Terri looked at Steve. "I appreciate it, really, but there's no reason why we can't stay at the house. That way I can help with some of the small repairs in the evenings."

"Terri," Benton began, "you're forgetting one very important thing. What are you going to do about Kelsey's asthma? We're going to stir up a lot of dust. There's going to be insulation fibers floating around as well. I'll need to wear a mask most days. You can't tame down the dust like we did the dogs. It's not just a safety issue. It won't be healthy for her to live in that."

Terri slumped back into the couch. "I never even thought about that." She stopped and patted Samantha's leg. "I'm not routing you out of your home. My insurance will pay for an apartment, or something, until the house is repaired." Her forehead wrinkled in a frown. "You know, I was so sure I'd finally found the path God wanted me to take. I thought this was my chance to do something special for Him. Maybe I got my signals crossed somewhere."

Callie sat down on the other side of her friend. "Terri, if you weren't feeling a little beat up right now, I wouldn't think you were human. But don't start doubting the choices you've made. This morning when you told me about your decision to be a foster parent, your face glowed with an excitement even flood waters couldn't douse. I, we all, think it's a wonderful thing you're doing, and we're all going to help you get over this speed bump."

Samantha bounced up and down on the couch in excitement. "Yep, we are. Just like you helped me and Iris last spring." She threw her arms around Terri's neck. "We wouldn't be a family today if it wasn't for you guys. Now it's our turn to repay the favor. Why should you spend the money on a strange place to live when you can be with friends?"

Terri hugged Sam back then pried the teen's arms loose. "You aren't going to take no for an answer, are you?"

"Not any more than you guys did when I tried to resist the help you were offering us."

Terri looked from Samantha to Steve. "You're awfully quiet. I understand Sam's desire to help, but I don't want you to agree to this just because she's determined to have her way. I'll be bringing another child into your house."

Steve pushed himself away from the doorframe he'd been leaning on and crouched in front of Terri. "Everything Samantha just said has my full endorsement. You need a place. We have a place. Don't be stubborn."

Terri searched his face with a defeated breath. "All right, we'll give it a try for a few days, but only if you promise to let me know if Kelsey is disturbing you."

Steve held out his hand in acceptance of her terms. "Deal."

"Yea!" Sam cheered. "Iris and I will come by after church to help you pack your stuff and haul it over to the house."

"Yea." Terri echoed in less than enthusiastic tones. "I think you're enjoying this just a little too much."

Sam's expression turned serious. "The fact your house is flooded, no way. This little bit of role reversal?" She smiled mischievously. "Every single minute."

8

Terri carried a box of shoes down the carpeted steps leading to Samantha's basement apartment, her progress only marginally hampered by the three-year-old holding on to the hem of her shirt as they descended. She added her box to the growing stack at the base of the stairs, wiped her hands on the seat of her jeans, and gave Kelsey an exhausted smile. "That's it, sweetheart."

"Not even close." Samantha came down behind them with an armload of clothes. "That may be the last load from your car, but it'll take us a dozen trips just to get your hang-up clothes down here."

"Only a dozen?" Iris dropped the load she carried. She looked at Terri. "I want to be you when I grow up. I like to shop. I've managed to put some serious dents in Dad's credit card over the summer, but I'm unworthy to stand in your presence. I've never seen anyone with so many shoes and clothes."

"True shopping is a skill, and I had a great teacher." Terri settled Kelsey at the small table tucked into a corner of the kitchenette. She poured a glass of milk and put two cookies on a paper towel. "Sit right here while I help the girls get the rest of my clothes out of Sam's car."

"Telwy be right back?"

"Right back," Terri assured her. She followed the girls up and out to the garage. Despite Samantha's dire predictions, it only took them three more trips each to get everything down the stairs.

Iris dropped a heavy garment bag on top of the stack. "Princess for a Day Bridal? What do you have in here?"

Terri moved to stop the inquisitive twelve-year-old, but she was just a moment too late. Iris lowered the zipper. "Oh," Iris exclaimed, parting the bag further. "Terri, it's beautiful. Yours?"

Samantha shouldered Iris out of the way and slid the zipper back into place. "Get out of there, nosy. What's wrong with you?"

Terri fought the heat flooding her face. "Someday," she answered Iris. "A girl has to be prepared."

Samantha frowned at her little sister and waved at the small mountain of dresses, skirts, slacks, and tops. "I'd say you're prepared for everything from a day at the beach, to a week at work, to a world cruise. I know it was my idea to bring all of your clothes over here so they wouldn't get all dusty, but I don't know where you're going to hang them. The boxes can be labeled and stacked against the walls, but…"

Terri took a step back. "It didn't look like that much when it hung in my closets. Mom would be so proud of me."

"Your mom?" Iris asked.

"Yeah, my shopping coach. That 'great teacher' I mentioned. She loved to shop. Daddy loved to fish. I combined their two hobbies into one. Her shopping skills, his patience. I can troll the mall all day on a Saturday looking for the perfect bargain." Terri looked at the stacks of clothes and shoes. "I never understood the concept of catch and release though. Maybe I should have worked on that more."

"Nah," Iris said. "Why spend the whole day doing something you love only to come home empty handed?"

Terri shook her head at the mess. "Mom's been in heaven for almost six years, but after I've spent the whole day shopping and finally find that *great bargain,* I like to think she looks down, gives Jesus a little nudge, and tells Him, 'That's my girl!'"

Sam laughed. "What a great way to look at it. I've never heard you mention either of your parents. Is your dad still alive?"

Terri's expression saddened. She shook her head. "No, I lost them both at the same time. They were in Hawaii on their second honeymoon. Dad had just gotten his pilot certification. He arranged for a day trip to one of the smaller islands. The small plane they rented had mechanical difficulties over some mountains. It took the search-and-rescue team three days to locate the wreckage. The medical examiner assured me that they died on impact."

Sam's eyes widened at Terri's explanation. "I'm so sorry."

Terri waved it away, using her shirtsleeve to swipe tears from her cheeks. "Don't worry about it. I don't talk about it because it still makes me cry, but I have a lifetime of good memories I can look back on. Hours spent fishing and shopping and just being loved. My dad was awesome, but Mom was my best friend. The three of us took a special vacation every summer when I was growing up. I have stacks of picture albums Mom put together over the years. I'll share them with you some time."

Sam nodded. When she spoke, her voice echoed

with her own loss. "It's hard to lose that part of your life. Good memories make it a little easier."

Terri agreed. "It seemed as if God had deserted me when it happened, but He always knows best. They were both Christians practically their whole lives. As much as they loved me, they would have been lost without each other. I know they're both in heaven waiting on me. They wouldn't come back even if they could.

"Beyond that, my story is a little like yours. You guys lived on your mom's insurance money until we located your father. My mom and dad left everything they had to me, including a large insurance policy. I found a note in Dad's things after the funerals. He told me to take what they left for me and make my life secure. Long story short, I bought both of the houses and started my business." She sniffed, a smile replacing the sadness on her face. "So, you see? Even though they're gone, they're still taking care of me. Between my business and my wardrobe, I do my best to make them both proud."

Iris hugged Terri when she finished. "That's so cool. Sad...but cool."

Terri hugged her back. "I know what you mean."

Sam took a final look around the cluttered apartment. "Well, you've got your work cut out for you to find a place for everything." She yawned, linking arms with her younger sister. "I think we're going to leave you to it. Iris and I are driving across the state line in the morning to check out the new outlet mall."

"Yeah," Iris interrupted. "You've given me a new shopping standard to live up to. I wish you could come along and share some of that coaching with us."

"Trust me." Terri closed her eyes in contemplation of the day to come. "I'd rather spend the day shopping."

"Is there anything we can pick up for you? I know you're going to have to get Kelsey some clothes. You could make us a list," Sam offered.

"No thanks, hon. I need to do it. The prospect of a little retail therapy will be a nice diversion after I deal with the mess at the house."

"OK," Sam said. "I need to retrieve Bobbie from Dad and get us both in bed. Tomorrow will be her initiation to marathon shopping. She needs her rest." She stopped at the foot of the stairs. "You have everything you need?"

"I think so." Terri enveloped both girls in a hug. "Thanks, you two, for all your help this evening. And Sam, thanks, really. This is the best solution, even if I was too stubborn to admit it at first."

"You're talking to the queen of stubborn, remember? Just make yourself at home. You know where most everything is upstairs if you need something." She paused at the door. "'Night, Kelsey."

"G'night." Kelsey waved at her new friends.

The door closed behind Sam and Iris. Terri sat down across from Kelsey. "It's been a long day, sweetheart. I bet you're pretty tired, huh?"

Kelsey yawned and rubbed at her eyes. "Nope."

"Yeah," Terri said. "I think it's just about bedtime for both of us. We have another busy day ahead of us tomorrow."

Terri washed Kelsey's hands and face and gave her a nebulizer treatment. She changed her into a clean T-shirt. "We really have to find some time to go shopping tomorrow. You can't live in T-shirts and flip flops the whole time you're with me."

"Colow." Kelsey yawned. "Books?"

Terri laughed. "It's good to know your priorities, sweetheart. Yes, we'll get some coloring books, drawing paper, and a big box of crayons while we're out. Will that work for you?"

"Tanks you, Telwy."

Terri gathered the child close for a hug. "Let's say your prayers and go to bed."

"Pwayews?"

Terri knelt beside the toddler bed they'd moved from her flooded house and patted the floor beside her. "Yep, prayers. Come here next to me." Terri bowed over the toddler and helped her recite the bedtime prayer her own mother had taught her so many years ago.

"Now I lay me down to sleep. I pray the Lord my soul to keep. If I should die before I wake, I pray the Lord my soul to take." She paused after every third or fourth word, allowing Kelsey a chance to repeat them. "God bless Mama and Daddy."

"God bwess Mommy and Daddy."

"Anyone else you want to bless?"

Kelsey thought for a second. "Bwess Fuzzy and Sara and Opie and Telwy."

Terri laughed. "Thanks, baby. I need all the help I can get right now." She stood and tucked Kelsey under the covers with her bear. "I'm right out here if you need anything. OK?"

Kelsey nodded. She pulled the bear close and stuck her thumb in her mouth. "'Night, Telwy."

"'Night, baby." Terri checked the nightlight and pulled the door closed behind her. She needed to tackle the mountain of clothes and boxes, but there was one more chore that needed to come first. A glance at her watch showed almost nine thirty. Longer than she probably should have waited, but not late enough to put it off until tomorrow. *What if they don't let me keep her?* Terri pushed that thought aside with a silent prayer for God's will in the situation and punched in Cindy Wilson's phone number.

"Hello."

"Cindy, it's Terri Hayes. I had a little trouble at the house." Terri filled in the social worker about broken pipes, the flooded house, and her altered living arrangements. "Is that going to be a problem on your end?" She closed her eyes and held her breath.

"No, but there are a few things we'll need to take care of. First, tell me about the apartment. Is there adequate space?"

Terri released a breath of relief. "Yes. Two bedrooms, just us."

"That should be fine," Cindy said. "I'll need to do an inspection, just for paperwork purposes. I'm leaving for a conference tomorrow after lunch, and I won't be back in the office until Friday. You know what needs to be done. If you can assure me that the safety issues have been resolved, we'll discuss what needs to happen next when I see you on Friday."

The ache between Terri's shoulder blades disappeared. "Thanks."

"For what?"

"I was afraid you'd want to place her somewhere else."

Cindy laughed. "Don't worry about it. Foster parents are people, too. Life happens. As long as you're good with the situation and Kelsey is safe, that's all that matters."

"Yes on both counts." Terri did her best to smother a yawn. "I'll double check for any safety issues and we'll talk on Friday. Have a good trip." Terri disconnected the call and refocused her attention.

One hurdle down, a mountain left to go.

****

Iris peeked out of her room. After a long day, the house seemed to be settling in for the night. All except for her. An idea was taking shape in her heart, and she needed Sam's participation and advice.

They would be alone most of the day tomorrow, but Iris's insides were tangled up in knots. If she waited, she'd never get to sleep. She tiptoed to the kitchen, grateful that her father's bedroom and office were on the second floor. If he saw what she was doing, he'd want to know what was wrong. He knew that only the most serious of problems warranted the cookies and milk tradition.

Iris assembled items on a tray. Two large glasses of ice-cold milk and a stack of chocolate sandwich cookies. Her steps were silent on the carpeted stairs, but her eyes watched her father's door for any sign of movement. She stood in front of Sam's room and scratched at the door, afraid if she knocked her dad might hear.

Sam opened the door and took a step back, allowing Iris to enter the room. After setting the tray down on the bedside table, Iris walked back to the door to look up and down the hall. Satisfied that all remained quiet, she closed the door and took a seat on the side of the bed. "We need to talk," she whispered.

Sam sat down and moved the tray to the bed

between them. "Cookies and milk? Is this serious?"

Iris nodded confirmation. "It has potential."

"You flunked your math test, and you don't know how to tell Dad?"

"No." Iris chewed her lip. "I need to ask you an important question."

"OK..."

"Do you love Terri?"

"Well that's a pretty silly question. She's sleeping in my bed."

Iris waved her hand in dismissal. "That's not what I meant. Do you *really* love her?"

Sam took a cookie, dunked it in her glass of milk, and stared into space for a few seconds. "Yes, Iris. I really love Terri. Why?"

Iris took a cookie for herself, separated the pieces, and licked out the cream before she dunked it. "Do you think she loves us?"

Sam reached over and softly rapped her knuckles against the side of her sister's head. "Are your brain cells on vacation?"

"What?"

"Brain cells. Are they with us? Because you just took a sharp detour into stupid, and you need to make a U-turn before you get lost out there. Of course Terri loves us." Sam frowned. "Where are you going with this?"

Iris got up again, opened the door a crack, and peered out. All clear. *Why is this so hard to say?* She sat back down and looked at Samantha. "Do you think Dad likes her?"

"*Iris.*"

"Quiet," Iris hissed. "Just answer the question."

Samantha took a deep breath and ate another

cookie. "Iris, I love Terri. She loves us, and I think Dad likes her fine. What's up with the twenty questions tonight?"

Iris gathered her courage. *Here goes nothing.* "I want Terri and Dad to get married."

"Have you lost your mind?"

Iris took a cookie and offered another one to Sam. "I don't think so." She got up and paced, finally reaching around her older sister to pick up a small framed picture of their mother. Her fingers traced the outline through the glass. "You know I miss Mom. No one could ever take her place. I wouldn't want anyone to try. But Dad's been alone for a long time. He needs to share his life with someone. That won't always be us." She met her sister's curious gaze.

"The way I see it, we have two choices. We can try and fix him up with someone we love, like Terri, or we can wait and hope he doesn't fall in love with the wicked witch of the west." She studied Samantha with raised eyebrows. "I don't know about you, but I like option one. It's simple logic."

Sam retrieved the picture, giving it her own silent study before returning it to its place on the bedside table. "Love isn't always logical." She nodded towards the picture. "They loved each other. They were good together, but love wasn't enough to hold our family together. Besides, who says Dad's even ready to think about trying again?"

Iris waved Sam's objections and questions aside. "I don't know that he is. But I know they're perfect for each other. I think we need to give this some serious thought while we have them stuck in the same house." Iris continued to look Sam in the eye. "And don't forget the most important difference between then and now."

Sam tilted her head in question and waited for Iris to explain.

"Mom and Dad didn't have God helping them with their choices. Terri and Dad do. I think that makes a huge difference." Iris handed her sister the last cookie. "Give me one good reason why it wouldn't work."

Sam took her time over the final cookie. Iris could almost see the wheels turning behind her sister's eyes as Sam weighed the pros and cons of her idea. While she waited for Sam to think things through, Iris checked her own mental list. Terri loved them. Hadn't she proven that about a dozen times over the last few months? Their father was a handsome, successful man. Did a worse option than Terri lurk around their corner? A vision of a green warty nose made her shiver. *We can so do this if Sam agrees.*

Sam's eyes came back to Iris. "I think I like it."

Iris let out a breath she didn't realize she was holding and pumped her fist in the air. "Yes!"

Sam moved the empty tray back to the table, and leaned back on her pillows. "But we can't be too obvious about what we're trying to do. Whatever happens, they have to think it was their idea." She sat up suddenly and grabbed Iris's fingers. "Sis, Terri really wants a baby of her own. How would you feel about that?"

Iris shrugged. "I've had my shot at being the baby of the family. I think playing the part of big sister would be fun. I could be the boss for a change."

Sam snorted. "That'll be the day." She tucked her long brown hair behind her ears. "Let's both give this some thought. I think we need to pray about it, too. I know Terri is depending on God to answer her prayer for Mr. Right. I mean, she already has a dress. It would be great if Dad turned out to be the answer to those prayers, but we need to be sure."

"I agree," Iris assured her. "But there's no reason we can't arrange for them to spend some time together over the next few weeks. I'm thinking some real family things. Picnics on the weekends and dinner for everyone at the table each night. We could take Bobbie and Kelsey to the zoo or the aquarium. Stuff to show them what a nice family unit we'd make."

"That's a good plan," Sam agreed. "You want to start?"

"What?"

"This is your idea, and we need to pray about it, so you start."

Iris took Sam's hand and bowed her head. "God, I guess You heard everything we just said so You know that we think Terri would make a great stepmom for us, and a good wife for our dad. Those things are important, but Your will is important, too, so we want You to have Your way. Help us bring them together if that's what You want."

Sam squeezed her sister's hand. "Amen," she whispered. She handed the tray back to Iris. "Take this downstairs and go to bed. We have a lot to do over the next few days. We can brainstorm some ideas while we're out tomorrow."

****

Ella hadn't spoken to him in almost twenty-four hours. Saturday night's tearful order that *he* not speak to *her* until Monday when he could report on his efforts to get Kelsey returned to them seemed to have been reversed in her mind.

Sean stared at the television screen in the spotless living room of their apartment. Ella had cleaned with a passion he hadn't seen since right before Kelsey was born when she'd been in a frenzy to get everything prepared. His meals had been served with downcast eyes and silence. She'd refused his help with even the heaviest tasks. Everything had been accomplished with tears on her cheeks and the animation of a zombie.

They'd known each other since they were five years old. Sean could never remember going two days without hearing her voice. She was making him pay, and he couldn't really blame her. He'd come home to find Ella on the sofa, a book open in her lap. When he sat on the other end, she'd shifted to angle her back to him. In almost an hour he never saw her turn a single page.

She hadn't asked where he'd been, and Sean hadn't volunteered the information. As much as he wanted to make her feel better, there was no point in getting her hopes up. He'd hold on to his newfound info until he saw how things went with the social worker tomorrow.

He turned off the television and sat in the darkness, paying little attention to the passing time until he heard the soft *snick* of the old digital clock as the one changed to a two. His heavy sigh filled the empty room as he stood and made his way to spend another lonely night in his daughter's bed. Sean stopped, his hand on the knob. He should probably check on Ella before he tried to go to sleep.

He opened the door to their shared room as quietly as he could. Ella's soft sobs froze him in the doorway. It was more than he could take. Sean moved to the bed, shoving toys and dolls to the floor. He gathered Ella into his arms and tried to soothe her with promises he only hoped he could keep. "Shhh, sweetheart. I'll make some calls first thing in the morning. We'll have her back by tomorrow. I promise. She's our baby. They can't keep her from us."

Ella didn't answer, but she didn't push him away. She snuggled close, finally accepting the comfort he offered. For the first time in two days he relaxed a little. The arm of his T-shirt wet from Ella's tears, his eyes damp with his own, he fell asleep.

****

Terri's eyes came open with a start. A mixture of crying and gasping from the next room brought her feet to the floor before her mind was fully awake. *Kelsey.* Grabbing the small bag of medications from the night table she stumbled blindly for the bedroom door. *Where's the stupid light switch?* More than a little annoyed at the total darkness of the windowless apartment, she led with her empty hand. Features of the room were catalogued in her mind. *Bed, door to the left, chest of drawers next to the door.* Something landed on the floor with a loud crash. *Great, let's wake up the whole house.*

The bare toes of her left foot slammed into the corner of an unfamiliar piece of furniture. Terri leaned against the wall for a second, everything forgotten in her own bright burst of pain. Another cry from Kelsey got her moving. Tears stung her eyes as she hopped the rest of the way to Kelsey's room on one foot. She yanked the door open and followed the dim glow of the nightlight to Kelsey's bedside. The child sat in her bed, crying and wheezing. Terri didn't take much consolation from the realization that if Kelsey had breath to cry, it signaled this attack was less severe than the earlier one.

The emergency inhaler went together properly on the first try. Terri pulled Kelsey into her lap and triggered the medication, watching as Kelsey grew calmer. She rocked her gently, waiting for the toddler's tears to subside.

"Is that better, baby? Did you have a bad dream?"

Kelsey buried her head in Terri's chest. "Bad doggies," she sniffled.

Terri closed her eyes, resting her chin against Kelsey's sleep tangled curls. She didn't know whether to laugh or cry. Those stupid dogs again. "Opie and Sara?"

"Bad doggies," Kelsey repeated, burrowing further into Terri's arms.

Before Terri could respond she heard the door at the top of the stairs open and Steve's voice in a loud whisper. "Everything all right down there?"

"Come on down," Terri invited.

Steve came down and knelt beside the small bed. "Sorry, I don't mean to invade your space, but I thought I heard crying and banging. I didn't want to knock in case I was wrong and you guys were asleep."

Terri shifted Kelsey back to the bed. The child was already drifting back to sleep. "She had a nightmare about Callie's dogs. They scared her earlier today. Change that to *terrified* her. I thought we'd moved past that, but I guess we still have some work to do on her subconscious. Once we got past the asthma attack, all she said was 'bad doggies.'" Terri looked up from her place on the edge of the small bed. "I'm sorry we disturbed you. It's exactly what I hoped to avoid."

Steve waved away her apology. "I wasn't asleep yet. I was working and came down for a bottle of water." He reached down a hand. "Come on. She's out."

Terri smoothed the hair from Kelsey's forehead and leaned over to kiss the peacefully sleeping child. Accepting Steve's hand, Terri rose to her feet and struggled to stifle a cry of her own as her injured foot took her weight. She sank back down to the edge of the bed.

"Ow, ow, ow!"

"What's wrong?"

"I kicked a piece of furniture when I tried to get to Kelsey. Hurts like the devil. I guess she won't be the only one sleeping with a nightlight from now on."

Steve took her hand again, pulling her up a second time. "Let's go take a look."

"It'll be OK." Terri let go of his hand and took a tentative step forward. She grabbed Steve's arm with a sharp intake of breath.

"Mmm hmm." Steve placed a hand under her elbow. "I'm sure it's fine, but let's humor my chivalrous nature, shall we?"

Terri limped to the small sofa, leaning heavily on Steve's arm for support. He left her there and went to turn on the bright overhead lights. Returning to the sofa, he sat down and patted his knees. "Prop it up here and let's take a look."

Terri put her foot in Steve's lap. She gasped in surprise when he pulled up the leg of her Tweety Bird pants.

"I don't think I've ever seen anything quite that

shade of purple," Steve said. He reached out a single finger to touch her swollen toes.

Terri realized his intentions and jerked her foot away. She batted at his hand. "Don't touch!"

"I didn't."

"You were gonna," Terri accused him. She lowered her injured foot slowly to the floor.

"Can you walk on that?"

"Of course I can."

Steve crossed his arms in obvious disbelief and settled back onto the cushions. "Show me." His eyes cut to the refrigerator across the room. "I never did get the drink I came down for. Why don't you grab us a bottle of water?"

Terri measured the scant distance for herself. She crossed her arms in imitation of his posture. "No thanks, but feel free to help yourself."

"That's what I thought." Steve patted his knee again. "Put it back up here. Let me have a closer look." At Terri's militant expression, he sketched an X across his heart. "I won't touch it, cross my heart."

Watching him with suspicious eyes, Terri propped her foot back on his knee. They both leaned over to get a closer look.

"They're pretty swollen. Can you wiggle them?"

Tears filled Terri's eyes as she made the futile effort.

"I'm thinking broken." Steve's tone was grim. "We need to get them X-rayed."

"We could just tape them. Surely you have some tape."

"You won't let me touch them."

"I'll let you."

Steve sighed. "I don't think so." He pulled her

pant leg back down and scooted out from under her foot, replacing his knee with a pillow.

"Where are you going?" Terri asked as he headed back up the stairs.

"I'm going to get Sam down here to stay with Kelsey. Then I'm taking you to the emergency room."

"Nope," Terri said stubbornly.

"Yep."

"Steve, no."

Steve put his hands on his hips. "Come over here and say that to my face."

When Terri didn't make the effort to get up, he traded a smirk for her scowl. "I'll be back in a few minutes."

Steve climbed the stairs, and Terri cringed when she imagined how she must look. Sleep-tousled hair, face devoid of makeup, hot pink sleep pants with bright yellow Tweety bird faces, the image of Sylvester the cat, emblazoned on her shirt. Pride kicked in. *Big deal, I didn't ask him to come to my rescue.* She glared up at him with a militant expression.

Steve turned with his hand on the knob. "You know, when you pout like that you look about twelve. It's actually kind of cute."

Terri searched for something to throw at him as he escaped through the door.

Three hours later Terri hobbled back down the stairs. Supported by Steve's arm on one side and a cane on the other, she took the steps one at a time, her progress impeded by the stiff and awkward boot splint encasing her left leg from toes to knee. Even on carpeted steps, the trip down the stairs must have been noisy.

Sam sat up with a stretch and a yawn. Her eyes

homed in on the splint. "Wow, that's an impressive piece of footwear. Broken?"

Terri gave a jerky nod.

Steve held up three fingers.

"Three?"

Terri stopped at the base of the stairs to catch her breath before answering Sam. "Yeah, the three in the middle."

"Oh no."

Terri sucked in a discouraged breath and looked at the clock. Four AM. She made her way to the sofa and lowered herself into the cushions. "Steve, you and Sam need to get to bed. I appreciate all you've done tonight, but I've disturbed your routine enough today to last for the whole time I'm here."

Sam put an arm around Terri's shoulders. "Don't be a goof. Do you need me to stay home with you and Kelsey tomorrow?"

Terri laid her head on Sam's shoulder for a second. "I appreciate the offer, sweetheart, but you girls have been planning this trip for weeks. I have insurance adjusters, furniture, and shopping to deal with. I'll be fine."

Sam motioned to the boot. "Can you drive in that thing?"

"Yes."

Steve cleared his throat. "Doctor says not for a week."

"Well, he's not the one with a flooded house, a new foster child to care for, and a business to run, is he?" She reached into her pocket, removed a small bottle of pain pills, and shook them at Steve for emphasis. "I have drugs. I'll be fine."

Steve snatched the pill bottle from her, used his

free hand to cup her chin, and forced her eyes up to meet his. "Drugs that say very clearly, 'not to be taken while driving.'" He, too, shook the bottle, matching her sarcasm for sarcasm.

Samantha eased between the two adults. "Whoa, guys, let's go to neutral corners for a second."

Terri dropped her eyes. "I'm sorry. It's just been a really long day. I need some sleep."

Forced to take a step back, Steve agreed. "Good idea. We'll deal with tomorrow, tomorrow."

Sam looped her arm through her father's, pulling him toward the staircase. "Do you need anything else tonight?"

Terri shook her head. "I'm good. Go on to bed, both of you." She pasted a smile on her lips and held it in place until the door closed behind them.

The independent façade slipped from her face the moment Steve and Sam left her. Toes throbbing, tears of pain and frustration trickling down her cheeks, she limped to the sink for a glass of water. Terri shook a pain pill into her palm, anxious for the relief it would bring. She popped it into her mouth, frowning at the door to Kelsey's room before she could swallow it. She spit it back into her hand. What if Kelsey had another asthma attack? Terri broke the pill in half and opened the doors to both bedrooms. Kelsey slept soundly; it was after four AM. Surely half a pill would take the edge off without knocking her out completely.

After swallowing the reduced dosage, she shuffled back to her borrowed bed. Feeling supremely sorry for herself, she plumped up a couple of pillows so that she could keep her foot elevated, per the doctor's instructions, and lay back. She closed her eyes and breathed a silent prayer as she fell into an exhausted, drug-induced sleep. *God, where have You gone?*

9

Terri turned over in the pitch-black bedroom and struggled to focus her sleep-blurred vision. Her eyes skimmed across the red numbers of the bedside clock. She squinted at the numbers. Almost nine? *I never sleep that late.* The internal clock that ticked in her head was so reliable she used her alarm clock more as a formality than a necessity. Tiny Tikes opened each morning by six. She was always the first one there. Today she'd need to rush to meet the insurance man by ten.

She shuffled from her room to Kelsey's doorway, peering into the shadows and listening for a second. All quiet. Maybe she could grab a quick shower before Kelsey woke and wanted her 'cwispies.' Once in the bathroom, she removed the boot and stepped into the shower.

The boot was temporary, given to her because she didn't have the luxury of staying off her feet for the next few days. It would give her some mobility, and she could re-tape her toes as needed. She added tape to her mental shopping list.

The soothing heat of the water chased the tension from her body and the cobwebs from her brain. She leaned her head against the wall while the hot water cascaded over her. Guilt nipped at the edges of her conscience. *I'm sorry, Father. I guess I was feeling a whole lot sorry for myself last night. I don't understand what's happening, but I know You have a purpose for everything*

You do. I need to hold onto those things today. I want Your will for my life. Help me find that. Help me find the future You have for me.

Back in her room, she searched through boxes for clothes and shoes. She tried several shoes on her right foot before finding one that balanced with the boot on her left. Mindful of the time, her hair and face got abbreviated attention before she went to wake Kelsey.

"Sleepyhead, it's time to wake up." Terri flipped on the overhead light, stopping when she realized there was no child in the bed. No child, but a note propped on the pillow. She plucked it up.

Kelsey and breakfast are both waiting for you upstairs. Steve.

Terri crumpled the note in exasperation. Steve had been clear at the party Saturday afternoon that he didn't want any more little ones complicating his life. Despite Terri's best efforts, Kelsey seemed to be intruding at every turn. Terri needed to figure out a way to fix that if they planned to live here for several weeks.

She grabbed her bag and her cane and made the slow climb up the stairs. Terri stepped into the kitchen and blinked moisture from her eyes as they worked to adjust from the dim light of the stairway to the sunlight streaming through the room's east-facing windows. Once her vision cleared, she found Kelsey seated at the table, obviously fresh from a bath and dressed in her single outfit. A dishtowel around her neck served as a bib and despite yesterday morning's denial, Kelsey seemed to be thoroughly enjoying a plate of pancakes. Steve, his back to Terri, sat across from the toddler with his own plate and a newspaper. Kelsey looked up and offered Terri a syrupy grin.

"Hi, Telwy. Steve made good cakes."

Terri limped around the table, dropping a kiss on Kelsey's head before sliding into an empty chair. "I can see that." She turned an apologetic smile toward Steve. "I'm so sorry. You shouldn't have gone to all this trouble. A couple of broken toes don't make me helpless."

"Not a big deal," Steve said absently, his attention focused on his daily Sudoku puzzle. "I figured you needed a couple of extra hours of sleep, so I had Sam go down and get her this morning. She gave her a bath and got her dressed before she left. All I did was fix breakfast." He pushed back from the table and retrieved a plate from the microwave. "Speaking of breakfast, you should have just enough time to eat before we have to leave."

"We?"

"Yes, we. The insurance adjuster is due at your house by ten, right?"

Terri nodded. "Why we?"

"The doctor said you don't drive for a week, so I'll drive you today."

"Steve, we had this conversation last night. I don't need you to wait on me. I'm sure you have better things to do."

Steve rinsed off his plate and loaded it in the dishwasher. "Are you always this stubborn, or is it something you save just for me?"

"I'm sorry if I sound ungrateful." Pricked by the gentle rebuke she heard in his voice, Terri rushed to apologize. "I'm not trying to be stubborn. I appreciate what you and the girls are doing for us, but you can't be at my disposal for a week, and I know you don't want Kelsey in your hair the whole time we're here."

She raised her hands in surrender. "I just feel like we're becoming a bigger imposition than you bargained for, and it hasn't even been twenty-four hours."

"Trust me," Steve said. "I won't be imposed upon if I don't want to be. I owe you much more than I could ever repay." His hand came up to stem her objections. "And before you jump on that bandwagon, I'm not doing anything for you out of obligation either. I have an ulterior motive that we'll discuss later when there aren't little ears around." He stopped with a pointed look in Kelsey's direction. "Are you finished, squirt?"

Kelsey nodded.

Steve removed the towel from around her neck and went to the sink to wet a corner of it. He wiped her sticky face and hands then took her plate to the sink.

"The doctor said you shouldn't drive for a week. Since you're determined to ignore his good advice, can we at least compromise? I can't be at your beck and call for a week, but I'm between projects right now, and I can give you a couple of days. Can we just go with that for now?"

"I'm sorry, again," Terri responded, more than a little chastened. "I guess this is my morning for apologies, three for you, one for God. That should just about use up my quota for the day."

"Why did you need to apologize to God?"

"I was feeling more than a little sorry for myself last night, and I told Him about it. You know, I remember sitting in your backyard less than forty-eight hours ago thinking about my life and feeling pretty satisfied. It's amazing how things can change in such a short time." She finished her breakfast and looked at Steve. "Thanks for breakfast. It was very good. I'd be grateful if you could help me with my errands today."

Steve added her plate to the dishwasher. "Now that didn't hurt too badly, did it? We better get going."

He stood Kelsey on her feet and bent down to make a quick inspection. He motioned in a circle with his finger. "Turn around. Let's make sure there's no syrup hiding somewhere."

Kelsey giggled and gave an obedient spin.

"I think you're good to go."

Kelsey wrapped her arms around his neck. "Tanks you."

"You're welcome, squirt." He held her close as he stood up. "Let's go get your bear."

"Fuzzy, yes!"

Steve started down the stairs with Kelsey in his arms. The sight of them together tugged at Terri's heart. What a shame that someone so naturally good with kids didn't have room in his heart for another child.

****

Sean prowled the Department of Human Services waiting area like a tiger in a cage. The jitters were back— not as bad as Saturday, but close. At least he had a reason for feeling that way this morning. Lack of sleep and the uncertainty of this meeting. Ella's quiet sobs had pulled him from his own disturbed sleep countless times during the night. But at least she hadn't pushed him away. Hopefully her acceptance of him in their bed last night meant she might be willing to forgive him. He shook his head. *If I mess this up, I can kiss that good-bye.*

He'd slipped from the apartment before Ella was awake this morning. She'd be angry that he'd chosen to come alone, but he wanted it to be a surprise when he brought Kelsey home. He planned to beg to accomplish that, and if begging failed, he intended to threaten legal action. With exactly fifty-eight cents in his pocket, Sean hoped Cindy Wilson wasn't smart enough to know how empty that threat would be. Sean's mind went back to yesterday's impromptu stakeout. There was always plan C. He really hoped humble did the trick.

The sound of brisk footsteps on the tile floor alerted him to Ms. Wilson's approach. She came forward to meet him. Her expression was neutral, but she stretched out her hand in greeting.

"Mr. Anderson. How may I help you this morning?"

Sean blinked. *How can she...humble, remember humble.* "I've come to pick up my daughter."

The woman crossed her arms and leaned against the wall in the empty hallway. "Really?"

Her cool question drove humble from his mind and boosted him straight to belligerent. "Yes, really. My wife is an emotional wreck. Neither of us has slept in two days. You had no right to come into our home and take Kelsey away from us."

"The laws of the state would disagree with you on that. Kelsey was removed for her own good and protection."

"Who are you to say what's *good* for my child? She's never spent a single night away from us. How can this be good for her?" Sean raked his fingers through his hair and tried for calm. "Look, I know the house was a mess when you were there, but Ella has spent all weekend cleaning. I know the argument sounded bad, but it was a onetime thing. We've been under a lot of stress since we moved here. Work's been slow, but it's picking up a little…"

"And the drugs?"

Sean jammed his hands in his pockets and leaned into the social worker's personal space, teeth bared in an innocent smile. "What drugs? The cops searched the whole apartment. They didn't find any drugs."

Cindy answered with her own smile and a shake of her head. "We both know you just got lucky."

Sean took a single step back. "I want my daughter. If you don't have her home by the end of the day, I'll be looking for a lawyer tomorrow." He waved to encompass the building. "I'll take you and this whole department to court. I have a right—"

Cindy took a step away from the wall and held up a hand to interrupt Sean's tirade. "You don't have any rights here, Mr. Anderson, but you do have opportunities. You have the opportunity to get drug and anger management counseling. You have the opportunity to enroll in some parenting courses. You and your wife have the opportunity to take advantage of services that will help you provide a better home for Kelsey where health, nutrition, and medical issues are concerned.

"We're not the *bad guys*, Mr. Anderson. We're here to help your whole family if you'll allow it."

"We don't need your help. We need our daughter."

Ms. Wilson took a deep breath. "Allow me to rephrase. Let's exchange the word *opportunity* with *requirement.* Now that action has been taken to remove Kelsey from your home, there are a series of *requirements* you and your wife will need to meet to get her back.

"Your threats of legal action don't impress or intimidate me. I've heard it all before and we're still here." She motioned down the hall. "Now, if you'd like to follow me back to my office, I have some forms and information sheets to get you started on the road to getting Kelsey back."

Sean pounded his fist into his other hand. "I want my daughter."

"I'm afraid you're going to have to prove that to me. You know where my office is." The social worker turned her back on Sean.

"I'm not jumping through anyone's hoops to get back what's mine."

Cindy continued up the hall. "Suit yourself, Mr. Anderson." The office door closed quietly behind her.

Sean watched her go, anger and despair fighting a vicious battle in his stomach. He leaned his head against the cool wall. *What am I going to tell Ella?*

****

Steve parked in Terri's driveway at exactly ten in the morning. The insurance adjuster had not yet arrived, so Terri left Steve to visit with the guys while she took the opportunity to run next door to Tiny Tikes for a quick check-in with her employees.

Kelsey held her hand tightly for the first few minutes, completely silent through all the explanations and introductions. Kelsey's eyes strayed to the various playgroups gathered in tempting clusters around the room.

"Kelsey, do you remember what I told you about going to school to play?" Terri asked.

Kelsey nodded, eyes glued to the group of little

girls playing dress up a few feet away.

"This is school."

"Weally?"

"Would you like to stay here and play while I go next door and see about the house?"

Kelsey's confidence fled at the prospect of being left behind. "Telwy play, too?"

"I think I have a few minutes. What do you want to play?"

The youngster didn't hesitate. She pointed at the little girls dressed in plastic high heels and rhinestone studded crowns. "Pwincess."

Terri allowed Kelsey to lead her to the play group and slowly lowered herself to the carpeted floor before introducing Kelsey to the other little girls. "Kelsey, this is Susie, Brinkley, and Maddie. Ladies, may we play dress up with you?" The other girls crowded around the new arrivals. Kelsey took a defensive position between them and Terri.

"Caweful. Telwy has a booboo."

Terri laughed and the next few minutes were spent in careful examination of her colorfully bruised toes. She finally waved them back to their play and used her cane to drag the box of costumes closer. Together she and Kelsey rummaged through until they both found glitter-encrusted crowns and ribbon bedecked wands. Kelsey completed her costume with a gauzy purple skirt and yellow heels. Fuzzy lay forgotten and abandoned in Terri's lap.

Terri was sitting in the floor, wearing her crown, holding a golden scepter and a teddy bear, completely involved in her newly appointed role of queen mother when Steve entered the center a few minutes later. She blushed hotly and whipped the crown off her head when Steve executed a perfect bow before her. "Your Highness, we await your presence at yon royal castle."

"Very funny." She accepted his hand and struggled to her feet. "Kelsey, I have to go next door for a while. Do you want to stay here and play?"

"Telwy be back?"

"In a little while."

"'K, bye."

Terri smiled at the easy dismissal. She dropped her royal finery in the box and allowed Steve to draw her free hand through the bend of his arm. They dodged around two little boys engaged in a sword fight with foam weapons.

"This is my first time in here. It seems like a happy place."

Terri turned to look around the room. Pride for what she'd built filled her heart. "We try to keep it that way. We have our share of tears, especially first thing in the morning. Mondays are usually the worst since the kids have spent all weekend at home. Some of them never quite get over that little bit of separation anxiety. As much fun as we try to make it, it's not home." She caught the eye of one of her employees and waved a silent good-bye, nodding her head in Kelsey's direction. They stepped from the air-conditioned center into the last dregs of summer humidity.

She blew her bangs out of her face as they walked across the yard. "Isn't there some universal rule about September being the beginning of fall? It's an oven out here."

Steve kept his hand under Terri's elbow as she navigated the three steps of her porch. "I don't think this part of Oklahoma got that memo."

After meeting with her insurance adjuster, Terri

spent the early afternoon directing the movement of her furniture. Like Benton, the adjuster had given her the good news/bad news routine. Her living room furniture was mostly ruined. There were a lot of wooden parts that had been exposed to the three-inch water for much too long. On the other side of that news, she had more than enough insurance to cover just about anything she needed to have done.

Since most of the furniture in her living room and study would need to be discarded, Terri had no reason to rent a storage unit. The ruined items were stacked in the garage to await the construction dumpster. Everything she thought might be salvageable simply went into one of the bedrooms. The electronics: TV, computer, and stereo system followed suit.

Terri spent most of the day in her study with the five built-in bookcases that held her beloved collection of books. Shelves covered the length of one wall, stretching from the floor to the ceiling, stacked with books that had been friend, companion, and entertainment, some from childhood. Terri had an e-reader she enjoyed using. But her Kindle would never replace the feel of a book in her hand or the memories of long days curled up in a quiet place with no noise except the soft rustle of turning pages.

She surveyed the upper shelves in gratitude, running her fingers over familiar titles before allowing herself to face the swollen, waterlogged volumes on the lowest shelves. The pages had soaked up water like a sponge.

Terri pulled the first of the ruined books from the shelf. Her eyes stung and her hand hesitated before dropping the dripping mess in the trash. When her phone rang she almost welcomed the intrusion.

"Hello."

"Terri, it's Pam. I am so sorry about your house. It's my day off. Is there anything I can do to help?"

Terri turned her back on the bookcases. "No, not really. I appreciate the offer though. The insurance guy just left. Benton, Mitch, and Steve are here. I'm sort of just directing traffic."

"Yeah, I heard about your toes, too. Bless your heart. Are you sure you don't need me to come over there?"

Terri paced the length of the room, her feet made a soggy noise on the wet carpet. Her eyes went back to the pile of books on the floor. Her response came in a single choked word. "No…"

"Oh, honey, what's wrong?"

"My books," she sniffed. "Some of them are ruined…"

"Not your mom's picture albums?"

"No, thank God. Those are on the upper shelves, but everything on the bottom is pretty much trash." She paused, rummaging in her desk for pen and paper to list titles she would need to try to replace.

"Terri…"

"I'm sorry, Pam. I'm just so frazzled right now. Can I call you back later this evening?"

"Sure. Call me sooner if there's anything you need me to do."

"Thanks, I will." Terri clicked off the phone and began to make a list. Her insurance would be replacing more than furniture and walls.

She called out to Steve as he walked past the door. He backtracked to join her in the study. He took in her tearful eyes and reached up to brush her cheek. "Toes hurting?"

"Not my toes. My heart." She motioned to the pile of saturated books. "They're all ruined."

He put his arm around her shoulder and gave her a small hug. "What do you need me to do?"

Terri took a deep breath. "I need boxes, lots of boxes."

"I can do that," he said. "I'll go see what I can find just as soon as I finish helping Benton move the fridge."

"Thanks," Terri answered softly and went back to her sorting.

Steve left soon after that to complete her errand. He came back with boxes, tape, labels, and since it was way past lunchtime, chocolate milkshakes. He didn't have to work too hard to convince her to join him on the porch for a break.

"Looks like you're quite a bookworm." He sat beside her on the porch steps.

Terri smiled. "I always have been. Being an only child can be a little lonely at times. I learned early on that a good book is a great companion."

"Yet you'd never heard of me before Pam found me last spring. I'm crushed."

"Well, I have to admit, I've never been a big reader of non-fiction. But," she hastened to assure him, "I've read them since, and at the risk of adding to that tremendous male ego of yours, I enjoyed them very much."

"Well, now that I've pulled a compliment out of you, I have something I need to discuss with you."

"The 'ulterior motive' you mentioned earlier?"

He nodded. "I want to write a story about you."

"Do what?"

Steve slurped the remains of his shake. "You heard

me. Well, not entirely about you but about the whole foster care thing."

"I'm listening."

"I've been praying about the direction for my next book. I've done stories about the work God can perform in the lives of drug addicts and alcoholics. I've told my own story now that I have my family back together. I want my next story to be from another angle. I want to visit the side that holds things together while God is working those miracles." He peeled away the damp napkin wrapped around his cup, wiped his mouth, and tossed cup and all into the large trash can beside the porch.

"I'd appreciate it if you could introduce me to your social worker. Let me go with you when you take Kelsey for visitation with her parents. I want to write a story that gives some hope to people who have allowed their children to fall into the system. Help them see the dedicated, loving people taking care of their kids while they work to get their lives back in order.

"You know as well as I do that accepting Christ into your heart doesn't solve all the problems we bring on ourselves. There are people out there who have given their lives to Christ, but whose kids remain in the system until, or if, they can prove themselves to a human judge."

Steve paused for a second, his lips compressed into a grim line. "It's not always a pretty picture. My daughters certainly didn't have a good experience, and even though Lee Anne did eventually end up with a family that cared for her, she saw a lot of negative things along the way. There are a lot of sides to tell. I think you and Kelsey would be great examples of how the system is *supposed* to work." He shrugged. "The idea is still a little vague and hard to explain. Does it sound like something you'd be comfortable helping me with?"

Terri sat quietly for a few moments before she answered. "Can I have a few days to pray about it? I'm so new at this. I need to get a handle on my feelings before I can give you an answer."

"Sure." He stood up from the porch steps. "Take all the time you need. I figure I've got you guys up close and personal for a few weeks. If nothing else, my natural charm is bound to wear you down eventually."

"Oh, you think?"

"Absolutely." Steve reached down to pull her to her feet, and she stumbled against him. His arms went around her to keep her steady and their eyes locked.

Terri swallowed hard as her heart thudded in her chest and heat flooded her face. The stress of the last few days and the attraction to him she was trying to ignore formed an uneasy mix, a complication she didn't have the time or energy to deal with right now. She forced her eyes away and took a step back.

"You don't know your own strength."

Steve took a step back as well. "Sorry. I didn't mean to pull quite that hard." He cleared his throat and nodded toward the house. "How much longer 'til you're done? We still have shopping to do."

More than a little flustered, Terri groped for her cane, anxious to put some more distance between them. "Now that the boxes are here, not too much longer. I'll pack and you can put that unexpected strength of yours to good use hauling the boxes to the bedrooms. We'll be finished in no time."

Terri got back to work, but she had to force herself

to concentrate on the job at hand. Her thoughts kept replaying that moment on the porch when such unexpectedly strong arms held her so securely. A girl could get used to feeling sheltered like that.

****

Steve worked quietly and struggled with his own thoughts. Terri had fit so comfortably against him. Almost as if she'd been made to occupy that spot just under his chin. It had been too long since he'd held a woman in his arms. He liked it...liked Terri.

He carried boxes on autopilot, his mind working to fit Terri back into the niche of friendship where she'd always resided.

Their hands brushed when he took the last box. The hair on his arms stood up, and his mouth went a little dry as he looked into her sparkling blue eyes. Who knew?

10

Six PM found Terri limping through the aisles of a crowded store. Kelsey rode, Steve pushed a loaded shopping cart, and Terri shopped. The experience carried none of its usual appeal. She was running on empty. This morning's pancakes were long gone and the afternoon milkshake nothing but a fond memory.

They filled WIC vouchers in the grocery department, lingering to pick up the various other food items necessary for the health and happiness of a twenty-first century three-year-old. Juice boxes, hotdogs, pudding and Jell-O cups, animal crackers and "cwispies." They followed the grocery department with a stop in toddler's clothing. Their cart held several new outfits for Kelsey along with a couple of pairs of shoes. Steve tossed a few more selections on top of those Terri picked out and shushed her when she objected.

"Consider it her consultation fee," he said.

"I haven't agreed to help you yet."

Steve winked at Kelsey as he plucked a large stuffed dog off the end cap of a clothing shelf. "It's only a matter of time." He handed the dog to the delighted toddler and left Terri standing in the aisle, hands on her hips, as he turned the basket toward the next department on their list.

Kelsey had been patient, but as the minutes turned into an hour she was getting hungry, tired, and whiny.

Terri brushed a hand through the toddler's hair and tried to distract her with conversation. "What did you have for lunch today?"

Kelsey wrinkled her nose in thought. "Soup and fishies."

Terri laughed, her own stomach growling at the mention of the simple food. "Yum. If you can be patient for just a few more minutes, we'll stop for pizza on the way home."

The mention of pizza pacified Kelsey for an additional fifteen minutes. They'd finally made it to the toy department to fulfill the promise of coloring books and crayons. Terri browsed the selection while Steve tried to entertain the three-year-old.

"What an adorable little girl."

Terri turned to find an elderly woman standing next to their cart. She carried a small basket filled with bread, bacon, and a few cans of vegetables.

She grinned as Terri turned. "I'm sorry. I know we teach our little ones not to talk to strangers these days, but I never could resist a pretty face."

The stranger turned her attention to the shelves of storybooks positioned next to the crayons. She picked one out and dropped it in her basket. "I have a new great-grandbaby," she told them with obvious pride. "You can't get them started on books early enough in my opinion."

She looked back at Kelsey with a smile and brushed the toddler's cheek with wrinkled fingers. "You're a beauty, sweetheart. I hope your mommy and daddy realize how blessed they are."

"She's...we're..." Terri began to object.

Steve put his arm around Terri's waist with a smile and pulled her snuggly to his side. "Thanks, we do." He held Terri close until they were alone in the aisle. There was a wide grin on his face when he released her. "Sometimes you just have to go with it."

Terri punched his shoulder. "Idiot."

"Telwy, I hungwy."

Terri tossed two coloring books and a drawing tablet into the basket and grabbed a big box of crayons. "I know, baby. We're done."

She turned, Steve turned, and his tennis shoe came down on her bandaged toes. Terri had no control over the tears that sprang to her eyes and overflowed on to her cheeks.

Steve grabbed Terri's shoulders. "Sweetheart, I'm so sorry."

Terri couldn't speak. It took all of her self-control not to cry out loud as she hobbled up the aisle, looking for a place to sit. She spotted a bench in front of one of the store's dressing rooms. Her knuckles were white on the cane as she sank gratefully down and rested her forehead on her hands. *Oh, Jesus, make it stop.*

Steve crouched in front of her. "Terri, I'm sorry. What do you need me to do?"

"Not your fault," she whispered. "Just let me sit here for a bit."

"Good idea. I'll take Kelsey, and we'll go check out. I'll call your cell phone once we have everything loaded. We'll meet you out front."

"Sounds like a plan."

She watched them go, dug her bottle of water out of her bag, and fished out a bottle of pain pills as well. Her hands continued to shake as she emptied two of the pills into her palm and swallowed them without a thought beyond hoping they were the fast-acting kind. Terri was still sitting there twenty minutes later when her phone rang. Steve's number flashed on the small display screen. "Hi."

"I'm right out front," he said. "Do you need us to come in and get you?"

"Nope, I'm good. I'll be right out."

Terri stood up and wavered for just a second before she found her balance. Her head was a little foggy, but her toes didn't hurt anymore.

****

Steve stood by the car as Terri limped out of the store. "Are you OK?"

"Never been better."

Steve helped Terri settle into her seat and hurried around to his side of the car. He buckled himself in and turned to face her. "Are we still going for pizza?"

She shrugged, her eyes at half-mast. "Whatever you guys want."

"Terri?"

"What?"

Steve searched her face for a few seconds, watching her struggle to keep her eyes open. "Terri did you take pain pills?"

"Oh yeah, and they're *real* good."

"On an empty stomach? I'll just bet they are. How many did you take?"

Terri took a deep breath and allowed her head to rest against the seat back. "Two," she whispered, losing the battle with her droopy eyelids.

Steve shook his head and put the car in gear. "Great," he mumbled, glancing at Kelsey in the rearview mirror. "Terri doesn't feel good, squirt. We need to take her home. I'll fix you some dinner when we get there, OK?"

Kelsey leaned forward and looked at Terri as she slept. "Poow Telwy."

"Yeah, poor Terri."

Steve parked his car in the garage thirty minutes later. His weary breath filled the silence. Kelsey slept in her car seat, head pillowed on her new stuffed dog—christened Sara—and Terri snored softly in the seat beside him. "Two sleeping females," he grumbled. He came around to Terri's door and reached in to unbuckle her. "Terri, we're home."

Her eyes never even fluttered. "That's nice." She made no effort to move.

Steve sighed in resignation. He maneuvered Terri out of the car and picked her up, fumbled briefly with the door, and carried her through the kitchen and into the living room. He stopped in front of the sofa and was about to lay her down when Terri reached out in her sleep, looped her arms around his neck, and snuggled her head against his shoulder. Her warm breath tickled his neck. Steve leaned his head against hers drawing in the fragrance of her shampoo and perfume.

He shifted her slightly, looking down at her face in the shadowed room. His eyes came to rest on her mouth, warm and inviting, and just inches from his. His decision was swift, the temptation impossible to resist. He angled his head slightly and captured her mouth with his in a gentle kiss.

Terri's lips parted beneath his in a small sigh as she kissed him back.

11

Terri's eyes snapped open. She forced a hand between them and pushed him back.

"What are you doing?" she sputtered.

"Satisfying my curiosity," he answered. "I've been thinking about kissing you most of the afternoon." He smiled. "I really liked it."

"Put me down."

He grinned smugly and swiped her lips with his a second time. "You liked it, too."

"Put. Me. Down."

Steve took the final step to the sofa and released her into midair.

Terri yelped as she fell into the cushions and bounced. She grabbed the back of the sofa and glared.

"You liked it, too," he repeated. He whistled as he walked out the door to the garage.

Terri lay back on the couch while the echoes of Steve's satisfied whistling rebounded off the walls around her. She pressed her fingers lightly to her lips and closed her eyes.

"Wow."

****

Sean navigated the cul-de-sac and eased his truck to a stop just beyond the house he'd watched so intently the day before. Early evening shadows shaded the property, but he still had plenty of light. No vehicles occupied the drive. No lights lit the windows. Exactly what he wanted. When the blonde and her bearded companion arrived home, they would turn into their drive well in advance of his position. They would have no reason to pay him any attention, but he had a clear view. He needed something...anything to take back to Ella.

His early morning return from speaking to Cindy Wilson had not been well received. Not only had his wife been upset that he'd gone on his own, the details of the failed interview had brought on another wave of tears and accusations. Sean's ears still rang with Ella's heartbreak, words and weeping that not even a day at work and the noise of hammering and power tools could drown out.

Ella had every right to be upset. He'd screwed up. He still resented the idea of a government agency telling him what he *would* do to get his own child back. Classes for this, classes for that, regulated once-a-week visitation. Seriously? They would do none of those things, except the visits, until he could explore other options. His wife disagreed, but Sean was still the man in his home.

Returning tonight with news that he'd seen Kelsey, that she was all right, and that he knew where she was and how to get her, would go a long way to restoring peace to his family. If his plan meant taking his Friday paycheck, packing everything they owned in the truck, snatching their child, and leaving Garfield in the dust, so be it. Sean hadn't asked for anyone's help or interference. Starving, after three days, for a glimpse of his daughter, he waited.

The excited barking of the dogs alerted Sean to an

approaching vehicle. He scooted down in the seat and watched while the black truck swung into the drive. The bearded man climbed out of the cab, pulled out a briefcase, and stooped to pet the dogs dancing around his feet. No Kelsey.

Man and dogs looked up at the same time. Sean squinted at the approaching car. *Kelsey has to be inside.* He watched as the blonde parked her car. The man opened her car door, extended a hand to help her out, and pulled her in for a quick hug. They walked to the front door sharing smiles and laughter that Sean couldn't hear. *Wait a minute.* He stared at the back door of the car, willing one of them to open it, to turn back to the car and help his daughter into the house. Neither of them paid Sean the least bit of attention as they entered their home, alone.

Sean pounded the steering wheel in renewed frustration. Where was Kelsey?

****

Thursday morning Terri walked through a construction zone that bore little resemblance to the home she loved. In just four days the floors had been stripped to bare concrete and the sheetrock and insulation removed to expose two feet of naked two-by-fours along all of the interior walls. It reminded her of a Victorian granny holding up her petticoats to cross a muddy street, her bony ankles, always so carefully concealed, briefly visible to the world. The image almost made her laugh. The front door opened and she turned as Benton took the steps down into the living room.

"Checking our progress?" His voice echoed in the

empty room.

Terri shook her head and laid her hand on the nearest wall. "I'm feeling a little bit like Ezekiel."

Benton raised an eyebrow. "What?"

Terri grinned at his confusion. "Son of man, can these bones live?"

Benton sat down on the living room steps, and Terri followed suit, lowering herself to the step leading to the kitchen.

"It's not as bad as it looks," he said. "I promise, when we get done, you won't be able to tell the old from the new."

"I'll take your word for that. But now that you've had a few days to get into it, I wondered if you could give me a better time estimate."

He studied her expression from across the room. "Something wrong?"

Terri gave a smirk and allowed her gaze to roam the room.

"Something besides the house," Benton clarified.

Terri considered the man sitting on the other side of the room. He was the husband of one of her best friends and thirty years her senior. If she confided in him, it wouldn't be the first time he'd acted as surrogate father since her parents' accident. But she also recognized the real friendship developing between him and Steve. She wouldn't put him in a difficult position because her own feelings were a jumbled mess. She waved his question away. "Not really. Just normal female impatience."

Benton shrugged. "It'll be a few more days before we can get the whole crew in here. Once that happens, three or four weeks should see it completed."

Four weeks? "Great," she said with forced

cheerfulness as she used the cane to lever herself to her feet. "That's much better than I expected." She took the step up to the kitchen. "I'll let you move on to your real job for the day. I need to get back over to the center."

Terri made her way back to Tiny Tikes in the big house next door. The prediction of three or four weeks didn't sound like such a bad estimate. Surely she could stay out of Steve's way for a month. Avoiding him for the last couple of days hadn't been too difficult. Her fingers traveled of their own accord to lips where the memory of Steve's stolen kiss still lingered...when she allowed herself to think about it. She struggled *not* to think about it because she was very afraid of the direction her heart wanted to take.

"Father, it can't be this way. You know my heart." She indulged in a muttered argument with God as she walked. "I'm willing to do the best I can to follow Your direction for my life, but it can't be this way." Terri stopped on the path and looked up toward heaven. "I want a family, a husband and children of my own. We both know I won't be happy with someone who doesn't want those things as much as I do. I like Steve, I really do, but he's content with what You've given him. There's nothing wrong with that. As much as I love Iris, Sam, and Bobbie, I want...*need* more." She opened the door to her business and allowed herself to be swallowed up by the voices of other people's children. Kelsey ran to her with outstretched arms.

"Telwy."

Terri stooped down to receive the energetic hug. "Are you having fun?"

"I play."

"Well that's a good thing." Terri pulled away from the toddler. She fought a losing battle to keep the tears of confusion from her eyes.

Kelsey put both hands on Terri's cheeks and cocked her little head to one side. "Telwy foot huwt?"

"No, baby, not my foot." She brushed a kiss across the child's forehead. "Better go finish your playtime."

"'K, love you."

Terri stood up. The child's innocent words tore at the crack in her heart. "I love you, too, baby," she whispered.

God, please don't ask me to give up my dreams.

She closed herself in her office, took a seat behind her desk, and prepared to give herself a good scolding. She had overreacted and participated in way too many pity parties over the last few days. So she'd had a few bumps and bruises, a little bit of opposition. It happens. *Grow up!*

And she needed to stop avoiding Steve. She was living in his house, for goodness sake. He'd offered a gracious solution to her problem and she was repaying him with rudeness. *You're attracted to him. You need to deal with it like an adult, not like a fourth grader hiding from a bully on the playground.* It was a single kiss, nothing more than that. She was doing a belly flop into the deep end of the pool to think one kiss meant the beginning of a romance, much less some dream-stealing future."

Terri sat back and a satisfied breath filled her office. Her little pep talks always did the trick. But she could not escape one fact. *I've been very rude to Steve.* She needed to do something to make up for that.

"I'll cook dinner for everyone tonight. It's been a long time since I had anyone to prepare a meal for. I'll stop by the store on my way home and pick up groceries. Lasagna, salad, and garlic bread should make everyone feel better. Throw in homemade brownies for dessert, and I should just about be forgiven." Pity party over and a plan for the evening in place, she began to sort through some of the mess left from the week before.

Most of the paperwork on her desk dealt with her projected expansion plans. A blueprint for the two rooms she wanted to add, cost projections, and decorating ideas. Tiny Tikes had grown into the most sought-after day care facility in Garfield, with a waiting list far greater than even her expansion plans would allow her to accommodate. She pushed it all to one side with a frown. *One project at a time.*

Terri shuffled more papers and uncovered her open Bible. She looked down at the passage of Scripture she'd read and highlighted before the dreaded home inspection just last Friday. Jeremiah 29:11. Her fingers brushed across the words, her voice a whisper as she read the verse aloud. "For I know the thoughts that I think toward you, saith the Lord, thoughts of peace, and not of evil, to give you an expected end." *I'm such a goof.*

"Father, how quickly we forget. Thanks for the reminder. Help me remember that every day is a step toward the future You have for me. Everything is in Your hands and that's the safest place for me to leave it. I love You so much."

Loved, scolded, and reminded of God's goodness, Terri returned to work with her smile firmly back in place.

****

Iris looked up from her bed as Sam stepped into

her bedroom, closed the door behind her, and leaned against it.

"Are you ready?"

Iris shut her American History book and rolled from her stomach to her side. "Ready for what?"

"To put operation SETH in motion."

"Seth?"

"Dad and Terri. Steve Evans and Terri Hayes. S-E-T-H. It's their initials."

Iris sat up and rubbed her hands together. "Ooh, I like it. What diabolical scheme do you have in mind?"

"Well, Terri is slaving away in the kitchen as we speak, but I think you really *have* to go to the library tonight, right after dinner. Don't you have an important test coming up?"

Iris grinned, patting her closed textbook. "Oh yeah, my history test. So good of you to remind me. Really lucky for you the library is open late on Thursday nights."

"Give me some credit, little sister. I did my research before I came up with tonight's scheme."

"And you're taking off to…?"

"I'm going to get ice cream with my new friend from school and her little girl. At the mention of ice cream, Kelsey is going to want to go, too. I will *graciously* agree to allow her to tag along, *just this once*. I'll volunteer to drop you off on my way with promises of an early return due to it being a school night for all."

"You're devious."

Sam shrugged. "I think Dad and Terri need a couple of hours to themselves. I'm not sure what happened, but Terri's been holed up in the basement for three days. If she's ready to come up for air, they probably need a little privacy to make it clean air."

"Agreed." Both girls jumped with a guilty start at the firm knock on the door.

"Smile pretty," Sam hissed.

Their father stood framed in the doorway, Bobbie riding on his shoulders, little hands clutched in her grandpa's hair. "Terri sent me to tell you guys to wash up for dinner."

Samantha smiled at her dad. "Great." She retrieved her daughter. "We're starving. Iris has been drooling ever since Terri mentioned the word lasagna."

Steve glanced back up the hall and lifted his face to sniff the air. "Yeah, it smells pretty happy in there. Anyway, five-minute warning." He turned back toward the family room.

Sam cleared her throat and frowned at Iris.

Iris hopped off the bed, scrambling to follow her father up the hall. "Dad, about tonight…"

****

Terri wiped the final drops of water from the countertop while Steve loaded the last of their dinner dishes into the dishwasher. She hummed a little tune as she worked. Dinner had received high praise by all and cleaning the kitchen with Steve felt so homey. If only…

Don't go there, she told herself and fell back on her mantra. *Just friends, just friends, just friends…*

"Thanks for the help." Terri folded the towel and laid it next to the sink. "I really should have discussed my plans with the girls ahead of time. We could have done this on a night when they didn't have someplace else to be." She reached for the pan of double-fudge brownies she'd made for dessert and sliced them into squares.

Steve shrugged. "Don't worry about it. I'm not sure what their plans are most evenings. It is a bit odd for all three of them, make that four since they took Kelsey with them, to leave at once. I guess it's a teenage thing. Staying home with the adults isn't a big priority." He poured them both a tall glass of cold milk to go with the warm brownies. "Dinner was terrific, though. Thanks." He carried both of the glasses to the table. "And missing dessert? That's entirely their loss."

"You're very welcome. I like to cook, and much of the time it's just me. I end up heating something from a can and eating over the sink."

Steve sent her a skeptical look.

"OK, the part about the sink was an exaggeration." Terri laughed and started to the table with the brownies. "But a can of soup..." She stopped with an indrawn breath and half-hopped, half-limped the rest of the way to the table. Dropping the plates, she yanked out one of the chairs, sat down, and began to massage her good foot. "Foot cramp," she explained through clenched teeth.

Steve sat down next to her and pulled her foot into his lap, running his knuckles up her instep.

Terri let her head fall back as the cramping muscles relaxed. "Thanks, it's been doing that off and on all afternoon. Broken toes on one foot, cramping toes on the other. I..." Her leg stiffened as a second cramp gripped her muscles. "Owww..."

Steve watched in apparent fascination as her toes curled downward of their own accord.

"Rub!" she said desperately.

He dug his fingers into her foot and worked to find the correct pressure points to relieve the cramp.

Terri finally sighed in relief. "OK, it's over, I think. I don't understand what's making it do that."

"It might have something to do with the fact that you're missing your boot, and I haven't seen you use your cane all evening. You're walking too much with all your weight on your good foot. It's called muscle strain."

"Thanks, Dr. Evans. I'll keep that in mind." She eased her foot to the floor and wiggled her toes experimentally. "That seems to have done the trick."

Steve patted his knee. "Let me rub the other one."

"You aren't getting your hands on my broken foot."

"It's your toes that are broken, not your foot. I promise to stay clear of any injuries."

Terri looked up at him from under her lashes, slowly raising her injured foot to his knee. She sighed in blissful satisfaction as his fingers began to knead gently. She reached for her brownie. "This is my idea of heaven on earth," she said. "A warm brownie, a cold glass of milk, and a foot massage. I planned tonight's dinner as a way to say thank you. Now really, thanks!"

Steve patted her foot. "Now that I've softened you up. Have you given any thought to what we discussed Monday?"

Terri's mind went immediately to a stolen kiss in a darkened room. "What...?" she asked in confusion, feeling her face warm with the memory.

"My book idea," Steve reminded her.

"Oh yeah, that."

"Yeah, that," he said, laughing at her obvious discomfort.

"Um, yes, actually I have. I don't see a problem with it. I'm having my first visitation with Kelsey and her parents tomorrow afternoon. I'll talk to Cindy and let you know what she has to say."

"Thanks. Remember to let her know that I'm not there to make personal judgments on anything or anyone. Nothing I write could be used to identify anyone later."

"I know she'll take all of that into consideration. If it's OK with you, I'll give her your cell phone number. She can call you directly with any issues that might need to be addressed."

Terri changed the subject. "I saw Benton this morning when he came by to make his morning check at the house. He told me Kelsey and I won't be in your hair for all that long. Just three or four weeks once they can devote their entire attention to my project."

"Terri, you guys aren't in my hair. I've barely seen you since Monday."

Terri finished the last of her dessert and stood to clear away the plates. "You're just saying that because I made dinner." She gave him a small smile. "Seriously? We both know Kelsey and I have disrupted your routine unmercifully. I'd apologize for that, but as sure as I do, something else will go wrong tomorrow, and I'll end up apologizing again." She stretched. "Speaking of routines, I think I'm going to take advantage of Kelsey's absence and curl up with my new novel. I bought the new John Grisham release the other day. I haven't even had time to open the cover." She reached for the door to the basement apartment.

"Terri."

She looked at him over her shoulder, watching his approach with nervous anticipation. When he reached her, he took her hand in one of his. With the other hand, he nudged her chin up so they were eye to eye.

When he spoke his voice was a husky drawl.

"About that *other* thing we talked about on Monday."

Terri stared into eyes so blue she could swim in them. This time she knew she was not mistaking his meaning. "Yeah…" She swallowed in an effort to clear her dry throat. "Yes."

He drew her hand up, and brushed a light kiss across her knuckles. "When was the last time you had a pain pill?"

"Yesterday," she whispered. "I'm feeling much better."

"Good, cause this time I wanted you completely conscious." He pulled her close and lowered his mouth to hers in a light, tender kiss. He held the kiss just long enough to make her want more, then held her in his arms, his chin resting lightly on her head.

Her heart tumbled long before Steve broke the brief embrace.

"'Night, Terri."

"'Night," she repeated and escaped through the basement door. She closed it behind her and leaned against it with legs barely willing to support her weight. Terri knew she had just stumbled head over heels into the deepest end of the pool.

12

"Mama, Daddy. Mama, Daddy. Mama, Daddy…"

Terri parked her car in front of the Department of Human Services office Friday afternoon and turned to look in the backseat. The straps of the car seat barely restrained the eager toddler who'd been repeating the "Mama, Daddy" litany for the full twenty-five mile drive from the day care center.

"Excited, baby?"

"Yes!"

Terri smiled. The happiness on the three-year-old's face chased away some of the nervousness she felt at this first meeting with Kelsey's parents. She unbuckled Kelsey and helped her climb out of the car seat. Stooping down, she brushed the wrinkles from the new pink dress and straightened the matching bow holding the majority of Kelsey's blonde curls up and away from her face. Taking the child's chin in her hand, she tilted her face back and forth and checked for smudges.

"I pwetty?"

"You're beautiful," Terri assured her. She stood up and reached for Kelsey's hand. "Hold my hand. Let's go see your mama and daddy."

"Yea!" Kelsey exclaimed, pulling Terri across the parking lot.

Terri hobbled, double time, in an effort to keep up, laughing all the way. The door opened at their approach to reveal Cindy standing just inside, pen sticking from behind her ear, day planner folded against her chest, awaiting their arrival. The caseworker did a double take at the sight of the boot and cane, but she kept her questions to herself. She crouched down to greet Kelsey.

"Well, Miss Kelsey, aren't you looking lovely today?"

"Telwy made me pwetty."

"Yes, she did." Cindy stood up and faced Terri. "What happened to you?"

Terri waved the question away. "Let's not get into the week I've had." She looked down at the bouncing three-year-old. "Kelsey's anxious to see her parents. We can talk about my problems later."

"Good enough." Cindy reached a hand down to Kelsey. "I think I have someone waiting to see you."

"Mama and Daddy?"

"You got it. Come with me." Cindy led the way down the hall to the visitation playroom. She opened the playroom door, and two young people scrambled quickly to their feet, holding their arms out to the toddler. Kelsey broke away and ran to grab both of them in an enthusiastic hug.

The female of the pair didn't try to hide the tears in her coffee brown eyes. She scooped up the child and held her close. "Oh, baby, I've missed you so much."

Kelsey rained kisses across her mother's face. She buried her hands in her mother's curly red hair and finished with a loud kiss on her mouth. She reached out to her father. "Daddy."

The man, no more than a boy really, held the child silently as Cindy and Terri joined them.

"Sean and Ella Anderson, this is Terri Hayes. She's

been looking after Kelsey."

Terri nodded at the young couple, puzzled by the frown the young man sent her way. She understood that it was an awkward situation for all, but she read more to his narrow-eyed stare than *awkward*. She opened her mouth, but what she started to say got lost beneath Kelsey's nonstop chattering.

"Telwy made me pwetty," the three-year-old said as she reached for her mother.

Ella held the child close once again while Terri and Cindy took unobtrusive positions on one of the sofas positioned around the perimeter of the room. "Oh, baby, you're prettier than pretty." She sat back down, cuddling Kelsey in her lap. "Tell me what you've been doing this week."

"Went shoppin' and had some fwies. Thewe wewe scawy dogs."

"Where did you see scary dogs?"

"Don't know. Went to chuwch." She scooted off her mother's lap and ran over to where Terri sat. "Suwpwise."

"Oh yeah." Terri pulled a folded piece of paper out of her bag and passed it to Kelsey.

"Tanks you," she said with a brilliant smile before retreating back to her parents. She held out the paper. "I make suwpwise fow you."

Sean spread the paper out on the knee of his faded blue jeans and traced his fingers over the scribbled drawing. His eyes held a suspicious hint of moisture when he looked up. "It's beautiful, baby."

"I colow fow you at chuwch."

"It's David and Goliath," Terri told them. "She colored it at church the other night and wanted to bring it to you."

Sean reached out a hand to cup his daughter's chin. "Thanks, sweetheart. We'll hang it in the living room when we get home."

Cindy stood up and addressed the young parents. "We're going to give you guys some privacy. We'll be sitting right outside the door if you need anything." Cindy motioned for Terri to follow her out of the room. The door closed behind them, and they seated themselves on a hard wooden bench next to the door.

Terri expelled a long breath. "Wow, that was…weird," she admitted.

Cindy gave a small shrug. "The first couple of visits are always the hardest, and I'll be honest with you, it's not going to be pretty when their hour is up and we have to separate them again. Sorry. It's a three steps forward, two steps back sort of thing at first."

Terri smiled in rueful acceptance. "Just one more thing to add to my week."

Cindy straightened her jacket and sat back on the bench, subjecting Terri to a silent study. "You and Kelsey seem to be getting along all right."

"Kelsey has been the single bright spot in my life this week."

"I know you had to move out of your house." Cindy nodded at the boot. "But it looks as if that was only the beginning."

Terri leaned back, blew her bangs out of her face, and recounted her week, start to finish. She motioned to her foot as the tale drew to a close. "Three broken toes. I've installed nightlights in every room of that confounded cave."

"You've had an interesting week. Doesn't seem to have upset Kelsey in the least."

"She takes it all in stride," Terri agreed. "We've

had a few moments that were less than stellar, but like I said earlier, she's been the highlight of my week. Having her to focus my attention on is the only thing keeping me sane."

"I'm glad to hear it. I know you were worried about keeping her through the move. Trust me. No one would hold it against you, with all you've got going on, if you needed to take a step back—"

"Don't even think about it," Terri interrupted. "If Kelsey were my own child, we'd just have to muddle through as best we could until things leveled out. Unless there's a reason on your end why our arrangement shouldn't continue as-is, I'd like to leave things the way they are."

"Hey, like I told you the other night. I'm good with the situation. I'm a great believer in the 'if it's not broke, don't fix it' rule. She's happy. You're happy. That's what we like to see."

Excited giggles filtered through the closed doors and drew Terri's attention to the playroom. "Tell me about her parents. They look awfully young."

"They are awfully young. They're both just twenty. Kelsey is three. I'll leave the math to you. The mother, Ella, is heartbroken at the situation. She's anxious to do whatever needs to be done to get her daughter back. Dad's a different story.

"Ella told me they were both juniors in high school when they found out they were having a baby. They ran across the border to get married, and then both dropped out of school. Pretty much a disaster looking for a place to happen. According to them, they were actually beating the odds until Dad's job went away a few months ago. They moved up here looking for work. They've both assured me that their fight the other night was an anomaly, something that's never happened before and won't happen again." Cindy shook her head, her expression pensive.

"Mom seems to understand that now that we're involved, they have to work the system and get some help in order to get their daughter back. Dad thinks we need to mind our own business, let them have her back now, and they'll get on with their lives.

"He showed up here bright and early Monday morning, making demands, threatening to get a lawyer. What gives us the right to take their child…?"

"Surely he understands…" Terri began.

"He doesn't understand anything right now. He's angry, his pride is wounded, and he's not allowing Ella to participate in any of the programs I've recommended." Cindy shook her head, dislodging the pen tucked behind her ear. She caught it as it slipped into her lap. "He'll come around. He doesn't have a choice. It's early days yet. This is the denial portion of the program. He doesn't have a problem. He doesn't need help. And if he doesn't cooperate, we'll pack up and go home. I've seen it all before. Today's visit will go a long way to reinforce the fact that he has to play by my rules now."

"But to put Kelsey in the middle of that—"

"I don't think he means to, and Kelsey staying with you will keep that from happening. I've been doing this for a long time now. My gut feeling? They're good kids. They sincerely love their daughter and each other." Cindy patted Terri's knee. "You wait and see. This is going to be one of our success stories."

Terri looked at the closed door to the playroom. *Father, heal this family.* "I hope so. Speaking of stories, I brought you something." Terri pulled a book out of her bag and handed it to the social worker.

"Oh, I've read this." Cindy turned the book over and tapped Steve's picture with a bright red nail. "He's a wonderful writer, and in the absence of my husband I feel free to say...*yummy.*"

"Yummy?"

"Look at that face, girlfriend, I think yummy fits."

Terri shook her head and cleared her throat. "He's my temporary landlord."

"Get out."

Terri sighed, trying hard to ignore the hero worship that sprang into Cindy's eyes. "He wanted me to ask you for a favor."

Cindy laid the book on the bench between them. "You're living with one of my favorite new authors. A drop dead gorgeous example of the male of the species, and he needs a favor from me? Terri, you need help."

"*Not* living with, borrowing an apartment from." Terri laughed. "There's a major difference."

"Semantics girl, semantics. What does he want from me? If it's not illegal or immoral, it's already his."

"You've read his books?"

"Both of them and eagerly awaiting the third," Cindy answered.

"How would you feel about helping him with the fourth?"

"Don't yank my chain."

Terri's laughter echoed through the empty hallway. "I'm being perfectly serious. He wants to do a story about people whose kids are in foster care. I'm the only foster parent he knows, and since he has Kelsey and me underfoot for a few weeks, I guess he thought we'd make good research subjects." Terri picked the book up and removed the business card she'd tucked into the middle. "Look, I don't know all the details about what he has in mind, but here's his cell phone number. He'd appreciate it if you'd think it over and give him a call."

Cindy allowed the business card to rest in her open hand. "This is Steve Evans's personal cell phone number? Steve Evans, the writer?"

Terri leaned her head back against the wall. "Cindy, you're the one who needs help. Just call him, OK? Let him explain what he has in mind."

Cindy tucked the card into the pocket of her day planner. "He'll hear from me before the day is over. In the meantime we need to set up a time to do a quick inspection of the apartment." She tapped her pen on the crowded pages. "I've got an hour free Tuesday morning at ten. Can you break free from the day care?"

Terri consulted her memory and didn't find anything that conflicted with the proposed time. "That works."

Cindy wrote down the address that Terri provided, zipped up the planner, and stood. "Time's up. Now comes the hard part."

She pushed open the door, and Terri followed her back into the playroom, almost bumping into her when Cindy stopped short in front of her.

Kelsey knelt next to her mother's leg. "God bwess Mama and Daddy, and God bwess Fuzzy and Telwy. Amen!" She jumped up. "Those my pwayews."

Terri watched in amazement as both of Kelsey's parents wiped tears from their eyes. She cleared her throat. "We say prayers every night before she goes to bed. I hope you don't mind."

Ella gave Terri a watery smile. "That's the same bedtime prayer my mama taught me. Sean and I met each other in Sunday school when we were just little guys. Neither of us has been inside a church in a long time though." She twisted one of Kelsey's blonde curls around her finger. "We've messed up in more ways than one. Thank you for taking such good care of our baby." She boosted Kelsey into her lap. "Mama and Daddy have to go home now."

Kelsey's mouth puckered. "Kelsey come?"

"Oh, baby, you're breaking my heart. I wish you could—"

Sean stooped down next to his wife and daughter. "Soon, sweetheart, real soon. Daddy promises."

"Just hush." Ella glared at him, her voice and her eyes equally layered in ice. "How can you promise her soon when you won't cooperate with anything we're being told we need to do?"

"She's our daughter—"

"Yes she is, but we don't deserve to have her right now." Ella rose with Kelsey still clutched in her arms and approached Terri with tears streaming down her face. "Thank you," she repeated. "For taking care of my baby." She untangled the toddler's arms from her neck and passed her off to Terri. The younger woman wrapped her arms around both of them. "Be good, Kelsey. I'll see you next week." A quick kiss to her daughter's cheek and she bolted from the room without another word.

Sean looked from his daughter to his departing wife. "Ellie…" he called and followed her out.

Their sudden departure took everyone by surprise. Several seconds passed before Kelsey realized they weren't coming back. "Mama, Daddy…" she howled, struggling in Terri's arms.

"Stay here with her," Cindy instructed. "I'll see if I

can catch them."

Cindy left the room, and Terri sat down, trying to comfort the distraught child. "Shh, Kelsey, it's gonna be all right."

"*Mama!*"

Terri did what came naturally to her. She held tight, rocked gently, and prayed hard. "We need Your peace, Father. Shh, Kelsey, shh. Father, have Your way. Help them help themselves. Show Kelsey's parents how to reclaim their family. Show me how to help..." Gradually Kelsey calmed down. With her face buried in Terri's shirt, the sobs became hiccups, subsided into sniffles, and finally vanished completely as she gave into the nap that she'd missed earlier in the afternoon.

Cindy came back into the room as the toddler nodded off. "I couldn't catch them. It's probably for the best if they stew on this over the weekend. It's a chance for the realities of the situation to settle in Dad's mind. I'll call them first thing Monday morning." Cindy focused her attention on Kelsey. "Poor baby. Is she OK?"

Terri smoothed the damp hair from Kelsey's forehead and kissed her before answering. "It's past her nap time." She looked into Cindy's face, tears filling her own eyes." I know you see this all the time, but how can people do it?"

"Do what?"

"How can people take the most precious gift God could ever give them and not cherish it?"

Cindy took a deep breath. "I ask myself that question every single day. I've yet to get a good answer." She stepped over and rubbed a hand over the back of the sleeping child. "But I'll tell you this. When I say my prayers at night, I thank God He made people like you who are willing to take a stand for these kids."

****

Sean drove them home while Ella stared out the window of his beat-up truck. Her little car, a well-used Honda, was nicer but hadn't had any gas in it in weeks. Tears lined both of their faces. Kelsey's final, hysterical "*Mama*" occupied the bench seat between them, a presence so real he could touch it. How had they reached this place? Sean put a hand on his wife's shoulder, and she yanked away from his touch.

"Don't," she hissed.

"Ella."

"Is this your plan, Sean? Is this how you're going to get our daughter back?"

Still reluctant to share his aborted snatch-and-run plans, and his obviously mistaken information as to Kelsey's whereabouts, Sean fell back on plan B. "I'm gonna get a lawyer…"

Ella continued to stare out the window. "We couldn't afford to buy new shoes for our baby. How are we going to pay for a lawyer?" She shook her head and used the tail of her shirt to wipe her eyes. It was a wasted effort. New tears replaced the old ones as she continued. "I love you, Sean. I got in your face, and I probably shouldn't have." She turned in the seat, allowing him to see the tears on her face and the heartbreak in her eyes. "Look, I'm sorry for the things I said the other day, but I'm not going to live like this. I'm not going to live without my daughter.

"You do whatever you think you need to do." Ella sat back, her arms crossed and her expression hard. "Hang on to your pride and your attitude and refuse the help that's being offered to us. I'll be calling Ms. Wilson on Monday and enrolling in whatever class she says I need to take to get Kelsey back."

"Ella, we're already good parents. We don't need someone to tell us how to raise our child."

"Listen to me." Her tone left little room for him to argue. "We've allowed our lives to fall too far. I'm willing to take my full share of the blame." She narrowed her eyes at him. "But you brought drugs into our home. Never again. I'm getting Kelsey back with or without your cooperation." The breath she released shuddered. "With or without you."

Sean's hands shook despite his grip on the wheel. He glanced at his wife. "Is that a threat, Ella?"

Ella turned her back on him. "Take it however you like."

13

Terri's traditional Saturday morning sleep-in time ended with loud banging on the door that separated the apartment from the kitchen upstairs. A glance at her alarm clock verified it was just past eight. She tossed back the covers and stumbled up the stairs. Thoughts of bodily harm and mayhem helped shred the fog in her brain and gave purpose to her climb. *Someone's about to die.* Iris's voice joined the pounding when Terri was halfway to the door. Terri yanked the door open and glared at the pajama-clad twelve-year-old.

"Morning," Iris said with a bright smile. At Terri's wordless stare she continued. "How's your foot feeling this morning?"

Terri swallowed, indulging in a mental count to five before she answered. "You woke me up, on the one morning of the week when I get to sleep in, to ask me about my foot?"

"Well, yeah."

Terri completed the silent count to ten.

"How is it?"

"Peachy," Terri answered and started to close the door.

"Great. Y'all need to get dressed. We're leaving in an hour."

"What?" Terri asked, more confused than she wanted to admit.

"Terri...the zoo today? Dad's taking us all to the zoo. We're leaving in an hour. Everyone's almost ready. Didn't he tell you?"

"I didn't see your father yesterday." *Made a concerted effort* not *to see him,* she added silently.

"Telwy, what's the zoo?"

Terri turned and looked at the toddler who'd crept, unnoticed, up the stairs behind her. Terri closed her eyes, knowing her plans for a quiet day at home had just been revised. "It's a place where they keep all sorts of animals."

Kelsey's eyes grew big. "Elapants?"

"Yes."

"Yea!" The toddler backed down the stairs on all fours. "I get shoes."

"Umm hum." She turned back to the door and looked at Iris. "I'm going to get you for this."

****

The door snapped shut in Iris's face. *Well, at least she didn't say no.* Iris untangled the fingers she'd crossed behind her back. Somehow it didn't work like it had in the past. Iris and Sam had told their share of lies to cover up their secret life before they were reunited with their father. But now that Iris had become a Christian, her conscience tugged at her heart over the lie. *Is it a real lie if it's not mean?* Iris took a deep breath and allowed the continued ache in her chest to answer her question. She looked up. *Sorry, but it's for a good cause.* Her conscience only slightly appeased, she headed for Sam's room. Operation SETH was in play for the day.

Sam waited in her room with her door cracked

open. She pulled Iris inside.

"Well?"

"Get dressed. Mission accomplished."

"Ohh, you're good. Ready for phase two?"

"On my way. Think good thoughts."

Iris stepped out into the hall and knocked on her father's bedroom door. "Dad, are you about ready?" When she received no response, she knocked louder. "Dad!"

The door eased open just a crack, and Iris found herself looking up into a single blue eye. "Iris, what is it?" Steve's voice was husky with sleep.

"You're not up and ready to go?"

"Go? Go where?"

Iris put on her most indulgent expression. "Dad! The zoo?" At her father's blank gaze, Iris continued. "You, me, Sam, and Terri...We're taking the babies to the zoo today. We talked about it a few days ago." This time Iris soothed her conscience with the truth. They had discussed a visit to the zoo. Months ago, not days, but her story this morning wasn't a *complete* lie. "Terri's up. She's getting Kelsey ready to go. Sam's dressing Bobbie. It'll take us an hour to get there so we need to leave at nine."

Steve scrubbed at his face. "Right. I must have gotten the dates confused. I'll be down in a bit." He closed the door between them.

She turned to see Samantha looking at her through a small opening in her own door. Iris gave her older sister a big smile and thumbs up before she went back downstairs to decide what to wear to the zoo.

****

White cumulus clouds played tag with the sun on a field of baby blue. The scents of roasted peanuts, cotton candy, and funnel cakes wrestled the air for superiority. It turned out to be a perfect day and the perfect place for an outdoor activity. Everywhere Terri and the family turned, they encountered bright fall colors and amusing animal shenanigans. The zoo walkways, already decorated for Halloween, boasted smiling jack-o-lanterns. Gauzy bats, ghosts, and witches swung from the trees. Terri gave serious consideration about bringing Kelsey back for some safe trick or treating in a few weeks. But that was for later. Right now she was doing her best to boost the toddler's courage for a more immediate adventure.

From their place outside the tropical parakeet habitat, they watched as Sam and Iris purchased small containers of clear nectar from a vendor and backed through the gate. Once free of the netting the girls lifted the liquid high into the air. The three-year-old watched with guarded interest as the birds zipped by in blurs of green, red, and blue. They swarmed around the older girls, hopping from head, to arm, to fist for the opportunity to drink from the small cups.

"See, Kelsey. They won't hurt you," Terri assured her. The birds perched on Iris and Samantha like animated Christmas ornaments. "We'll buy some food if you want to give it a try."

Kelsey, her confidence already cresting from her earlier experiences of feeding the baby goats in the petting zoo and a short ride on the back of an aging elephant, nodded her head in excitement. She crawled from the rented stroller. "I feed biwds."

Terri laughed and fished quarters out of the pocket of her jeans. She handed her camera over to

Steve who was minding Bobbie in a second stroller. "Get some pictures for me, OK?"

"Sure thing."

Terri took Kelsey by the hand and went to purchase a couple of containers of food. Kelsey didn't hesitate. They pushed open the door to the exhibit and were immediately surrounded by the small, multicolored birds. She held the tiny plastic cup straight up and was quickly rewarded when two of the birds landed on her outstretched arm. Her mouth formed into a delighted "O" as the birds drank daintily from the cup in her hand. Kelsey reached out a tentative finger and stroked the brilliant feathers. "Telwy, watch."

"I'm watching, baby."

"So pwetty."

Samantha and Iris, cups empty, came back their way. "How's this for awesome?" Iris asked.

"Pwetty biwds."

The older girls laughed in agreement on their way to the gated entry.

"Where are you guys going?" Terri asked.

"Back out to get more food." Iris answered.

"I'm empty too," Terri told them. "Stay here with Kelsey, and I'll go out and send your dad in for his turn."

Iris and Sam turned to where their father aimed a camera in their direction from the other side of the fence. All three girls were quick to strike a humorous pose for the camera's benefit. Steve was laughing at the picture on the computerized display when Terri joined him and retrieved her camera. "Your turn. Take plenty of food."

Steve bought as many of the small cups as he

could carry and pushed his way through the gate to join the three girls. Amid a flurry of wings, he passed containers to Iris and Sam. He handed the final cup to Kelsey, picked her up, and held her high over his head.

Terri watched the obvious affection between the two and the crack in her heart widened. Her camera captured the moment as Kelsey wrapped her arms around Steve's neck and delivered a loud, sticky kiss to his cheek. Kelsey leaned back to look up at the sky, her small arms stretched wide as Steve swung her around in a wide circle. Her delighted squeal filled the air. "Yea!"

Oh, Father, if only he could see what I see... Terri smothered the small moment of sadness under a cheerful smile as everyone came back to the strollers.

Iris dug the zoo map out of her pocket and checked their location. "The new primate enclosure is just over the hill."

"Lead on," Steve said. He settled Kelsey back in her seat. "Want to go see some monkeys, squirt?"

"Yes, monkeys!" Kelsey bounced up and down with excitement.

Terri shook her head. "You are a monkey." She leaned on the stroller as they walked up the hill, allowing it to take some of the weight off her foot.

Steve motioned to the boot. "How're you holding up?"

"Fine. This thing has so much padding it's like walking on a cloud."

Kelsey pointed. "Monkeys!"

Terri and Steve increased their pace a bit. "I won't have to worry about getting her to sleep tonight," Terri said.

"I'm glad she's having a good time." Steve looked

over the awning of the stroller he pushed. Bobbie was sound asleep. "This one's missing the whole day."

Terri patted her camera. "We have plenty of pictures. I got some wonderful shots of her and Sam on the elephant."

"Do you think they remember anything at this age?"

"Who knows? We'll remember for them." She laughed as the older girls raced to the entrance. Large cages housing spider monkeys, marmosets, and other small breeds fronted the double doors and were filled with swinging, chattering primates. "They're having as much fun as Kelsey."

"Yeah, I'm glad Iris got me up this morning." He paused, his eyes on his daughters. "At the risk of sounding sentimental, these are the sorts of things I've always regretted not sharing with them. I still don't remember agreeing to come today, but it's been a lot of fun."

Terri drew her eyebrows together and frowned. "Iris got you up? She told me this was your idea."

Steve brushed aside her confusion, backing through the door with the stroller. "I don't guess it really matters who thought of it as long as everyone is having a good time."

Terri's questions melted away as they pushed through the doors. The monkeys had always been her favorite, too. The older girls quickly vanished, swallowed up by the crowd, leaving Terri and Steve to wheel the strollers around the glass-fronted exhibits at their own pace. They finally came to a large enclosure housing a mother gorilla and her young offspring. They took seats on the bench, allowing Terri to rest her foot for a few minutes. Kelsey took the opportunity to get out of the stroller for a closer look. She climbed up on the padded ledge in front of the glass.

"Telwy, a baby."

"Just like you."

The young gorilla dislodged itself from its mother's arms and crept over to the glass to get a better look at the human child. Kelsey laughed in delight and flattened herself against the glass. Terri watched in amazement as the small ape struck a similar pose. She laughed aloud as the *children* pressed against the glass, hand to hand and face to face, and exchanged loud kisses through the glass. Terri fumbled for her camera and flashes went off all around her as everyone hurried to take advantage of their hilarious pose.

"Monkey see, monkey do." Steve scooped Kelsey up and onto his shoulders. "Come on, squirt. Lots more to see."

Streetlights burned in the darkness by the time they got home. The zoo had been followed by dinner, before the two-car caravan finally wound its way back through the residential streets. The babies were worn out after the full day on the go. Even the naps Bobbie had taken in her stroller throughout the day had not sustained her into the evening. Terri opened the front door and stood aside as Sam and Steve each carried a sleeping child into the house.

"Night guys," Sam whispered. "I'm just going to put her straight to bed. It won't hurt her to sleep in her clothes for one night."

"Ditto," Terri agreed, reaching for Kelsey. "She can have a bath in the morning."

"Get the light and the door." Steve nodded at the cane in Terri's hand. "I'll take her down for you. I know your foot must hurt after being on it all day.

You'll break more than your toes trying to carry her down the stairs using that thing."

Terri smiled her agreement and turned toward the kitchen.

"Dad, Terri," Iris called. When the adults turned around, the flash of a camera blinded them briefly.

Two adult voices intertwined. "What?"

"One final picture from our day." Iris smiled mischievously. "I had a great time."

Steve sent an indulgent smile toward his younger daughter. "Imp. Go get ready for bed."

Steve followed Terri down the stairs and into Kelsey's room. Terri pulled back the covers and removed the toddler's shoes. The three-year-old didn't twitch a muscle when Steve laid her down, tucked her in, and kissed her forehead. "'Night, squirt," he whispered. Terri followed with a kiss of her own, and after switching on the nightlight allowed herself to be led from the room.

Steve continued to hold Terri's hand, pulling her up the first four steps with him. He turned to face her, leaning his hands on the wall, imprisoning her shoulders between them. "Thanks."

Terri's heart beat so hard she was sure he could probably hear it. She refused to meet his eyes, afraid of what he might see in hers, even in the dim light of the stairwell. "For what?"

"For sharing the day with us. I really enjoyed it. We make a good team."

"Oh, well. We enjoyed it, too."

"Terri?"

"What?" Her question came out as a whisper.

"Look at me."

She raised her head and his lips met hers in a

gentle kiss. The lightest of touches, just lips, nothing else. When he broke the contact, he looked at her intently. "I really enjoy doing that."

Terri couldn't deny him the truth. "Me, too."

"Then why are you avoiding me? Why do you hide down here for days every time I kiss you?"

Terri lowered her gaze. "I'm not avoiding you."

Steve forced her eyes back to his with a firm but gentle hand under her chin. "Terri...?"

Terri shook her chin loose and leaned her forehead against his chest. "You jumble my feelings," she admitted. "I'm having a hard time sorting everything out right now."

"Have I done something to hurt your feelings?"

"Steve, no. I'm sorry if I've made you feel that way." She swallowed around the lump in her throat. "I'm just not sure where God is taking me right now. It scares me a little. I need a plan. I work better with a plan. When I don't have one, I'm confused." Terri closed her mouth on her own babbling.

Steve smiled in the muted light. "I confuse you?"

She would have sworn he sounded more than a little satisfied at the thought. "A little."

Steve took the cane and tossed it back down the stairs. He took a half step closer and captured her mouth with his a second time. A little firmer, a lot warmer. Terri's breath grew shallow and her hands came up to rest flat against his chest. Steve took the kiss deeper for just a second before he stepped away.

"I'm not confused, Terri." The brush of his whispered words caressed her ear.

She didn't answer him. He'd stolen her voice along with the kiss.

His satisfied grin flashed once more before he

leaned down for a final kiss. "Sit with me at church tomorrow?"

All she could do was nod as he left, closing the door between them.

14

Steve loped barefoot down the stairs and into the kitchen a little later than normal on Monday morning. Fresh coffee waited on the counter along with his favorite cup. He filled the oversized mug, held it in both hands, and took a deep breath of the strong brew he preferred. The rich fragrance seeped into his system and began the job of kick-starting his morning. The first chapter of his new book had weighed heavy on his mind most of the day yesterday, and after everyone else went to bed, he'd retreated to his office for a few hours of writing.

Cradling his cup, Steve leaned back against the kitchen cabinets and savored the morning with a deep feeling of contentment. His house was quiet, his coffee hot, and his heart overflowed with gratitude for all God continued to bless him with.

The home he shared with his daughters was a huge step up from the home he'd worked so hard to provide for his wife, Lee Anne, and their babies so many years ago. He'd been blessed back then as well, but too blind to see it and too foolish to appreciate it. Steve shook those thoughts aside. Dwelling on the past accomplished nothing, but an occasional trip back kept him thankful. Thankful God had forgiven him for the mistakes and sins of his youth, thankful for his successful writing career, and thankful for a second chance with his daughters. He didn't feel worthy of any of the blessings God had poured into his life, but much like the rich brown brew in the coffeemaker, he didn't intend to waste a single drop.

He took his first cautious sip of the steaming coffee, commemorating his late night with a wide yawn and a sigh of satisfaction for a productive evening. With a sincere prayer of gratitude for caffeine, he poured the rest of the pot into an insulated carafe and headed back to his private domain. His office bore little resemblance to the bedroom it was originally designed to be. Bookcases lined the walls on two sides. Books tended to overflow onto the floor, especially when he was researching a project. An oversized desk dominated the space and faced large windows that looked out on to the street. No shades, no blinds, no curtains. Nothing to obstruct his view. He'd positioned the desk so he could look out those windows while he worked. The world at large, even this small-town slice of it, provided Steve with a constant source of inspiration.

This morning he stood in front of his windows, watching the almost autumn wind ruffle the leaves of the trees that lined the neighborhood street. Fall colors had appeared overnight, jeweled tones of emerald, ruby, topaz, and amber flickered in the sunlight. A quiet morning in a quiet town. He knew some would label Garfield boring, especially after the excitement and constant action of Chicago. But Steve's whole body hummed with anticipation this morning. His life had no room for boring when he stood on the brink of a new project.

He picked up the stack of papers from his desk and re-read what he'd printed off before calling it a night. He'd been praying for a couple of months about direction for his next book. Terri's decision to become a foster parent had sparked an idea to life. Having her and Kelsey here had fanned that spark into a flame.

Foster parents, social workers, the dreaded *system*. There were so many negative meanings attached to those things. There didn't need to be. A shudder crept up his spine. His imagination conjured images of his hands around the neck of the perverted piece of scum that had been foster parent to his daughters for a short time. He forced a deep breath.

Even the negative experience his daughters had endured didn't mean the system was flawed. People were people everywhere you went and in every situation you could encounter. Steve hoped to use Terri and Kelsey as living proof that the system worked. He knew he couldn't tell this story without touching on the bad and the ugly, but he intended to focus on the good.

Terri's social worker had called him late Friday afternoon. He knew she planned to visit with Terri in the morning. Steve planned to be gone. He wanted this first meeting on neutral ground. They'd arranged to have lunch later this week. Steve hoped he'd be allowed to accompany Terri on Friday when she took Kelsey to visit her parents. The memory of his conversation with Cindy Wilson made him grin. He appreciated the people who read and enjoyed his books; it's why he wrote them. But he didn't think he'd ever get used to being viewed as a *celebrity*. The undisguised hero worship in her voice had humbled him greatly.

Steve Evans, ex drug addict, homeless vagrant, and displaced family man had come a long way with God's help. *Far enough?*

Terri's presence in his house had awakened more in him than an idea for his next story. Steve had been surprised to discover a longing to share his life with someone. Not just anyone. Terri's laughter haunted his thoughts. Something subtle and peachy floated in the air when she left the room. The days seemed to drag from morning until dinner time when he could see her again. The feel of her lips beneath his, her smile, the way her body fit against his, like the missing piece of a long neglected puzzle. He leaned back in his chair and raised his eyes toward the ceiling. "Morning, Father. Thank You for the morning and a fruitful work session last night. I feel like I have Your direction for the story now, but I need Your direction in something else today. You gave me everything I could need for happiness a long time ago, and I threw it away. But You have proved to me You are a God of forgiveness and second chances. You gave my daughters back to me when I had almost given up hope. Now I feel hope of a different kind stirring in my heart. I think I love her, Father. I think I could have another shot at all the things I missed. God show me Your will and speak to Terri's heart as well. I know she's looking to You for her future. If it's Your will for me to be a part of that future then please show both of us."

Steve picked up his Bible and allowed it to fall open to the portion of Scripture God had for him today. He read Lamentations 3:21-25. *This I recall to my mind, therefore have I hope. It is of the Lord's mercies that we are not consumed, because his compassions fail not. They are new every morning: great is thy faithfulness. The Lord is my portion, saith my soul; therefore will I hope in him. The Lord is good unto them that wait for him, to the soul that seeketh him.* Steve laid his Bible down and wiped moisture from his eyes. "Thanks, Father. I'd call that a green light." He picked up the phone book and found the number to Garfield's only florist.

****

Terri looked up at the knock. Wesley, the retired gentlemen who ran deliveries for the florist, stood in the doorway of her office. She could barely see him, obscured as he was by the huge vase of roses he held.

"Is that you behind there, Wesley?" she teased.

"Yes, ma'am. Got a delivery for ya."

"Those are beautiful. You can leave them in here. I'll make sure they get into the proper hands."

Wesley came into the room, placed the vase on her desk, and handed her a card. "Those would be your hands, Ms. Hayes."

Terri looked from the card, to the flowers, and back to Wesley. "For me?"

"That's what they said at the store." He touched the bill of his tattered baseball cap in a polite farewell. "Enjoy."

Terri laid the card on her desk and sat back in her chair, relishing the suspense along with the surprise. *For me?* Her fingers stroked the velvety texture of soft orange petals edged with red. They were perfect, a good two days from being completely open. They would grace her desk for days. A smile bloomed on her face. How long had it been since she'd received flowers? *Way too long.* She prolonged the anticipation by burying her nose in the bouquet and inhaling their fragrance. She smiled. An odd disappointment layered over the excitement. They smelled like roses. Something their color should smell like orange sherbet.

152

Her heart hammered as she reached for the envelope and slid out the card. *Steve*. A blush heated her face behind a wide smile. She should have known. That man was just full of surprises.

As the two singles in a group of married friends, she and Steve had been paired up a lot in the past few months. She'd warned her friends to forget any matchmaking attempts. As far as she could tell, they'd complied with her instructions. Terri saw no point in lying to herself. There was no getting away from the fact that she liked Steve. In the privacy of her office and thoughts, she could even admit to some feelings that went beyond "like." He was a handsome, successful, *Christian* man, and a good kisser.

Her thoughts re-wound to the moment on the stairs Saturday night. Make that a terrific kisser. Steve hit four out of the top five traits on her husband wish list. It was stubborn number five that caused her such confusion and made her head hesitate when her heart wanted to rush forward at warp speed. The fifth?

I want a man who wants to have children with me.

The chime on her computer interrupted her thoughts. She looked at the mail icon on the desktop and clicked it open.

Terri, I told the florist to send you something that would bring the sunshine into your office. I hope they made a good choice. I haven't forgotten that I owe you a pizza. Would you go out to dinner with me on Thursday night? Steve.

P.S. Yes, I'm asking you on a date.

She typed her response.

Steve, the roses are beautiful. Orange tipped in red. It's almost like they're on fire. I'd say I have enough sunshine in here to last me a month.

Terri's fingers paused on the keyboard. Her mind went back to the scene in Steve's backyard. The moment when all of her mild fantasies had narrowed to one sharp reality. Steve already had all the family he wanted. She bowed her head. "Father, forgive me if I'm being selfish, or ungrateful, or just plain stubborn in wanting my own way. I don't mean to be. I've waited so long for You to bring the right someone into my life. I look at the dreams I have for myself and I hesitate. Help me remember that if this is Your will for me, I won't give up anything."

A half-remembered Bible verse flooded her heart. Something about not worrying about tomorrow because today's troubles are enough to worry about— *Isn't that the truth?*—and God always knew what you needed. She grabbed up her Bible and thumbed through the concordance until she found what she was looking for. Matthew 6:31-34.

Her whispered voice filled her empty office. "Therefore take no thought, saying What shall we eat? Or, What shall we drink? Or, Wherewithal shall we be clothed? (For after all these things do the Gentiles seek:) for your heavenly Father knoweth that ye have need of all these things. But seek ye first the kingdom of God, and His righteousness; and all these things shall be added unto you. Take therefore no thought for the morrow: for the morrow shall take thought for the things of itself. Sufficient unto the day is the evil thereof."

Thanks Father, I needed that. She finished her message. *I'd love to have dinner with you on Thursday night. Terri.*

She took a deep breath and hit the send button.

****

Terri and her friends sat at Callie's dining room table after Bible study Monday evening. There had been much debate about Jephthah's rash vow to offer the first thing to come out his door as a burnt offering in exchange for victory in the battle against the children of Ammon. Some people held the opinion that her father's careless words had cost this young girl her life. Other's felt she'd simply lived out her normal life span as an unmarried virgin. Two weeks of study had yielded no conclusive evidence over the fate of Jephthah's daughter. Their study group was as divided as the armies of Ammon and Israel. They'd finally agreed to disagree and move on to a new subject for next week.

Terri sat back and brushed her hair from her forehead. "No wonder you wanted me here tonight. I know that Jephthah's daughter was my choice, but I'm glad we're moving on to a new topic next week."

Callie laid fresh dessert plates and a stack of plastic containers on the table next to an uncut amaretto-almond cheesecake. "I was just giving you a hard time about playing hooky last week. I like it when we disagree. It makes me think."

"Is that why you suggested Job's wife as our new topic?" Pam asked with a grimace. "I'm cringing already."

"I just think she gets a bad rap," Callie insisted. "All we ever hear about is how she told Job to curse God and die." She looked around the table at her friends. "I've never heard anyone discuss the fact that it was also her children that died and her lifestyle that was reduced to nothing. In addition, let's not forget the fact that she cared for a sick husband for an undetermined amount of time. Is there anyone here that doesn't know how tedious that can be?"

Terri raised her hand with a grin.

"Smarty," Karla laughed. "You know, Callie, you're right. I never thought about it like that. She definitely held out through the whole better-and-worse, sickness-and-health, richer-and-poorer thing. She gave him, what, ten more children when it was all said and done. Any woman who survives twenty pregnancies without killing the man responsible deserves to be remembered for more than a single negative statement. Just nursing a sick man is enough for me to think about saying a lot of stuff I wouldn't really mean."

"Amen, sister," Pam agreed and then amended hastily. "Not Harrison. When he's sick, he closes himself in the spare bedroom, and I have to check on him occasionally to make sure he's still alive. But, Alan? If he got a splinter, he thought he was dying. Moaning and crying, convinced the whole world had turned against him. Always *too tired* to do anything I wanted to do. Even now, the kids say all he does is sit around." She shrugged. "That was then; this is now."

"How is Alan?" Callie asked.

Pam shrugged. "Jeremy and Megan came home from their summer visit with all these stories of his new girlfriend, Kate, the latest in a parade of women in and out of his life over the last few years. From all accounts this one, at least, has him attending church again."

"That's a good thing, right?" Karla asked.

"I hope so, if for no other reason than for the kids. Their relationship sounds pretty serious. If he's planning to bring a *stepmother* into their lives, I'm all for her being a Christian."

"How would you feel about that?" Callie asked. "Alan getting remarried."

"I'll send him a note of congratulations and a sympathy card to her." Pam paused. "Seriously? More power to him. I've got Harrison, and I'm happier with him on a bad day than I ever was with Alan on a good one." Pam sat back and closed her eyes. "Can we change the subject? Cheating ex-husbands are not my favorite conversational topic."

"I kissed Steve," Terri winced at the blurted admission. "I mean…well...he." She fanned her face with a napkin. "I must be losing my mind," she moaned.

"Stop right there," Callie said. She finished cutting the leftover cheesecake. Four slices went onto plates for immediate consumption. The remaining four went into containers for the men waiting at home. "Karla, go get that fresh pot of coffee out of the kitchen. I think we're going to need caffeine."

Once fresh plates and cups were in place all around, Callie motioned to Terri. "Dish it up, girlfriend. You can pick up back at the kissing part."

Terri swallowed back her embarrassment. Maybe talking out some of her confusion would help clarify what she was feeling. "It wasn't so much that I kissed him, as he kissed me. I can, however, make a reasonable claim of diminished capacity, since I was only partially conscious. At least the first time."

"Whoa, *first time?*" Karla asked.

"Explain 'partially conscious,'" Pam demanded while Callie rested her chin in her hand and studied Terri with amused blue eyes.

Terri laughed at her friends. "What part should I explain first?"

"Mine," Pam insisted, "I think we really need to understand the 'partially conscious' part of this equation."

"It was last Monday afternoon," Terri began. "We'd spent the whole day working at the house. Then we had to take Kelsey shopping. I hadn't had anything to eat most of the day and when Steve stepped on my toes—"

"Your broken toes?" Karla asked.

"Yep."

"*Ouch!*" Pam cried.

"Yeah, anyway, he stepped on my toes, and while I waited for him to get our stuff checked out and the car moved around, I took a couple of pain pills—"

"Hold up," Callie interrupted. "You, the person who can't take an aspirin without falling asleep, took *two* prescription pain pills...on an empty stomach?"

"Oh, Callie, I know I shouldn't have, but it hurt so badly. All I could think about was just getting it to stop."

Karla waved a hand in front of Callie. "Will you let the girl finish? She was in pain and she took pills." She faced Terri. "And?"

"Well, it gets a little fuzzy at that point. I guess I fell asleep in the car, and Steve had to carry me into the house, because the next thing I remember is being kissed while he had me up in his arms."

"Is he any good?" Pam asked.

Terri closed her eyes on a sigh. "Even half conscious I can testify to his ability in this area. Good enough that I kissed him right back."

Pam sat back and fanned her face. "Wow."

Karla inched her chair closer to the table. "Since you mentioned that this was the first time, are we to assume kissing Steve has become a habit?"

"I don't think I'd use the word *habit*, but there have been two other encounters that ended in kissing. And I have to tell you, the man is only getting better with practice."

"Double wow," Pam muttered.

"I think I'm being courted," Terri confirmed. "He sent me flowers at work today, and we have a date Thursday night."

"Flowers?" Callie asked. "What kind?"

"Roses. Wait," Terri said. She rummaged in her bag for her phone, "I took a picture." She brought the picture up on the small screen and passed the phone across the table.

"Those are beautiful," Callie said, passing the phone to Karla.

"The picture doesn't do them justice," Terri verified. "He said something about bringing sunshine into my office."

"Flowers and poetry? He's a goner," Callie assured her.

Terri nodded but felt the small frown gathering between her eyebrows.

Callie reached over and took her hand. "What?"

"I'm not sure I want him to be a goner," Terri admitted.

"Sweetheart, why not?" Callie asked.

"Yeah, why not?" Pam echoed. "He sounds like the answer to your prayers."

Terri threaded her fingers through her hair and stared at the table for a few seconds before answering. "That's just it. I don't know if he is." She got up to pace the room. "He's successful and funny and handsome. Plus he's a Christian. You don't find a combination like that every day. But I'm not sure I see our futures going in the same direction.

"I want a family. He's already got one. He's got his career. I've got my business. We've got three houses between us…"

"Terri, stop it," Callie said. "You're generating obstacles where there aren't any."

Terri sat back down. "I know." She played with the slice of dessert on her plate. "But this is all happening too fast, and I'm just messed up. Forget what I said about careers and houses. That's just me being silly. But the family thing's a major issue for me. I love Iris and Sam, and you guys know how I feel about Bobbie, but I want a family of my own, and I just can't see Steve starting over at that level."

"Wait a minute," Karla requested. "He loves kids. He's crazy about Bobbie, and he seems to be doing fine with Kelsey, too."

Terri sighed again. "Bobbie is his granddaughter. *Granddaughter*, guys, and Kelsey is just…a temporary blip on his radar. If it weren't for the situation with my house, he probably wouldn't have spent ten minutes with her. So neither of those situations can compare to the lifetime commitment I'd be asking him to make if we got married and started a family."

"Have you talked to him about your issues?" Callie asked.

"Not yet," Terri answered, her voice oozing sarcasm. "But it's high on my list of conversation starters for our *first* date on Thursday."

"Point taken," Callie admitted.

This time Terri reached out and took Callie's hand.

"I'm sorry. I don't mean to be snippy. I'm just so confused. My heart's telling me one thing. My head's telling me another. I've been praying about it and thinking about it, and trying *not* to think about it." Her glance took in all of her friends, finally settling on Karla. "He made his feelings on the subject of more children crystal clear at Sam's party. That's why I was sulking in the kitchen. I meant what I told you, about putting any dreams of a future with Steve behind me. But every time I turn around, he's right there." She sat back. "Will you guys help me pray? I don't think this is something I'm going to be able to work out on my own."

Callie patted her hand. "That's why we're here." She reached out to Karla who reached out to Pam. Pam closed the circle by taking Terri's other hand. "How do you want us to pray?"

"For God's will in this whole thing. If this is right, it'll work. But if it's not, I don't want our friendship divided over a failed romance. Love is precious and unfortunately falling is simple. Staying there's the hard part. I'm afraid we're going to end up hurting each other."

15

Steve parked his SUV in front of Terri's house. He had a lunch meeting with Cindy Williams today. The social worker had called to let him know she'd been delayed and to offer him the opportunity to reschedule their appointment. He was anxious to outline his project for her, and they'd agreed to a one o'clock lunch instead of the eleven o'clock time originally scheduled.

Unexpected time to kill and the knowledge that he could find two of his best friends hard at work in Terri's house were his excuses for heading in this direction. He assured himself that the possibility of seeing Terri in the middle of the day had little to do with his choices. Even if they didn't already have a date tonight, he would have seen her at dinner.

Dinner. Steve shook his head. He didn't know what had gotten into his daughters lately, but Samantha and Iris were cooking up a storm every night and insisting that Terri and Kelsey join them. Stacks of new cookbooks littered the kitchen counter, and he found a new shopping list on his desk each morning. When questioned, the girls informed him that cooking was an important skill for a woman. With their mom gone, they'd decided to teach themselves. His daughters wanted to know how to prepare more than the hamburger helper, spaghetti, and sloppy joes they'd mastered months ago when they'd been living on their own. Steve had two jobs in regard to their latest hobby: shopping for supplies and eating what they put in front of him. *Kids.*

Thoughts of his dinner date stirred something in Steve's gut and turned his hands sweaty on the steering wheel. It had been twenty years since he'd pursued a woman. His schedule for today was busy enough to keep him occupied, but maybe he should pencil in a trip to the florist. He didn't want to appear over eager, but he didn't want to look like an under achiever either. When he'd dated Lee Anne they'd both been college students with limited finances. Now...

A tapping on his car window snapped him back to reality. Mitch stood next to the car, thumbs tucked into the bib of seemingly stiff and obviously new denim overalls. Steve rolled down the window with a smirk. "Well, Farmer Brown."

"Don't go there," Mitch implored him. "I promise you, I've already heard all the jokes this week."

Steve remained silent as he dug a coin out of his console. He flipped the quarter out the car window.

Mitch watched it fall at his feet. "What are you doing?"

"I just wanted to see if you could bend over to pick that up without breaking in half."

"Ha Ha." Mitch ignored the coin and leaned into the window. "Karla was so enthused about getting me out from under her feet she went shopping for new work clothes. This is her idea of what *construction guys* wear. It wouldn't be so bad if she hadn't starched the daylights out of them. These things could stand in my closet without a hanger." Mitch shrugged. "Anyway, you OK?"

"Yeah. Why?"

"Well, you've been sitting out here in a parked car staring into space for fifteen minutes. I figured I better check on you."

"Oh," Steve looked at his watch, "I guess I've got some things on my mind. I came by to see how the house was coming along."

It was Mitch's turn to smirk. "Some*thing* on your mind or some*body*?"

"Excuse me?"

"Bud, you weren't just staring into space, you were watching the day care center like a cat watches a goldfish in a bowl. The *somebody* you have on your mind went to the store earlier for some supplies. She took Karla with her. Who knows when they'll be back."

"I came by to see you and Benton."

"You just keep telling yourself that."

"Mitch, I…" He stopped when Mitch began to whistle a warped version of a wedding march.

Steve sighed in resignation. "That obvious?"

"If we were living in a cartoon, there'd be blue birdies circling your head."

"Very funny. Is Benton here?"

"He went to Subway to get us some lunch. He should be back shortly if you want to hang around for a few minutes."

Steve took another look at his watch and calculated the distance and the lunchtime traffic he was likely to encounter. "I better not. I have an appointment in about forty-five minutes. Just let him know I stopped by."

Mitch pushed himself back from the car. "Will do." He started back to the house.

Steve rolled up the window with a grimace as the

poorly rendered wedding march filtered back into the car. He was five miles down the road before he realized he was humming the same tune.

****

Steve paused at the deli counter to order the chef salad Ms. Wilson had requested along with a loaded hoagie for himself. He filled two tall glasses with iced tea and settled at a small corner table to wait for his guest. He sipped his drink and indulged in a few minutes of people watching. The main lunch crowd had thinned out, but enough late diners remained to keep him entertained.

A young mother with two small children sat across the room, her salad largely ignored, her attention focused instead on the little boys who seemed more interested in playing than eating. Two businessmen in suits sat near the back. Their mouths boasted polite smiles that failed to reach their eyes. Their body language appeared tense. All was not going well at their table. A slender lady with dark brown hair, similar in build and coloring to Terri, sat with her back to him. Steve started in surprise when she stood to leave and turned in his direction. She was *very* pregnant. She laughed with her friend and patted her rounded belly. *Certainly not Terri.* But his errant mind pasted Terri's face on her shoulders. His fertile imagination took flight. *Hmmm...boy or girl? My eyes, Terri's nose? Curly hair or straight?* Steve shook off the image. *Get a grip, Evans.*

The chime over the door sounded. A forty-something black woman headed toward his table. He stood and held out his hand. "Ms. Wilson? Steve

Evans."

She clasped his hand with a brilliant smile. "Please, Mr. Evans, call me Cindy.

Steve smiled in return. "Only if you'll call me Steve. I'm looking forward to working with you. I work easier with friends."

Cindy took her seat. She propped her elbow on the table and put her chin in her hand. "Wow, I have a celebrity for a friend. Steve it is, but you'll have to excuse me if it takes a while for me to get used to the idea. You're the only celebrity I've ever met."

Steve laughed. "I have to admit, I'm a little intimidated at the thought of being called a celebrity," he said. "In a world obsessed with reality TV, I'm a writer who's more blessed than I deserve to be. End of story."

"Maybe so, but we're all entitled to have a personal hero or two. You'll just have to get used to it." Conversation lagged as a young waitress arranged their lunch order on the table. Cindy drizzled dressing on her salad while Steve ripped open a bag of chips.

"I have a better idea," Steve said, intent on getting back to their business. "How about if we just agree to be two friends working on a project together?" A few beats of silence greeted his suggestion. Steve watched Cindy's face transform from smiling to serious. His lunch guest straightened in her seat, crossed her arms, and met his eyes with a probing stare. He leaned back in his chair and crossed his arms. "Wow."

"Wow?" she asked.

"How do you do that? Are you even aware that you do that? Hero worship to hard professionalism in the space of a heartbeat. Talk about intimidating."

The social worker tilted her head, never breaking

eye contact. "Honey, you haven't seen *intimidating.*"

Steve caught himself wanting to squirm under her unblinking consideration.

"Why do you want to work with me, Steve?"

"I thought Terri…"

Cindy shook her head. "I know what Terri told me. But if you expect to get close to any of my kids and their families, you're going to have to convince me of your motives." She took a long drink of her tea. "I like you. I'll admit to being a fan of your work, but those things will not get you what you want. What's driving you towards this project?"

Steve considered her question for several seconds. How could he explain something that wasn't one hundred percent clear to him just yet? Thoughts and explanations were examined and discarded as he stared at the far wall. "The good, the bad, and the ugly," he finally said. "I've got experience with two of those scenarios. Terri is a likely candidate to show me the third. I think it's a story worth telling."

Cindy's expression moved to intrigued. "I'm going to assume you're putting Terri and what she's doing into the *good* category." At Steve's nod she continued, "I need you to tell me about the other two."

He took a deep breath. This wasn't ground he'd expected to cover today. "My wife was a foster child. Lee Anne's mother gave her up at the age of five because she couldn't care for her. A noble sentiment, but that abandonment scarred her on a level she never fully recovered from. Lee Anne was,"—he searched for the right word—"precocious. She had an above-average intelligence that made her restless and difficult to deal with. No one recognized those gifts until she went to college. Her nature was perceived as rebellious, so instead of being adopted and nurtured, she bounced from foster home to foster home. She was never mistreated or abused, but her experience was unproductive."

Cindy nodded. "The *bad*."

"Well, indifferent, at best." Steve took a drink and worked to keep his expression neutral as he continued. "When my wife died, my daughters went into foster care as well. The woman had been a friend of Lee Anne's, someone she thought she could trust. Helen's husband, Richard, was not so trustworthy." He drank again, surprised at how his hand shook at the memory. "He did not succeed in his attempts to molest my daughters, but he has much to answer for if our paths ever cross."

"The *ugly*," Cindy provided. She studied him across the table. "Are you going to use your story to malign my agency, Mr. Evans?"

"Of course not, but I do intend to tell the truth. Every story has two sides, and a good book tells both. I need your help to show me the good. To show me that the system works, that the good outweighs the other two options."

Cindy nibbled at her salad for a few moments, obviously weighing her decision. She picked up her glass and touched it to his. "That's a challenge I can accept. I'll have to clear it with my superiors, but I don't see them standing in your way."

Steve raised his own glass in salute. "I hoped you'd say that. I depend a great deal on God's direction for the stories I tell. I really feel Him pulling me along on this one. I think the job Terri's taken on is a valuable one. It's not just about cute little babies needing a temporary home. Some of these kids have been damaged by the lives they've led. These caregivers are warriors, and I want to tell their story."

Cindy nodded. "You're absolutely right. And it's not just the kids our foster parents are forced to do battle with. Sometimes the families of these children are more difficult than the children themselves." She looked at Steve intently. "Please don't think I'm negating Terri's effort in any way. She just happened to draw the long straw this time. Kelsey is an easy child to care for, and I have a very positive feeling about the outcome of this case. If you'd rather, I can put you in touch with people who've had much more difficult experiences."

"I appreciate that. I certainly want to speak to everyone you can recommend, but I think Terri and Kelsey will be my base story." He laughed. "They're sort of captive at my house right now. Makes for easy research."

"Yeah, I heard that story, too." Cindy looked at her watch and shoved the remains of her salad away. "Man, this has turned into *one of those days.* I'm going to have to run. I'll talk to my boss and give Kelsey's parents a call as well. I'll let you know tonight about attending visitation tomorrow. You have release forms?"

Steve nodded. "Standard fare for interviews."

"Just make sure they sign one. In the meantime I'll see what I can do about putting you into contact with other people who might be willing to work with you."

"Cindy, I'm so grateful for your help. Your name will appear in bold letters in the acknowledgement section of the book."

"Oh well, gee. That's nice, but not really necessary." Cindy shifted in her seat, her voice hesitant when she continued. "I do have one favor to ask before I leave."

"Name it."

She reached for the huge bag hanging on the back of her chair and pulled out copies of both of his published books and an ink pen. "I've read these and I loved them. I was hoping that you would autograph them for me."

Steve accepted the books and her pen, his laughter ringing through the nearly empty deli.

****

Iris trooped down the stairs of the basement apartment Thursday night, schoolbooks and iPod in hand. She stopped at the bottom of the stairs, offering a smart salute as Terri came from Kelsey's bedroom. "Reporting for babysitting duty as requested, ma'am."

Terri grinned. "Thanks, sweetheart. I appreciate you staying down here while I'm gone. I feel better about her asthma knowing you're down here and not all the way upstairs."

"Not a problem. It's more than a little cool to get paid for babysitting and not have to leave my house."

"OK, you remember what I showed you about her meds and the nebulizer?"

"Yes."

"I left my cell phone number on the table."

Iris cocked her head in Terri's direction, fished her cell phone out of her pocket, and waved it. "It's on my speed dial, has been for months. We went through all of this on Monday."

"I know, but I'm still a little new at this mommy stuff. Just let me run through my list."

"OK."

"I just tucked her in. She knows I'm going out and that you'll be here if she needs anything. I tucked Fuzzy and Sara in bed with her. She should be down for the night."

"Got it," Iris assured her.

Terri took a deep breath and picked up her bag. "How do I look?"

Iris studied Terri's pale blue dress and matching flats. "Terrific. What happened to the boot?"

"The doctor gave me permission to go without it for short periods of time as long as I keep the toes taped and use the cane. He assured me that my toes will tell me when I've over-done things." Terri ran a hand over the skirt of her dress and focused on her feet. "Iris, can I ask you a serious question?"

"Sure."

"You know this is a date, right?"

"Yeah."

"That's all right with you? Me dating your dad."

"Yeah."

"Just that simple? Yeah."

"Terri, I'm not a baby. You guys like each other. I'm cool with that. I love you both enough to want you to be happy." Iris shrugged. "If being together makes you happy then, yeah, it's just that simple."

Terri pulled Iris into a hug. "Sometimes I miss the simplicity of life at twelve."

They both looked up at the knock from the kitchen side of the door.

"Oh, let me." Iris raced back up the steps. "Yes?" she asked, opening the door just a crack, doing her best to restrain a smile at the sight of her dad in shirt and tie holding a single red rose in his hands.

"Is Terri ready?"

"Yes, but you'll need to come down and escort her up like a proper gentleman."

"Out of the way, brat," her dad said.

She opened the door wider, making room for her father to descend the stairs.

He handed Terri the rose as he took the final step down.

She sniffed at the bright red bloom. "Wow, two trips to the florist in one week. I'll bet you're Millie's new favorite person."

"I'm working on it, but I'm more concerned about being your favorite person."

"You're working on that, too," Terri admitted with a smile.

Iris came down behind her dad and held out her hand for the flower. "I'll put this in some water for you." She turned with her hands on her hips, pulling herself to her full height. "Now you kids go have a good time. Drive safe and call if you can't make your weeknight curfew."

"Yes, ma'am," Steve answered. He grabbed Terri's hand and helped her up the stairs. On the top step, he swung her around and looked down at his daughter. "Iris?"

"Yes."

He didn't say anything as he lifted Terri's chin and kissed her right on the mouth. He winked down at his grinning daughter. "I wouldn't count on that curfew thing."

The door closed behind them, and Iris grabbed for her cell phone. Sam and Bobbie were upstairs in Sam's room.

"Get down here," she yelled into the phone when

Sam answered. "I have a *major* SETH update."

****

Terri struggled to pull a sip of the thick chocolate milkshake through her straw. She shivered and lowered the cup to her lap as Steve parked the car in the drive. The streetlights revealed his eyes on her.

"Are you cold?"

Terri smiled at his question. "That wasn't a cold shiver. That was a contemplative shiver."

"What are you contemplating?"

"The effects of your milkshake habit on my waistline."

Steve tipped his head to one side and studied her with open admiration. "I don't see anything to worry about from over here."

"Yet," Terri muttered, reaching for the door handle.

Steve stopped her. "Can we just sit here for a bit and talk? There's not a lot of privacy in there."

Terri shifted back in her seat and spooned up another bite of her shake. "Sure, 'til one of the girls starts flashing the porch light."

"Flashing the...why would they do that?"

Terri laughed. "My parents used to flash the porch light on and off when my dates brought me home and we lingered too long in the car. You never got that treatment?"

"Nope."

"Lucky you."

Steve took her hand. "I enjoyed tonight. Do you think we could do it again?"

"We've been seeing each other pretty much every

day. Aren't you getting a little bit tired of me?"

He lifted her hand and kissed her fingers. "Nope. I kind of like it."

Terri swallowed past the lump in her throat caused by his lips on her hand. "Steve, where are we going with this?"

"I'm trying to work that out for myself. I messed things up pretty good once upon a time. I haven't been seriously interested in a woman in a lot of years." His lips brushed her knuckles again. "I have to admit that my attraction to you is a pleasant surprise. I want you to know I'm praying about things. I want God's will for both of us."

"That's just about the nicest thing a man's ever said to me."

"Oh? Then I guess I can just forget all the mushy things I've been working my way up to."

Terri laughed, reaching for the door handle again. "I don't think so. I'm a girl. I like mush."

They walked to the door, and he hesitated before putting the key in the lock. "Spoken or unspoken?"

"What?"

"Mush, do you prefer spoken or unspoken?"

The balmy fall evening, the sight of his blue eyes glowing in the semi-darkness, and the pounding of her heart combined to transform the simple wooden porch into a romantic oasis. "Surprise me," she whispered.

Steve raised his eyebrows and took her shake. He placed both drinks on the porch rail and cupped her face in his hands. He tilted her head and bent slightly to brush his lips against hers. "You didn't answer my question," he reminded her, his voice husky in the dark.

Terri lost the capacity for thought. "Hum?"

"Can we do this again?" he whispered against her lips.

She managed to get one word past her constricted throat. "Yes."

Steve didn't say anything. He buried his hands in her hair and allowed his lips on hers to do the communicating.

16

Steve allowed himself to be pulled down the driveway by the excited toddler.

"C'mon. We huwwy," Kelsey said.

He laughed at the child's impatience. After waiting a week to see her parents, she refused to allow anything to slow her down. Not her chauffer—he glanced back at Terri—or her pack mule. "Pick it up back there," Steve called out to a lagging Terri. He buckled Kelsey into the car seat. "The princess is impatient."

Burdened with both Fuzzy and Sara, Terri followed at a slower pace, boot back in place and still forced to use the cane. She opened the rear passenger door on her side of the vehicle, and arranged the two large stuffed animals beside Kelsey's car seat before settling herself in the SUV's front seat. "Ready when you guys are."

Kelsey began her singsong mantra. "Mama, Daddy…Mama, Daddy…Mama, Daddy…"

Steve turned his key in the ignition. "Is she going to do that the whole way?"

"Probably."

Steve rolled his eyes, put the car in gear, and cranked the radio up a bit. Once the car was pointed toward the interstate he took Terri's hand, entwining their fingers. "I had a good time last night." The blush that stained her cheeks made him smile.

"So did I."

"Would you like to try for something a little more substantial than pizza?"

"Like?"

"Dinner and a movie, tomorrow night after our picnic. I already have Iris on standby to babysit. After spending the day at the lake with the kids, I think we're entitled to some time to ourselves."

"Oh really? One date and you're already taking me for granted."

"I prefer to think of it as being prepared. I used to be a boy scout, you know?"

Terri snorted. "I'll just bet you were."

"You don't believe me? Remind me to show you my collection of merit badges sometime."

"Thanks, but I'll take your word for it."

"I really was. There's a lot we don't know about each other." He rubbed her knuckles with his thumb. "We could explore some of those things tomorrow night, if you say yes."

They rode for a few minutes, hands comfortably clasped, the music from the radio punctuated by Kelsey's excited babbling. When Steve turned into the parking lot of the Department of Human Services center, Terri squeezed his hand and pulled free. "What time?"

Steve's smile broadened at her delayed response. "The movie starts at seven thirty. I'll pick you up, like 'a proper gentleman,' at five thirty. That way we don't have to rush our dinner exploration." He parked the car, got out, and freed Kelsey from the car seat. Terri came around to join them. Hand in hand they walked to the entrance.

Kelsey twisted back to the car. "Sawa and Fuzzy."

"They need to stay in the car," Terri said.

When the toddler's lip jutted out in the beginnings of a pout, Steve scooped her off the ground and tossed her over his shoulder fireman style. "They're asleep, squirt." He tickled her ribs with his free hand. "Let them have their nap, and we'll all go for ice cream later."

Kelsey patted Steve's back, giggling from her upside down perch. "OK."

"Thanks," Terri whispered.

"Not a problem. It's just one of the things you'll have to get used to. Women of all ages find me irresistible."

Terri didn't have a chance to answer before the door opened, and Cindy rushed out to greet them. She acknowledged Terri with a quick smile, holding her hand out to Steve.

"Steve, how nice to see you again."

Steve swung Kelsey back to her feet and released her to Terri. He took Cindy's out stretched hand in both of his. "Thanks again for arranging this for me."

"My pleasure." Cindy gave him a warm smile. "You be sure to let me know if there is anything else I can do to help you with your project."

Steve released Cindy's hand and she bent down to speak to Kelsey. He looked at Terri over Cindy's back and shrugged. "It's a curse."

Terri narrowed her eyes and shook her head at him. "Jerk," she mouthed playfully as Cindy led the way to the playroom and held the door open. Kelsey raced through. Her parents stood to meet her eager hugs. The three older adults remained in the hall to allow them a few minutes of privacy.

Cindy turned back to Steve. "I talked to them

about what you want to do, and they've both agreed to speak with you. How do you want to handle it?"

Steve pulled a piece of paper and a tiny recorder out of his shirt pocket. "I'd like to observe them as a family for a few minutes, get a feel for the situation." He held up the paper. "Then I have questions to ask individually if they will. Interviewing them separately keeps their responses from being clouded by each other's answers."

"That should work fine," Cindy agreed. "You can use my office for your interviews." She looked at her watch. "I can't stay, I have another appointment. Let me show you which office is mine before I leave."

Steve held out his arm. "Lead on."

****

Terri sat on the hard bench outside the playroom door. Cindy accepted Steve's arm with a girlish giggle. Terri rolled her eyes as they disappeared down the hall. *Irresistible, indeed.*

When Steve returned alone a few minutes later, Terri stood to meet him. "Did Cindy take off, or did you leave her sitting at her desk in a besotted swoon?"

Steve grinned. "Besotted? Are you jealous?"

"In your dreams."

Steve glanced up and down the hall. Obviously emboldened by the fact that they were alone, he pulled Terri abruptly into his arms and kissed the smirk from her lips. He held her tightly, looking down into her face. "Besotted...smitten...infatuated. Do any of those adjectives apply to you, Terri?"

The sudden intensity of his gaze seemed at odds with the smile that played around his mouth. The combination left Terri breathless. She took an unsteady step back, touching her lips with the tips of her fingers. "I don't know," she whispered.

Steve nudged her back to the bench. "Well, now you've got something to think about while I'm working. Something else we can talk about tomorrow night."

Terri watched him enter the playroom, not quite ready to accept what her heart kept trying to tell her head.

****

Sean and Kelsey had the playroom to themselves once Ella left for her private interview with Steve Evans. Sean colored a picture with Kelsey and fumed. He didn't have a good feeling about this whole interview thing. He selected a red crayon and tried to isolate his feelings.

Pride? Well, there was definitely some of that. His problems were his own. He didn't feel the need to share them with a stranger, much less have them published in some book for the world to see.

Intimidation? Oh yeah, *lots* of that. Mr. Big Shot Author. So smooth, so accommodating, just oozing education. *And*, Sean just knew, doing his best not to let him or Ella see how pathetic he thought they both were. Steve Evans was everything Sean would never be. Polished, successful, and confident in his own skin.

Nagged to death? Ella had done nothing but nag at him for two weeks, when she'd spoken to him at all. Every time he looked at her he saw tears in her eyes. He loved his wife. He'd never wanted some subservient woman afraid to express an opinion, but a man had limits. A man needed to be a man. He'd lost that. He would never have agreed to this interview nonsense if not for Ella's begging. She was so sure their cooperation would help get their daughter back.

Helpless? On every level, and that was not something a man should ever have to deal with.

Embarrassed? Sean closed his eyes. He could be straight with himself. He'd messed up. But he could fix it if everyone would just get out of his business and give him a chance.

Sean watched Kelsey's hand move back and forth on the page of the coloring book, her fingers clenched around a fat green crayon. His heart ached. *What if I can't get her back?* He pushed that traitorous thought aside and tried to focus on what his daughter was saying.

"Daddy, Steve said... Steve did... Steve took... Steve played... Steve read..."

Steve, Steve, Steve. The red crayon snapped in Sean's fist. His vision clouded as one emotion took center stage. Anger. He'd be hanged before he let another man take his place in Kelsey's life.

****

The slap of flip-flops sounded on the tile floor. Terri looked up from her book. Ella and Steve were returning from their interview. When Steve had escorted Ella to Cindy's office twenty minutes earlier, Kelsey's mother looked solemn and withdrawn, trailing behind Steve like a condemned prisoner. Now, as they returned, Steve had her hand drawn through the bend of his arm. They acted like old friends, laughing and talking together.

She caught herself shaking her head in amazement—again. She forced her attention back to the book in her hand, watching from under lowered lashes as Steve handed Ella a business card and received a quick hug in return. Terri turned the page with a mental shrug. No way would she feed Steve's ego by openly acknowledging his self-proclaimed *irresistibility*. Even if those claims appeared to be true.

The playroom door opened again, and Sean accompanied Steve to Cindy's office. Where Ella had been somber and quiet, Sean was cocky and loud. He walked next to Steve with an exaggerated swagger, telling an old joke with just a little too much enthusiasm.

"Hey man, did you hear the one about the blonde whose crop failed?"

Terri followed their progress until they rounded the corner. A burst of forced laughter was all she heard of the tired punch line. The old adage about opposites attracting seemed applicable in this situation. She silently wished Steve luck with Kelsey's father. It did not look as if his attitude had improved much in the last week.

She closed her book, curiosity getting the better of her. Steve had invited her to sit in on the interviews but she'd declined. Now she reconsidered her decision, justifying her change of heart by telling herself that she could help Kelsey better if she understood more of the situation. After a brisk knock on Cindy's door, Terri pushed into the office.

Steve sat at a small conference table with his questions and a release form in front of him. His recorder rested in the middle of the table. He leaned forward on his elbows, carefully going through the legalese of the release from.

Sean lounged in the chair across from him, legs stretched out, well-worn athletic shoes crossed at the ankles. His hands hung limply from the arms of the chair while he stared at the ceiling.

They both looked up when she entered the room, Steve with a welcoming smile, and Sean with an insolent grin. Steve motioned to the chair next to him and refocused his attention on Sean. "Did you understand all of that?"

"Yeah, man. I'm not stupid." Sean's tone was one of boredom.

Steve pushed the form and a pen across the table. "Didn't mean to imply you were. Just sign and date it at the bottom."

Sean rocked forward, signed the form with a careless flourish, and slid it back to Steve. "Now, can we get this over with?"

"Do you mind if I record our conversation?" Steve motioned to the recorder. "It's easier for me if I can play it back while I work."

The younger man gestured casually at the small machine. "Whatever."

Steve pushed the record button, leaning back to study Sean for a few seconds. He opened his mouth but stopped before he spoke. Terri saw him nod his head before he laid his list of questions aside. "You don't want to do this, do you?"

"I hope you didn't use all of your fancy college education to figure that out."

Steve shrugged, motioning to the closed door. "You're not tied to that chair, Sean. Feel free to leave."

Sean sat up and faced Steve and Terri seated across the table. "You'd like that, wouldn't you? Well,

I'm not going to give anyone any more excuses to poke their noses in my family's business. Ask your stupid questions."

"We'll get to that," Steve assured him. "But let's take a few minutes to get acquainted. Tell me a little about yourself. What do you do for a living?"

Kelsey's father studied Steve's face as if looking for some hidden meaning. "Construction when it's available, which it hasn't been lately. My dad had a construction business, but it went belly up a few months ago. That's why we moved here. I thought this would be a good place to find enough work to support my family." His snort of disgust filled the room. "Talk about a waste of time."

Steve considered the insolent young man for several seconds before he responded. "You've given Ms. Wilson permission to talk to me about your case and she has. From the outside looking in, it seems pretty straightforward. You're a high school dropout with no steady employment. At least part of the money you do manage to earn is being funneled into a potential drug habit. You're bordering on abusive behavior with your family. They removed Kelsey from your home because of your conduct, suspected drug use, and neglect. Ms. Wilson has given you a set of conditions to meet for you to get Kelsey back, and you're refusing to cooperate." Steve leaned forward. "Did I leave anything out?"

The younger man's chair overturned when he shoved to his feet. He leaned across the table, bracing himself on arms that shook with suppressed emotion. "That's a load of *crap!*"

Terri jerked back slightly at his outburst, but Steve gave no ground in the face of Sean's angry display. "By all means please set me straight."

Sean backed away from the table, righting his chair and sliding it under the table so that he had room to pace. "I love my wife and daughter."

"I have no doubt of that," Steve agreed quietly. "Good people are trying to help you get her back."

Another rude noise met Steve's comment. "You call it helping? I call it interfering. Look," he swung his chair around and straddled it backwards, "I messed up, but I can fix it. I just took a drug test and you know what? It's going to come back clean, guaranteed. They've got no proof that I was doing drugs. I've given Ella permission to sign us up for whatever"—he waved his hands in the air, searching for a word— "idiotic parenting course they want us to take. I'm cooperating with you." He stopped and gave Steve a cheesy smile. "See?"

The smile disappeared and his eyes drooped at the corners. "My temper got the best of me the other day. I've never laid a hand on my family in anger, but I'll take their anger management course if that's what they want. And when all of that's done, I'm taking my family, and I'm blowin' this town. There's not a single one of these people that knows anything about me or my problems. All they've done is make a bad situation worse."

"That's an interesting point of view," Steve conceded.

"That's God's truth," Sean confirmed.

Steve's expression hardened. Terri frowned at what she saw building behind his eyes.

He leaned forward and slapped the table in front of Kelsey's father. "You're an idiot."

Sean sat back in surprise. "What?"

Steve reached over and turned off the recorder. "You're an idiot," he repeated.

Terri kicked him under the table, but he ignored her.

"Do you know what I see when I look at you? I see myself fifteen years ago. Make no mistake when I tell you that's *not* a compliment."

"I don't have to listen to this." Sean stood and turned to the door.

"No, you don't. But if you're smart, you will." Steve plowed ahead despite the pressure Terri applied to his arm. "You need to open your eyes and take a long hard look in the mirror, Sean. We both know you're playing with drugs. If you think you can control it, handle it, or fix it, then you need to think again.

"I've been where you're sitting. I thought I could control it, too, and I only wish someone had *interfered* in my life before I lost every important thing God ever gave me." Steve took a deep breath. His voice sounded calmer when he continued. "You know what I've been doing for the last two weeks, Sean?"

Sean shook his head warily.

"I've been reading bedtime stories and playing hide and seek. I've kissed booboos and given piggyback rides. I've done those things with *your* daughter." Steve leaned back and draped an arm around Terri's shoulders. "We went to the zoo last weekend. We fed the birds and rode an elephant. We laughed at the monkeys and shared an ice cream cone. At the end of the day, I carried *your* daughter into *my* house, tucked her into bed, and kissed her good night. You missed out on that." Steve rocked forward. "*You* will *never* get those moments back." Steve gave a seemingly careless shrug. "When Kelsey looks back on those moments in her life, moments she should have shared with you, she's gonna see my face, not yours."

Sean had bowed his head in the face of Steve's lecture. When he looked up, moisture gleamed in his eyes. "I'm not you, and I don't need your help—or anyone else's—to take care of my family."

"That's a lie, son. You might not recognize it, but I do. It's the same lie I told myself the night my wife threw me out of our house. It's the same lie I told myself every day for five years when a drug addiction had me living on the street while my daughters grew up without me." Steve's voice gentled. "Sean, Ella told me that you both have strong religious backgrounds. I don't need to tell you that Jesus loves you, but maybe you need to be reminded that He can help you when you can't help yourself."

Sean stood up and pounded his clenched fist on the table. "Yeah, He's been a big help so far. I'm out of here." He reached for the door again.

Steve stopped him. "I gave Ella my card. Please call me if you change your mind."

The younger man stormed from the room without answering.

Steve sat at the table with his head bowed. Terri stared at him in stunned silence. She had no name for the mix of emotions she felt at Steve's outburst. If she spoke now, she'd regret it later. She left the room and followed Sean back to the playroom.

She was still there twenty minutes later when Steve came looking for them. Sean and Ella had gone, their leaving just as traumatic for Kelsey as last week's good-byes. Terri sat, rocking the toddler, tears running down both of their faces.

Steve found them there and sat beside them. He

reached out for Kelsey. Terri tightened her hold on the child. "Will you take us home?" she whispered.

"Terri, I…"

Terri shook her head. "Just take us home."

17

Steve sat on the small couch in the basement apartment while Terri put an exhausted Kelsey down for her afternoon nap. He rested his head in his hands. No one needed to tell him that Terri was upset, but he hoped she would tell him why. He replayed the scene in Cindy's office. The truth and nothing but. His shoulders hunched when Kelsey whined about the ice cream he'd promised her earlier. Terri's response was an indistinct murmur.

Terri came out of the bedroom and closed the door firmly behind her. Beyond her request for him to bring them home, she hadn't spoken to him. Steve didn't think he wanted her to say anything just yet. She continued to the foot of the stairs.

"You need to go home, Steve."

"I am home."

Terri crossed her arms. "Let me rephrase my request. You need to leave my apartment."

Steve got to his feet. He made it to the first step before Terri reached out and touched his arm.

"What were you thinking?" she asked. "In five words or less can you please tell me what you hoped to accomplish this afternoon."

Steve paused on the step. "Save his life."

Terri put her hands on her hips and looked up at him. "I trusted you. You asked me for my help. I willingly gave it, and you betrayed my trust at the first opportunity." She took a step back. "How could you do that?"

Steve frowned. "How did I betray you? I get it that you're angry. I'm not sure I understand why, but you can't call it betrayal."

"Yes, I can. I have a responsibility to that little girl in there. It's not just about taking care of her while her parents work out their problems. It's about being part of a complete process, at least it is for me. Everyone working together to find a solution that brings her family back together. That includes encouraging Sean and Ella to get the help they need, not driving them away from it."

"Driving them away?" Steve struggled to control his tone. "Weren't you listening? I was trying to witness to that kid. Did you miss the part where I 'encouraged' him to remember his Christian roots? I can't believe you took offense at that."

"Steve, you don't have to rip someone apart to witness to them. You used to share your testimony at shelters and missions. Is this the technique you used?"

Steve sputtered. "Technique? I don't have any technique other than the truth. I can't count the times I prayed for God to give me the chance to stop one person from making the same mistakes I made. All the meals I helped serve, all the testimonies I gave…I can only hope I made a difference somewhere. I'll never know for sure. But I do know from bitter experience that if Sean doesn't get a grip on his life, he's going to face much worse than what I gave him today."

"You can't possibly know that."

"I know he's walking the same road I traveled. I could draw him a map. Allowing Jesus back into his life is the only thing that's going to help him."

Terri shook her head and paced away from the stairs. "I agree that they need to renew their relationship with God. I don't object to your witness. It's your method that offends me. You called him an idiot. Twice."

Steve came back down the steps. "Terri, have you ever known a drug addict?"

"Not that I can remember."

"Then pardon me for saying this, but you don't know what you're talking about."

His statement earned him an incredulous stare.

"You're in over your head on this one." He reached out and took her shoulders in his hands. "Terri, you have a wonderful, gentle relationship with God. It's one of the reasons I love you, but you don't know anything about the other side."

She wretched her shoulders out of his hands. "What other side?"

Steve ran his hand through his hair. "The side that you can't deal with while you're wearing kid gloves—a truth that's not always pretty and soft, but hard and tough. I've been in his shoes. I wish someone had loved me enough to call me an idiot. I wish someone had taken the time to warn me about what I was about to lose in a way that made me open my eyes and see reality for myself."

Terri held up her hand to stop him. "I was there. I heard what you both said. Did you miss the part where he said he'd just taken a drug test that he knew would come back clean? Cindy said they didn't find any drugs the night they took Kelsey away. Maybe we've all misjudged him. Or even if he was experimenting, it sounds like he quit. I know the boy has a bad attitude, but that doesn't make him a drug addict or an idiot."

"Don't be naïve."

Terri bristled. "Naïve?"

Steve continued. "You can take my word for it. He's doing more than experimenting with drugs. No one misjudged him, and he hasn't stopped—not for good. The fact that he can pull his habit back long enough to pass a drug test only tells me this is the perfect time to get tough with him, before he destroys himself and drags Ella and Kelsey down with him."

"You're just full of tact today, aren't you? I'm going to ask you again. Please leave. As far as your story, I don't think it's a good idea. Kelsey and I won't be involved in it any further. I think you should pursue another project."

"That would be my business, sweetheart, not yours," Steve reminded her.

"Your business? You want to build a fence around your business while you're thrashing your way through mine? It doesn't work that way."

"Terri, look—"

"No, you look. We need to give each other some serious space for a few days. I'm afraid that I've allowed my feelings for you to cloud my judgment. I have Kelsey to consider. I have to put her welfare first." Terri crossed her arms. "Please let Sam and Iris know that Kelsey and I will eat our meals down here for now. You can explain my decision in whatever way seems best to you, but I think for now, we need to stay out of each other's way."

"What about our picnic at the lake tomorrow?"

Terri pushed her hand through her hair. "I forgot about that," she admitted. "I promised we'd go, and I don't want to disappoint the girls. But Steve, this whole mess is a closed subject."

Steve went up the stairs two at a time. He stopped at the top, his hand on the knob. "I don't want to leave things like this. I don't want to think about you sitting down here angry with me. Nothing is going to be accomplished by us retreating to separate corners to brood. We'll have to talk this out eventually."

"Maybe so, but not today." She raised her hands in a halfhearted gesture. "I'm not angry, but I'm firm about not participating in your project. I'm done with that. I'm genuinely sorry if that makes *you* angry. I'm not going to 'brood' about anything. I'm going catch up on my Bible reading, and then I'm going to pray for some direction in this whole mess. Sean and Ella need our prayers, now more than ever. God's the only answer I can help them find."

He stared down at her for a few more seconds. "I'm sorry if you were offended by my tactics this afternoon, but we both know that there's more going on here than what happened today. Every time we take a step forward in our relationship, you find a reason to take two steps back. I need you to help me understand the real issues."

When Terri didn't answer he turned the doorknob. "I'll see you tomorrow," he whispered. On the kitchen side of the door he leaned his head against it and closed his eyes.

"Jesus, that could have gone better. Forgive me if I got ahead of You or spoke out of turn to Sean. I'm not egotistical enough to think I have all the answers, but I know I'm on the right track in both my project and my feelings for Terri.

"I looked at that boy today and I saw myself. Thank You for turning my life around. Maybe I got carried away. Please help me use what You've given me to help him."

He knocked his head against the door a couple of times, sifting through their conversation. "I think I just told Terri that I love her. It got so mixed up in the argument she probably didn't even hear me. Father, please give us both some direction." He took a step back and stared hard at the door. *Did she say she had feelings for me?*

****

Terri sat with her Bible open in her lap, contemplating the verses she'd just read in the thirteenth chapter of First Corinthians.

Charity suffereth long, and is kind; charity envieth not; charity vaunteth not itself, is not puffed up, Doth not behave itself unseemly, seeketh not her own, is not easily provoked, thinketh no evil; rejoiceth not in iniquity, but rejoiceth in the truth; Beareth all things, believeth all things, hopeth all things, endureth all things.

Her favorite verses, but today they brought her no comfort. She pulled her feet up onto the sofa and rested her forehead on her knees. "Father, Steve is right about one thing: the relationship I share with You has always been a gentle one. I'm not saying I've always lived a perfect life, or I haven't faced trials, but loving You is all I've ever known. I'm grateful for that. I don't think that makes me 'naïve.' I think that makes me incredibly blessed. I know there's a dark side to this world that I've had very little contact with. I'm not foolish enough to view the world through rose-colored glasses, but isn't it just as wrong to jump to the worst conclusions about people? I'm sorry if I'm acting like a stubborn child. I'm just trying to understand."

She shifted and stared at the door separating her space from Steve's. "What I saw today wasn't patient, kind, or gentle. It was...mean. Forgive me if I'm in the wrong, especially if I'm getting in the way of what you're trying to do for Kelsey's family. I don't want to be angry with Steve. I just need You to help me understand. I need some direction, Father. I need Your help to find Your will for us in this whole situation."

Terri sat alone with her thoughts for a little longer. At last, twitchy and needing to see about dinner for Kelsey, she got up and went into the kitchenette. Her eyes fell on the single red rose Steve had given her last night. *Just last night?* She reached out to stroke its petals and her hand froze in place. "Did he say he loves me?" she whispered to the empty room.

****

Terri prepared picnic food the next morning, smothering a yawn with her shoulder as she packed sandwiches into baggies. She'd spent a confused and restless night. Every time she closed her eyes she saw Steve's face at the top of the stairs, asking her not to be angry with him. And somewhere, a casual "I love you" echoed in her memory. She pushed the voice aside. *You're taking it out of context,* she scolded herself harshly. *"One of the reasons I love you" doesn't equal "I love you." You're only a making a bad situation worse by taking a few carelessly spoken words and blowing them out of proportion. Besides, you don't want it to equal "I love you," do you?*

She packed cookies and apples into the cooler, mulling that hundred-thousand-dollar question. *Of course not,* her head responded. *Maybe...*her heart whispered. The inability to carry on an honest conversation with herself was a sad thing. The door at the top of the stairs opened, saving her from further soul searching.

"Terri, are you about ready?" Iris asked, descending the steps.

She closed the cooler. "Yep. Ask your dad to come down and take this ice chest up. I'll get Kelsey and the beach bag and meet you all in the driveway.

"You OK?"

"Yeah. Why?"

"You look a little tired is all."

Terri tried unsuccessfully to stifle another yawn. "I'm fine. Just didn't sleep very well last night."

"Well, grab an extra beach towel. You can stretch out under a tree and take a nap later."

"That's my plan," Terri assured her. "It's September—we don't have many warm days left. Got to take advantage while we can. Go on and get your dad. I've got to drag Kelsey away from her toys. She's determined to take everything she owns to the lake 'to see a fish.'"

Iris shuddered.

"What?"

"Fish. I've done my share of swimming in a pool but never the lake. If I get nibbled on by a fish today, I'm done."

Terri laughed as she walked behind the twelve-year-old. "Chicken," she teased. "It's not so bad." She pinched the back of Iris's arm. When Iris shrieked, Terri laughed harder. "Feels sort of like that."

****

Iris frowned as she spread her beach towel next to Sam's. She retrieved a soda and a sandwich from the cooler and stared out at the water where Terri and her father played with the younger children. Dad had Bobbie in an inflatable swim float and was engaged in a game of splash. Fifteen feet away, Terri had Kelsey in the water with a life jacket. She demonstrated swimming motions to the bobbing toddler. Kelsey's giggles rippled across the water as she tried to duplicate the moves.

The adults had been polite to each other when contact couldn't be avoided, but they studiously ignored each other as much as possible. *Together but miles apart.* Tiny pinpricks of sunlight danced on the lazy waves of the lake. She nudged her sunglasses into place and plopped down beside her sister.

"Something's up."

"Yep," Sam confirmed. "This is not what I expected today. Any ideas about what's wrong?"

"Not a clue." Iris unwrapped her sandwich. "Dad put me on standby Kelsey duty tonight. But that was yesterday. He hasn't mentioned it since. Terri looked tired and pale this morning. Said she hadn't slept well."

"Yeah, and she and Kelsey missed dinner last night."

"Well, they were fine Thursday night. Dad made a point of kissing her right in front of me."

"So you said, but you'd never know it now." Sam rested her chin on her drawn up knees, watching the lack of action in the water. "Something must have happened while they were together yesterday."

"All they did yesterday was meet with Kelsey's parents." Iris crumpled the sandwich wrapper in frustration. "Drat! It was going so well. Should we push it?"

"Maybe just a little. It's your turn for kitchen duty. What do you have planned for dinner tonight?"

"Nothing special. With the picnic today and Dad asking me to sit tonight...I didn't think dinner would be an issue."

"OK." Sam's gaze rested steady on the lake. "I don't think we can afford to push too hard. We've done pretty well so far at keeping our conspiracy under the radar, but we have to do something to get them talking again." Terri and Kelsey turned in their direction and began wading to the shore. "Ask her about sitting tonight so we can judge her reaction, and then just follow my lead, cross your fingers, and pray really hard."

Terri and Kelsey waded out of the water. "Done so soon?" Iris asked.

Terri picked up a towel and wrapped it around her waist. "Kelsey needs to visit the little girl's room."

"Are you having fun, Kelsey?" Sam asked.

"I swim. Watch." Kelsey flailed her arms around in exaggerated paddling motions.

"Wow," Iris said, "that's pretty good." She turned to Terri, trying to sound nonchalant. "Terri, Dad said something about needing me to sit for you guys tonight. Do you?"

Terri bent her head and wrapped a second towel around Kelsey. "I don't think so," she answered quietly. "I've opted for a quiet evening at home after being out all day."

"Oh, good," Sam said without missing a beat. "Could you help me with something tonight? I promise it won't require you to leave the house."

Terri relaxed visibly. "Sounds like just what the doctor ordered. What did you have in mind?"

"I want to learn how to make lasagna. I've looked at some recipes, but they all sound so complicated. Yours was so good the other night...can you help me? We can make a list when we get home and send Dad to the store. We'll have a girl's night in the kitchen and make Dad babysit while we cook."

"Surely you girls don't want lasagna again so soon. It's only been a week or so. I think there's still a slice in the fridge."

"Are you kidding me?" Iris asked. "I'd eat lasagna twice a week if I could get it. I love it." She smiled at Terri. "Especially yours!"

"Please," Sam coaxed.

Terri prepared to carry the barefoot child up the hill to the bathhouse, her sigh of frustration not quite buried under the effort of picking Kelsey up. "Sure."

The girls held their peace until Terri disappeared through the restroom door. Then Iris grinned and high fived her sister. "Yes!" they whispered in satisfaction.

"What are we celebrating?" Steve asked.

Iris jumped guiltily and turned to face her father. He stood behind them, water dripping onto the sand that had muffled his approach. "Nothing," she assured him. "Just...good news on a project we're both working on."

18

Terri made the transition from her Sunday school class to morning worship in the sanctuary. She settled at the end of a pew crowded with friends she'd known all her life and allowed her defenses to relax a little. The emotional roller coaster her life had become over the last few weeks had her exhausted.

Imagination aside, Steve had never been a serious romantic consideration in her life. Yes, they'd spent a lot of time together over the last few months. Yes, she would admit to being very fond of him. Yes, she found him physically attractive. *And yes*, a smaller internal voice continued, *he has the ability to turn my insides to jelly with a single touch*. If questioned on a witness stand, she would be forced to plead guilty on all counts. Nothing wrong with any of those things, she admitted to herself, but the last two weeks had only served to wrap everything in layers of complication.

As her life stood right now, she was more than willing to pretend the last two weeks hadn't happened. *Oh, that's gonna work*, she thought with a muffled snort. She didn't want to see Steve, but she was forced to live in his house. The fact that she didn't want to hurt Sam and Iris forced her into more time with Steve. Last night's dinner flashed through her mind. The hours of strained smiles and small talk had only given her heartburn.

Taking care of a foster child should have occupied

all of her free time, but said child *adored* Steve. Even in church, she found no peace because there, too, three rows in front of her, sat Steve. Everywhere she went, everything she did, everyone she knew seemed to have joined forces in some galactic conspiracy to link her with Steve.

Terri took a breath and resolved that today things would start to change. The praise and worship team began to sing. Her eyes closed and she attempted to lose herself in the music. She lifted her face to heaven and raised her hands in worship.

Jesus, You are so faithful. Help me forget about all the bad stuff this week and focus on You this morning. I feel like I've lost my direction. I don't know where You're leading me anymore. Please shine a light on my path.

A light touch fell on her arm, and Terri opened her eyes. She blinked in confusion. "Ella?"

"Can I sit with you?"

"Ella, you shouldn't have come here. I mean…"

The younger woman nodded. "I know. Don't worry. I'm not going to make a fuss to see Kelsey. It's breaking my heart, but that's not why I'm here."

"Why…?" Terri trailed off. She scooted over to make room for Ella as Pastor Gordon stepped to the pulpit.

"I needed to come to church this morning." Tears shined in Ella's eyes. "This was the only one I knew anything about. I really need to talk to you when service is over."

Terri nodded absently, her mind lost in a maze of possibilities. *Jesus, she can't be here. There's got to be some rule about her being here, but how can I not listen to what she has to say? I'm really going to need some help here.*

****

Terri's friends milled around her once service was dismissed. She pulled Ella back down to their seats. "I have to know why you're here."

"I needed to talk to you and Mr. Evans. This was the only way I knew to reach you today."

"Ella, I know you have Steve's card if you have questions about his book. If this concerns Kelsey, you should have called Ms. Wilson. If it was urgent she would have contacted me. This is not going to help your situation." She looked up at Steve's approach.

He bent down next to the pew. "Ladies, is there a problem?" he whispered.

Ella directed a watery smile at Steve. Her lower lip trembled. "I'm so glad you're both here." She took a deep breath, tears overflowing her eyes. "Sean's gone."

Frustration fled, replaced with compassion. Terri took Ella's hand. She glanced at Steve, her eyes cold. "Oh, Ella. I'm so sorry."

"We need to take this someplace more private," Steve suggested.

"Yes," Terri agreed, "and I need to pick up Kelsey." She squeezed Ella's hand. "You understand that I can't let her see you this morning?"

"I know, Ms. Hayes. I've made a real mess of things. I don't deserve to see her right now."

Terri closed her eyes against the pain she saw on the younger woman's face. "Steve, I'm going to take Ella back to Callie's classroom. Could you please have Iris get Kelsey and send them home with Samantha?"

"I'll take care of it," he assured her. "I'll meet you in the back in a few minutes." He laid his hand gently on Terri's shoulder in a silent show of support. Terri shrugged it off.

"Thanks," she hissed at him through clenched teeth and a forced smile. "For everything."

Terri ushered the younger woman through the back hall, going the long way around to avoid the nursery. As they waited for Steve to join them, Terri could see that Ella was making a brave effort to control herself. Both women looked up when Steve came in and closed the door behind him.

"The girls are all on their way home." He took a seat next to Terri, reaching across the table to take Ella's hand in his. "You're among friends here. We want to help if we can. Tell us what's happened."

Ella sniffed, and Terri handed her a handful of tissues from the shelf behind her. She and Steve waited while Kelsey's mother decided where to start.

"I want you both to know I understand it was wrong of me to just show up here this morning." Ella shrugged. "I needed to come to church. Steve told me I'd be welcome here when I was ready." She looked into their faces with tear-filled eyes. "I'm *so* ready. I talked to Jesus last night for the first time in a long time. He took me back. I wanted to tell you in person." She looked at Terri. "Ms. Hayes…"

"Terri, please."

"OK," Ella answered shyly. "Terri, I don't want you to think this is just an act to help me get Kelsey back. I know I've screwed up. I know I have to prove to God and myself that I'm worthy of the gift he gave me. I can't tell you how much I appreciate the way you're carin' for my baby." Her voice broke, and she paused for a few seconds, the struggle for composure evident on her face. "For introducing her to the things I've neglected."

Terri grabbed a tissue for herself and wiped her eyes.

Ella continued, "It meant so much for me to come to church this morning. I'd like to come back. I promise I'll do what I need to do to avoid my baby 'til Ms. Wilson says I can see her." The younger woman stopped as her voice cracked. She took a couple of deep breaths. "Will you pray about it? I don't want to make things worse than they already are."

"I'll call her this afternoon," Terri assured her. "She'll be thrilled. I'm sure she'll see it as a positive step. I'll ask her what arrangements we need to make to keep us all out of trouble."

"Thank you," Ella whispered.

Steve nodded his agreement. "This is wonderful news, Ella. What about Sean?"

Ella looked down at the table and sniffed loudly. "He's gone." She focused her attention on Steve. "I don't know what you said to him on Friday, but it hit him real hard. He's been brooding about it for the last couple of days. He was gone when I came home from the store yesterday afternoon. I didn't hear from him all night."

Terri looked at Steve through narrowed eyes before turning her attention back to the younger woman. "Oh, Ella."

Ella looked up. "He'll be back. He just needs some time to think. He really is a good man." She looked up with fresh tears on her face. "I can't remember a single day while we were growing up that we didn't love each other. We've been playmates and soul mates our whole lives. I know how dumb that must sound to you, but we always knew we were meant to spend our lives together." She paused, her expression turning thoughtful. "When we found out I was pregnant, we didn't know whether to be happy or terrified. We were both just sixteen, barely juniors in high school. We understood we were going to have some ugly moments with our families, but we knew everything would be fine as long as we had each other. It was pretty scary, but not having our baby was never an option."

The younger woman's eyes went dreamy with memory.

"We didn't tell our parents, we left on a date one Friday night and didn't stop driving until we crossed the border into Mexico and found a priest to marry us. By the time we got home on Sunday, they'd pretty much figured everything out for themselves. They weren't happy about what we'd done, but it was done." Ella wiped her streaming eyes and added another tissue to the growing pile on the table in front of her.

"It hasn't been easy, but we've worked hard, and we've made our own way. We didn't blow off our educations. We both have diplomas. Sean took and passed his GED and went to work with his dad. I studied for my own test while I waited to have the baby. Our parents both offered us space in their homes, but we rented a small apartment instead and made a home for ourselves. We've never asked for any help. That's why it's so hard to accept it now." Ella stopped for a few seconds.

Terri glanced at Steve. He listened with his head bowed and his eyes closed. Terri hoped he was thinking about the damage his words had done to this young family. She averted her eyes when his snapped open in her direction.

Ella clasped her hands on the table in front of her. "The night Kelsey was born was the most wonderful night of our lives." She met Terri's gaze and then Steve's. "I know how things must look to you, but Sean loves his daughter. This isn't all his fault. I have to accept my share of the blame. I've been so worried about our finances, sick with migraines from the worry, unable to look for part time work because I was sick..." She tucked an unruly red curl behind her ear and looked across the table, her eyes full of pleading. "We haven't been very good for each other or Kelsey for the last few weeks. I cringe when I think about the conditions we were living in. I know it's not an excuse, but it's so easy to become depressed and overwhelmed when you have no money in your pocket and no God in your life.

"We both lost our tempers the other day. It just got to be too much. But I swear it was the first time, and for me, the last. I'm beginning to think it might have been the best thing that ever happened to us." She pulled herself up from where she sat, her shoulders squaring. "That's over now. Sean will have to come to his senses just like I have. I know once we put our lives back into God's hands, He'll provide for us and help us get our daughter back."

Steve studied Ella for a second before he spoke. "Ella, I hope you're right, but I have to tell you from experience, his choices will not be easy ones, and they will by no means be a sure thing."

Ella smiled sadly. "Sean has a lot of thinking to do. Not just about the situation with Kelsey. He's got a call on his life," Ella confided. "That's something else we've both always known. He worked a lot with the youth group back home when we were growing up.

Our pastor took him out of that position when we got pregnant. I know our pastor made the right choice, but it broke Sean's heart. He's been running from God ever since.

"We made a mistake, but human mistakes can't erase my husband's call to the ministry. Underneath everything Sean is now, there's a preacher. I have to trust God to work it all out. It's the only hope we have left."

Terri and Steve reached for her hand at the same time. Ella smiled and held out both hands.

"We'll be praying for you both," Terri said.

"Thank you," Ella whispered. "Do you think I could come back to service tonight?"

"Absolutely," they both answered at once.

****

Steve watched Terri walk through the parking lot of the church. She limped slightly, her eyes on her feet. If he knew her, and he was beginning to, she was contemplating Ella's soul-bearing confessions and blaming him for every problem short of global warming. She reached out to open her car door and jumped when Steve cleared his throat from the other side of her car. He smiled at the startled look on her face. "Sorry. I need a ride home."

Terri looked across the lot to where Samantha had parked her new Mustang.

"I sent everyone home in the SUV since they had two car seats to deal with. I forgot to get Sam's keys before they left."

Terri unlocked the doors with a shrug and settled herself behind the steering wheel. She turned the key in the ignition, staring straight ahead while Steve climbed in beside her and buckled his seat belt. Silence filled the space between them as she pulled out of her parking spot and turned the car toward Steve's home.

"It's past lunch time," Steve commented. "Why don't you pull through the Sonic? My treat."

"I will if you want something. I'm not hungry."

Steve didn't answer, just watched her thoughtfully as she drove. They stopped at the light of Garfield's main intersection. The Sonic sat two blocks down to the right.

"If you want Sonic, speak now…"

Steve shook his head. "That's fine. I'll get something at home."

Terri simply nodded and continued through the light.

Steve took a deep breath. "Terri, after what we just heard, you can't still be mad at me."

She drove in silence for a few more blocks. "I told you Friday that I wasn't mad. I meant it then and it's still the truth now. I'm confused. I just need to try and sort things out."

"What are you trying to sort out?" Frustration edged his voice. "God's doing the sorting. Ella's rededicated her life. I'd think you'd see that as positive progress."

"What I see is a young woman sitting in church by herself." When she spoke her voice was laced with weariness and all the blame he'd imagined. "What I see is the fact that her husband is off somewhere licking the wounds you inflicted. What I see," she finished, "is the fact that he would have probably been with her this morning if you had treated him with a little more consideration and a lot less animosity."

"You still don't get it, do you?"

"I guess not. I wanted to give you the benefit of the doubt, wanted to believe your harsh tactics would reach him, but that doesn't seem very likely right now. It looks like your words only pushed him further over the edge. I think we both need to pray that Ella's right, and he's just off sulking, or your estimation of Sean's future may just prove to be prophetic."

Terri turned into the drive and slammed out of the car before Steve had a chance to respond. He sat and watched her go into the house.

"God, that has to be the most stubborn woman You ever created. If I didn't love her, I'd be happy to strangle her. I know You're working things out, both with Sean and Ella and for Terri and me. I trust in Your plan, but do You think You could hurry things up a bit? I'd really like to get back to the courting portion of the program and put this disagreement behind us."

He took a couple of calming breaths. "Thank you so much for working a miracle in Ella's heart. Please speak to Sean as well. If he really is running from Your call in his life, show him the futility of that. Help him do what he needs to do to find Your will in his life and pull his young family back together." A shudder ran down Steve's spine as he contemplated the alternatives.

19

Sean picked up scraps of wood and trash, trying to look busy while he waited for the rest of the crew to drive away from the partially constructed house on Monday night. Once the last truck had turned the corner he retrieved his sleeping bag, ice chest, and portable radio from his pickup and made himself comfortable in his temporary home.

As a home it left a lot to be desired—sheetrock, studs, a cement floor, and a roof, but as long as the weather remained mild and his boss didn't find out he was camping on the job site, it gave him some time and much-needed space to think.

Three nights now and he was still thinking. Three nights and that writer's words still rang in his head. *When Kelsey looks back on those moments in her life, moments she should have shared with you, it's gonna be my face she sees, not yours.*

Sean jumped up from his sleeping bag, his tennis shoes silent on the bare cement floor as he paced. His imagination painted Steve's face on a discarded cardboard box. He kicked it across the room with all the fury he could muster.

He stood in the middle of the twilight-shadowed room, chest heaving from emotions he couldn't name, fists clenched at his sides. The house echoed with his anguished curse. Sean flopped back down on the sleeping bag and dug in the ripped corner seam for the single joint he'd been staring at for three days. Oh, how he wanted to light it up. How he wanted to find a little peace from those words he couldn't get away from. How he wished he'd never lit the first one.

The pills had gone in the trash and he hadn't had an energy drink in days. *Lesson learned.* But this? He held the joint in his open hand. So much relief in such a small package. Sean lowered his head to his upraised knees. He crushed the cigarette in his hands with clenched fingers. *Oh God, what am I supposed to do?*

****

Terri sat in the corner of Pam's breakfast nook and brooded. How had her life gotten so complicated? She looked up when Karla and Callie scooted in with her, Callie across the table, Karla on the bench beside her. Pam was seeing out the last of the ladies who'd come to her home for their Monday night Bible study. She'd be back in a minute for their traditional sharing of the leftover dessert and gab session. Her three friends better have lots to talk about 'cause there wasn't a thing in Terri's life she felt like sharing.

Pam came back into the kitchen. "OK, ladies, I can make a fresh pot of coffee. I've got iced tea and Cokes in the fridge. Name your poison." Soda was the unanimous response. Pam distributed the cans around the table before she slid into the booth next to Callie.

Callie popped the top on her drink, propped her chin on her fist, and stared across the table.

Terri squirmed under the intensity of her friend's attention.

"You've got dark circles under your eyes, and we haven't seen a smile all night. What gives?"

Terri played with the unopened can of soda. "I'm just tired." She shrugged. "This whole repair thing and driving back and forth every day, coupled with a toddler to care for. I guess I'm not sleeping very well."

"Umm hum," Pam mumbled. She sat back and crossed her arms. "Noticed you had a visitor in service yesterday."

"I noticed that, too," Karla chimed in. "Between your mystery guest and the fact that Steve sat by himself in both services, I could hardly pay attention to Pastor Gordon's sermon."

"Yep," Callie agreed. "Add in the way you and Steve hustled that visitor out the side door plus the dark circles and surly disposition, and I think we have a bigger problem than just being tired."

Terri looked up. Her gaze moved from Karla, to Pam, to Callie. She shifted to lean back against the wall. "I'm trapped."

"Like a rat in a cage, girlfriend," Pam confirmed. "We've got questions. You've got answers. Start talking."

Karla slipped an arm around Terri's shoulders. "We're sisters here, Terri. We're not being nosy. We're not after the latest gossip. You're unhappy and we want to know how we can help you."

Terri rested her head against Karla's shoulder and closed her eyes. "I don't even know where to start. Everything's so messed up."

"Well," Callie suggested, "let's start where we left off last week. You had your first official date with Steve on Thursday. Did he show up in dirty clothes and take you to McDonald's instead of the pizza place?"

Callie's question drew a genuine smile from Terri.

"No. He showed up at my door with more flowers. We had a wonderful time."

"Did this encounter also end in kissing?" Pam asked.

Terri straightened in her corner. "Pam!"

"Hey, I'm married to a lawyer, remember? And by the established rules of cross examination, this is an acceptable line of questioning since the witness, you, brought it up first. Do I need to remind you of your previous testimony?"

Terri leaned forward, licked her lips, and tossed her hair. "Actually, it did," she answered with a wicked grin. "Slow, passionate, hands in my hair, full mouth contact."

"Halleluiah!" Karla lifted her soda can in a toast.

"And we've been arguing ever since," Terri muttered beneath the clank of soda cans.

"About what?" Callie asked.

Terri took a deep breath. "The visitor you saw yesterday was Kelsey's mother."

"Wow." Callie's eyes crinkled at the corners. "I mean, is that even allowed?"

"Not really," Terri answered, "but since she didn't see Kelsey, it's not important." She dismissed that line of questioning with a wave of her hand. "What's important is that when we went for Kelsey's visitation on Friday, Steve went with us. Under the pretense of gathering information for his new book, he completely ripped Kelsey's father to shreds. He was rude and belligerent. He called him a drug addict, which we have no proof of, and read him the riot act about his treatment of his family. The poor kid left the room in tears. Ella, Kelsey's mother, came to church yesterday to tell us he'd been missing for a couple of days."

Terri sipped her soft drink, allowing time for her words to soak in around the table. "Friday's confrontation was one of the ugliest things I've ever seen. You just don't treat people like that. Especially someone you're trying to help. Then, when we got home on Friday, we had this huge argument about what he'd done, and he had the nerve to call me naïve."

"Let's put your argument with Steve on hold for a few minutes," Pam suggested. "If Kelsey's mother showed up yesterday morning to tell you that her husband was missing, why was she there last night?"

"That's the only good news in this whole mess," Terri answered. "Ella came to tell us that she's rededicated her life to Christ. They both have Christian backgrounds, and she's realized she needs God back in her life to be the wife and mother she was meant to be. I think we'll be seeing a lot more of her at church. I've cleared that part of it with our social worker."

Terri closed her eyes and allowed her head to fall against the high back of the booth. "I don't know what to do or what to think. It's such a huge mess, and I'm sitting smack in the middle of it." With a resigned shrug, Terri glanced at her watch. "You guys need to let me out. I've got to get home. Iris is watching Kelsey, and she has school tomorrow."

Pam held out her hands to her friends. "Let's have prayer before we go. What's Kelsey's father's name?"

"Sean."

"Father," Pam began, "thank You for another good day. We thank You in advance for Your blessings tomorrow. We give You praise for speaking to Ella's heart. Lord, please keep Your hand over Sean. We don't know everything about the situation, but we know he needs You. Keep him safe while You speak to him. Bring him back to his family where he belongs.

"Father, have Your way in every part of our lives. We prayed last week for You to direct Terri and Steve's relationship. We ask for that again tonight. Let there be peace and wisdom for both of them. In Your name we pray. Amen."

"Amen," her friends echoed from around the table.

Karla scooted out to allow Terri's escape. "I'll walk out with you."

They said their good-byes and Terri trailed Karla out of the house.

Karla leaned against Terri's car. "You know I love you, right?"

"Of course."

The older woman nodded. "That's good. I just wanted to make sure, 'cause you can take what I'm about to say two ways, and I want you to temper what you hear with the knowledge that I love you." Karla reached for Terri's hand. "I think you're wrong."

Terri stepped back "What?"

Karla kept Terri's hand firmly in hers as she continued. "I'm not going to call you naïve, but I am going to remind you, with all the love in my heart, that you've never been in this position before. You've lived a sheltered life, and you're one of the most tenderhearted people I know. Those aren't bad things, but they can put you at a disadvantage if you're not careful."

Terry studied her feet and tried hard not to resent the fact that Karla seemed to be on Steve's side.

"I've got thirty-one years on you, sweetheart. I've seen a lot more of the world than you. I'm betting on

Steve's instincts here. I think you need to trust him, and God, in this situation."

"Karla, it was horrible."

"I don't doubt that. But I want you to promise me you'll try to think about it from his perspective. I think you'll see things a lot clearer."

Terri nodded even as her heart nosed-dived further into confusion. "I'll try."

"That's all you can do." Karla pulled her in for a hug. "It's going to be all right. We're all praying, and God won't let you down." She released Terri and crossed to her car. "See you later."

Terri made the short drive back to Steve's house. She parked the car and rested her forehead against the steering wheel as she felt tears prick the backs of her eyes. A few deep breaths controlled the tears. When she straightened she stared at her reflection in the rear-view mirror. *God, what am I missing that everyone else seems to see so clearly?*

20

Terri tiptoed out of Kelsey's room, making every effort not to wake the grumpy toddler. Today had not been a good day. Kelsey had acted out at every opportunity, her normally sunny disposition giving way to temper tantrums, whining, and even a few fights with some of the other kids at day care. She'd been placed in time-out at least three times this afternoon. When Terri's refusal to join Steve and the girls for dinner had resulted in another throw-myself-on-the-floor-until-I-get-what-I-want meltdown, along with a rejection of her favorite soup and sandwich dinner, an early bedtime seemed like the only answer. Kelsey had fallen asleep almost before her head hit the pillow, worn out either by her own behavior, or stressed on some level by the continuing tension between Terri and Steve. *Is that even possible?*

The buzzer on the dryer sounded, and Terri held her breath until she was sure Kelsey would sleep through the noise. So many worries, so many chores, and a chance to do it all over again tomorrow. Terri stopped in her tracks at the small niggle of dissatisfaction that brushed against her heart. *Really? What's wrong with me?* There didn't seem to be any logic to her feelings these days. Tiny Tikes was her pride and joy, a business she'd built with her own determination and sweat. She loved it and each of the children she cared for. Her hand lingered on the growing stack of little-girl laundry as she added a fresh shirt, still warm and fragrant from the dryer. *Is this how mommies feel?* This mixture of emotions in their hearts, a sense of time slipping away while the child you love sleeps in the next room. *While the man I love is upstairs...*

The door at the top of the stairs opened. Her heart lodged in her throat. *Steve.*

"Terri?"

Terri fought with disappointment at the sound of Iris's voice. "Come on down."

Iris descended with two plates in her hands. "I know you guys had dinner down here. But I brought you dessert. I made a chocolate pie."

The evening's battles with Kelsey had postponed her own dinner. Terri's mouth watered at the thought of the rich dessert. "That's quite an undertaking for a novice. I'm impressed."

The youngster shrugged. "Pre-made crust, instant pudding, and whipped topping. Not much of a challenge, but it tastes pretty good. Anyway, I brought a piece for you and Kelsey."

"Kelsey's already in bed. She had a hard day today. But I haven't eaten, and this looks scrumptious. Join me?"

Iris pulled out a chair. "Don't mind if I do."

Terri reached for the drawer to get a couple of forks. Her cell phone rang, and her hand went to her pocket instead. She smiled when she read the display.

"Gary!"

"Hey, doll face. What's up?"

She giggled at the old endearment. "Not much. What are you doing?"

"Looking for a dinner date."

"You're in town?" Silence greeted her question.

"Well, duh. Tonight?"

"Yep, I'm going back first thing in the morning. I'd love to see you."

Terri looked at the clock. It was just a little after eight. A visit with an old friend might be just what she needed to snap her out of the mood she was in. "Where and when?"

"Noticed a new Chinese place on Main Street. Are they any good?"

"Very, actually, and they're open 'til ten."

"Meet me there in thirty minutes?"

"Hang on." Terri put her hand over the phone. "Iris, can you sit with Kelsey for a little bit?"

"I guess, but—"

"Great." Terri went back to the phone. "I'll be there."

"Keeping the rug rats overnight now?"

Terri grinned. "Not normally. It's a long story. I'll tell you when I see you. Bye." She closed the phone, picked up her pie, and stuck it in the fridge. "I promise I'll have it for dessert."

"You're going out in the middle of the week, this late?"

"Are you twelve or forty? It's barely eight on a Tuesday night. I'll be home before your bedtime. Did you have something else you needed to do?"

"No, not really. Who's Gary?"

"An old friend," Terri said on her way to the bedroom to change. "A very special old friend."

****

Iris paced. "A very special old friend." She rewrote the sentence in her head. Very special old *boy*friend.

Has to be. She nodded. Terri had been giggling on the phone, and that sappy smile… She never smiled at Dad that way, at least not lately. This was bad, very bad.

Dad and Terri still weren't talking. Five days now and there was no end in sight and no clue from either of them about what had caused the fight. No reason to color it pretty. It was a fight. And now Terri had a date with another guy. *There has to be something I can do.* She pulled out her cell phone and punched in Sam's number.

"Why are you calling me? Are you too lazy to walk up the stairs?"

"Rag on me later, Sam. Just listen. Terri just left on a date."

"Dad and Terri—"

"Not Dad, just Terri."

"Ohh, not good."

"Ya think? What are we gonna do?" Several seconds of silence met her question.

"Where did they go?" Sam finally asked.

"Chinese place here in town." Iris waited. She could almost hear the gears turning in Sam's head. If anyone could come up with a plan on the fly, it was her sister.

"I'm going to bed."

Iris held the phone away and looked at it in disbelief. "You're doing what?"

"Calm down, sis. Bobbie's stuffy with a cold. Give me ten minutes to get her snuggled down with me. Isn't tomorrow snack day in your home room?"

"Yeah. I've got a box of brownies I'm going to make as soon as Terri gets back."

Sam giggled. "I bet they'd rather have eggrolls."

"What?"

"Iris, do I have to spell it out for you? Once I'm in bed, give Dad an emergency call about the eggrolls you need for class tomorrow. If I'm already in bed, he'll have to go get them for you. This could work to our advantage. If he sees Terri with another guy, maybe he'll get a clue."

Iris nodded while her sister talked. "You're a genius." She looked at her watch. "You're on the clock. Get tucked in."

****

Terri stepped into the softly lit restaurant. Excitement lightened her mood. There'd been a time, before his company transferred him out of Garfield, when she had considered Gary *the one*. Her eyes scanned the booths. *There he is.* She took a second to study her old friend. Gary had been gone for almost six months, but he hadn't changed. Still tanned, his curly blond hair gelled ruthlessly in place. New York City must agree with him. He smiled in her direction and stood to meet her. His arms locked around her in an enthusiastic embrace.

"Look at you," he said. "How can you look so beautiful on such short notice?"

Terri laughed up at him. "After the day I've had, you have no idea how much I needed to hear that." They scooted into the booth across from each other.

Gary nodded at the tall glass in front of Terri. "I took a chance and ordered your drink. Still Diet Coke, right?"

"Yep, thanks." Terri helped herself to the bowl of Chinese noodles in the center of the table. "I didn't have dinner, and I'm starving." She pushed the menu to one side without opening it. "I can highly recommend the cashew chicken with lo mien noodles."

The waitress descended on their booth. Terri placed her order and after a quick study of the menu, Gary did the same. "I'll have what she's having."

"And we need a bowl of your garlic sauce," Terri requested as the young Asian woman prepared to leave.

Gary settled back in the bench seat. "Catch me up."

Terri rubbed her face and smiled across at him. "I don't even know where to start."

He grinned. "The cane and that attractive piece of footwear might be a good place."

"Oh, that's just a small part of a very long story." She proceeded to fill him in on leaking appliances, broken toes, foster parenthood, and housing repairs.

"Wow," he said when she'd finished. "You're finally a mommy."

Terri felt her heart swell. He got it. All the news she'd just shared and he picked out the most important thing without having to be told. Not like a certain thick-headed writer. *Not going there.* "It's wonderful. She's wonderful. We're a wonderful team. Can you tell I'm totally, absolutely in love?"

"Yeah, but what happens when you have to send her home?"

"I'll cry," Terri said honestly. "But hopefully there'll be a sense of accomplishment that outweighs the tears. I know I can't keep her. I'm praying for God to heal her family, so I'll have to be happy when He answers that prayer." Terri looked at her nearly empty plate, food delivered and consumed while she talked. Gary had always been a considerate listener. "Enough about what I've been up to. How's New York?"

Gary's blue eyes frowned across the table. "I hate it."

"Oh, I'm sorry."

"Not your fault. The metropolis hustle and bustle is just too much for this small town guy. I'd come home if I had a home to come home to."

Terri finished her last bite of noodles and chicken. "There's a half a page of rentals in the classifieds if you're serious."

"Not what I meant." Gary reached across the table and took her hand, his expression suddenly serious. Terri felt her brows rise under her bangs at the look on his face. "Can I come home to you, Terri Hayes?"

Terri stared at their linked fingers. Heat flooded her face. "Gary?"

"Choked you right up, didn't I?" Gary rubbed his thumbs across her knuckles. "This isn't a proposal, Terri. I'd like it to be, but I won't do that to either of us." He turned her hand over and played with her fingers. "I know we called our relationship quits because we felt like God was sending us in different directions. Maybe we were hasty. The company is opening a new office in Oklahoma City, an easy commute from Garfield. They've offered me a leadership position if I want to make the move. I can keep the job I love. You can keep the business you've worked so hard to build. *We* can make a home together and fill it up with babies. I've been miserable without you." He pulled her fingers up and kissed them. "More important than that, I love you. I always have. I guess I had to spend some time without you to see what was right in front of my face."

****

Steve fumed as he parked the car. Eggrolls at nine thirty at night? *How is it possible to forget something like that?* He stepped out of the car and up onto the empty sidewalk. He pointed the remote at his car and paused, recognizing the car two spots down from his. Terri? *Wish I'd known. I'd have called and saved myself a trip.* The door squeaked when he pushed it open. Iris had phoned ahead, and the order should be waiting for him at the counter.

He was halfway to the register when his feet froze to the old wooden floor. Terri sat in a dark corner booth snuggled up to a man he didn't recognize. Jealousy slammed into his chest and drove the air from his lungs. Steve strode toward Terri's table. *Not on my watch.*

His jaw clenched as he approached his target. The stranger had just lifted Terri's hands to his lips. *Who is this joker and why was Terri allowing him to slobber all over her?*

"So this is where you ran off to."

"Steve. What are you doing here?"

Steve was only mildly gratified when Terri yanked her hands into her lap like a guilty child. He wished the lights were brighter so he could gauge her expression more clearly. He didn't answer her question, turning instead to face her friend. He held out his hand. "Steve Evans."

The stranger cleared his throat and took Steve's hand in a firm grip. "Gary Carr."

"Nice to meet you, Gary. New in town?"

"No, Garfield born and raised. I've been away." Gary paused and the look he directed at Terri turned

Steve's stomach. "Just catching up."

Terri took Steve's attention. "Is there something you wanted?"

Steve shook his head. "Nope, just picking up an order." He turned back to Gary. "I better get to it. Will you be in town for long?"

"Unfortunately, no. My flight back to New York City leaves bright and early in the morning."

New York? The muscles across Steve's shoulders relaxed. *Good riddance.* "Too bad," he said aloud. "Have a safe trip home." With a nod in Terri's direction he went to retrieve Iris's eggrolls.

****

Terri and Gary walked from the restaurant a short time later. Gary opened the car door for her but pulled her into his arms before she could sit. "Will you think about what I said?"

"Gary, I—"

"Shh." He laid a finger across her lips. "I know I took you by surprise. Just give it some thought. We were working on something very special before I left. I think we can have that again." Gary cupped her face in his hands and lowered his mouth to hers.

Terri allowed herself to sink into his kiss and felt...absolutely nothing. She murmured a good-bye, closed the door, and started her car. *What's wrong with me? I've waited for this moment my whole life. A handsome, successful, Christian man had just proposed to her.* Well...yes, she decided, it was a proposal and she...she felt nothing. *A good-looking man, one she cared for, wanted to make babies with her, and all she could think about was the one who didn't. Steve*

Evans, the man with all the family he wanted, the man she could barely stand to look at just now…the man who melted her into a puddle every time he touched her.

She stopped at a red light and looked out the windshield at the star-filled sky. Her whispered prayer filled the car. "Were You listening to that, Father? You just gave me a chance to have everything I've ever wanted, tied up in a pretty silver bow, and I'm not even considering it. I'm so confused. Have I missed Your direction somewhere in this mess? Because I'm lost." A single tear slipped down her cheek. *What's wrong with me?*

21

Iris plumped up her pillows Wednesday morning and settled back against the headboard of her bed. Outside her window the sun was just beginning to peek over the rooftops. Her alarm would go off soon, which was fine since she hadn't slept much anyway. She couldn't forget the look on her dad's face when he got back with the eggrolls. Sort of sad and scary at the same time. On the other hand, Terri had been just plain sad when she came in.

Iris covered her eyes with her folded arms. *And grownups think kids are goofy when it comes to dating.* She leaned over and pulled out a pink legal pad from under her bed.

Project SETH was underlined in purple ink at the top of a page followed up with notes about outings and family dinners. Flowing hearts containing her father's and Terri's names decorated the margins of her list. Such a simple plan, so clear and logical in her twelve-year-old mind. The problem? So far the adults had proved to be far more thick-headed than originally anticipated. The scheming had been fun for both of the girls, but fun wasn't getting the job done. She drew another heart as she considered the next step in their plan. They needed help and advice. Iris hoped she knew where to find it.

To get it, she needed an excuse to stay home from school. Just being tired wouldn't fly with her dad, especially with two dozen eggrolls sitting in the fridge. A mental examination of her whole body followed. Surely there was a headache, toothache, or hangnail she could capitalize on. *Nothing.*

She shook her head. What if Terri really liked this guy? What if she and Sam couldn't pull this off? She rubbed her belly as the thought made her stomach do painful flip-flops. Every time she thought about Terri's date last night she felt a little nauseous.

Nauseous? Well, duh. She wouldn't even have to lie. She threw off the covers, stuck her tablet under her arm, and went to enlist Samantha's help for the day.

A few minutes later a sleep-disheveled Iris knocked lightly on her father's bedroom door. "Daddy."

The door opened on the whispered word. "What's up?"

Iris put on her most pitiful expression, thought about *Gary* and rubbed at her midsection when the uncertainty produced the necessary twinge in her gut. "I'm not feeling very well this morning." *The whole truth and nothing but.*

Dad rested a hand on her forehead and felt for a fever. "What hurts?"

She continued to rub her belly. "I don't feel well…" She allowed her explanation to hang vaguely between them.

"Oh," he said, obediently jumping to the intended conclusion. "It's a *girl* thing." He ruffled her hair. "What about all those eggrolls and your party?"

Iris shook her head. "We'll have them for dinner. I don't even want to think about food right now."

"OK, I'll call the school office for you. Take a couple of aspirin and go back to bed for a while. Do you need the heating pad?"

"I think I'll be OK without it," she croaked. Her voice almost broke with the effort it took to sound believably pathetic. "Thanks, Dad." She started back to her room, but in an apparent afterthought turned back to face her father. "If I'm feeling better by lunch time, can I go out with Sam for a while?"

"Sam's not going to class either?"

Iris took a deep breath and frowned against the *pain* in her belly. "Bobbie isn't feeling any better. They're sleeping in."

Her father shrugged, totally oblivious to the plot unfolding around him. "Go on back to bed, sweetheart, and see how you feel later. I'll be gone most of the day myself. I've got some research interviews to do."

Iris nodded, loitering in the hall until the door closed between them. "Yes!" she whispered, pumping a victorious fist in the air. She made it to the landing before a large ache in her heart replaced the small one in her stomach. With her feet on the top step she looked up at the ceiling. *What's up with this? I didn't tell a single lie. Why are You poking at me? All I did was trick him…a little.* She pursed her lips as the ache tightened a bit before it subsided. Her breath huffed out into the empty hallway. *Got it. It doesn't have to be a lie to be dishonest. Sorry.* This being a Christian stuff sure got complicated sometimes.

****

Iris sounded whiny, even to herself. "We can't tell them everything. They'll just tell us to mind our own business."

The sisters sat at the kitchen table, alone in the

house except for the sleeping Bobbie.

"Well, this is, sort of, our business. Our dad, our house, our future." Sam used Iris's own arguments against her. "Besides, Callie and the others want Terri to be happy just as much as we do."

Iris remained unconvinced but remembered the episode in the hall earlier. They needed help and they had to be honest to get it. She finally nodded in agreement. "Whatever."

Sam took out her cell phone and punched in a number. She put the phone on speaker and placed it on the table between them.

"Hello?"

"Callie, it's Sam."

"And Iris."

"Hey, girls. What can I do for you?"

Iris chewed her lip, crossed her fingers, and prayed. *Please, please, please…*

"Can you take a long lunch today?" Sam asked. "Iris and I really need to talk to you."

"Probably." Callie's puzzled tone came through the phone. "What's wrong?"

"Nothing's wrong in a bad way," Sam assured her quickly. "Iris and I just need some advice on a…project…we're working on."

"OK. Where do you want to meet?"

"Is anyone at your house today? We need a quiet place to talk, and I'll have Bobbie with me. We'll bring lunch."

"Benton will be working at Terri's all day," Callie informed them. "You girls are making me very curious."

"I promise it's nothing serious," Sam said. She placed her crossed fingers on the table next to Iris's.

"What are the chances of Pam and Karla joining us?"

"Wow," Callie answered. "Terri isn't invited to the powwow?"

"We'll explain when we get there. Can you call them, or do I need to?"

"I'll call them in a bit. I'm sure they'll be as intrigued as I am."

Sam nodded. "Thanks, Callie. What do you guys want for lunch?"

"Cheeseburgers and fries all around. I've got tea and soda at the house. Is eleven thirty OK?"

"Perfect," Sam said. "See you in a bit." She disconnected the call and yawned widely. "I'm going back to bed for a while. Be ready to go at ten forty-five."

Iris grinned. "I'm already feeling much better."

****

Iris stared at the three other cars in the driveway as Sam parked the Mustang. *Maybe this isn't such a good idea.* "I think I've changed my mind."

Sam shook her head. "Too late. You said it yourself. We need help. If they say no, we're on our own and no worse off than we are now."

Iris gathered bags of food while Sam collected Bobbie. "I guess."

Callie opened the door as the girls mounted the porch steps. She stepped out and took the baby. "Come here, precious."

"Have you guys been waiting long?" Sam asked.

"Five minutes. Just long enough to get the door unlocked and let Karla and Pam in the house." Callie led the last of her visitors into her dining room.

Iris dragged her feet. This wouldn't be their first serious conversation around Callie's table. It probably wouldn't be the last. But it might turn out to be the most important.

Samantha settled Bobbie in the highchair with a sippy cup, french fries, and small pinches of hamburger bun. Food for the grown-ups was distributed. Iris could almost feel the questions radiating from the women.

Sam cleared her throat. "Thanks for breaking free for us today."

Callie waved it aside. "Not a problem. We were having a slow day at the clinic." She dipped a fry in ketchup while Karla and Pam offered their own assurances.

Karla unwrapped her lunch. "Both you girls skipping school today?"

Sam shook her head. "Bobbie's cold kept me up all night. I couldn't have stayed awake in class if I'd wanted to."

"Dad thinks I have cramps," Iris confessed.

"Excuse me?" Callie asked.

"Dad thinks I have the cramps."

Iris squirmed beneath the older woman's blue stare as Callie the friend became Callie the Sunday school teacher. "You lied to your father so you could skip school?"

Iris shook her head. "The word 'cramps' never came out of my mouth. He jumped to that conclusion all by himself."

"He jumped, or he was pushed?"

"Well…"

"That's what I thought." Callie's stern look caused Iris to shrink in her seat. "I think someone needs a

232

refresher course in honesty."

Iris rushed to defend herself. "Well, I couldn't very well ask his permission to skip school so we could come over here and discuss his love life. Could I?"

Pam choked on her drink. When the coughing fit passed, she wiped her streaming eyes with a napkin and studied both of the girls. "Life is never boring with you two around."

Callie sat back with her soda. "All right. Out with it."

Sam took a deep breath and forged ahead. "We want Dad and Terri to get married."

"They're perfect for each other." Iris jumped in. "They both need someone to share their lives with, and since their lives directly intersect ours, we thought it would be great if Dad married someone we already love."

"Like Terri," Callie supplied.

"Exactly," Sam said, picking up the explanation. "We've turned it into a real project. It even has a name. SETH."

"Steve Evans, Terri—"Iris began.

"Hayes, their initials," Karla finished. "Very catchy."

"We've done everything we can think of to bring those two together over the last couple of weeks," Sam said. "We wanted them to see what a nice family we could make so we engineered trips to the zoo and the lake."

"We're spending *every* night in the kitchen, "Iris complained. "We thought family dinners would help, so we bought some cookbooks and told Dad we wanted to learn to cook. The only thing I've learned," Iris whined, "is I don't like it very much."

Sam tossed a fry at Iris. "Baby," she muttered. "Anyway, we thought we were making some progress. They actually had a date Thursday night—"

"Dad kissed her right in front of me," Iris interrupted with a whisper.

"Yeah," Sam said, winding down. She propped her elbow on the table and rested her chin in her hand. "And five days later they can't say two words to each other and won't spend ten minutes in the same room together. All they do is stare at one another when they think the other one isn't looking."

Iris threw caution to the wind. "I think something's really wrong. Terri had a date with some guy named Gary last night. What are we going to do?"

Pam reached across the table to pat Iris's hand. "Don't worry about Gary. He's living in New York. If she saw him, it was just a friendly visit between old friends. Nothing for you to worry about."

"Thank goodness."

Sam leaned forward and addressed Callie. "You're the one who taught us to take advantage of the opportunities God gives us."

Callie raised an eyebrow over her hamburger.

"This opportunity is quickly passing us by," Sam finished. "We're only going to have her there for another week or so. Will you guys help us?"

Conversation around the table ceased. Iris watched as looks and nods were exchanged between the three women.

"Yes," Callie answered for all three.

Iris took a second to process the simple answer. "You will?" she asked and received three nods in response.

"You don't think we're being goofy and we should

just mind our own business?" Sam asked.

"Nope." Callie wiped her mouth. "I… we… agree with you."

Karla rose and began to collect discarded wrappers. "We've all noticed the affection growing between Terri and your dad over the last few months."

"But we've been under strict orders from Terri not to try any matchmaking." Pam sipped her drink. "She told us to leave the matchmaking to God."

Callie nodded her agreement. "We've abided by her wishes. And despite Terri's noninterference directive, they've fallen, hard, for each other. I think we all agree. It's a match made in heaven."

"That's a good thing, right?" Iris asked.

Callie laughed, "Well, good, bad, or indifferent, at least we're all on the same page."

Sam took Bobbie out of the highchair and wiped her hands and face. "Has she told you guys what's wrong? The tension between them is thick enough to cut with scissors."

Callie's answer was hesitant. "Yes…"

"But there are confidences involved," Karla finished. "Things they're going to have to work out for themselves."

"Have you girls been praying about the situation?" Pam asked.

When both girls nodded, she continued, "That's about all any of us can do right now. They're both grown-ups, and unfortunately we only get more hardheaded as we get older. Keep doing what you've been doing—dinners, outings, and praying. The rest will fall into place when it's time."

"But they're fighting," Iris persisted.

"I know," Callie assured her. "But as far as I'm

concerned that's just another indication they're headed where we all want them. If they didn't care enough about each other to fight, they'd just go their separate ways and be done with it. Fighting is a big part of learning about each other. Benton and I had some doozies when we were dating. Still do." Callie sipped her drink. "I've got a good feeling about this. I think this disagreement will resolve itself pretty quickly."

Callie looked at her watch. "As far as the help you asked about, we're praying about it, too. We'll talk to Terri about some of the things she's hesitant about when the opportunity presents itself. If she can be nudged in the right direction, we will. Will that work?"

"Well, short of marching them to the altar at gunpoint, it'll have to," Sam answered, obviously disheartened.

"Patience girls," Callie advised. "We're all going to have to be patient."

Iris sat back and crossed her arms. "I hate that word."

****

Steve pushed through the front door, juggling a box and the mail, a satisfied smile on his face. Advance copies of his third book had arrived. He shoved the door closed with his foot and hurried to set the box on the kitchen table. It opened to reveal twelve neatly stacked copies of *Reunited*. His smile broadened when he turned the book over to study the picture on the back cover. Bobbie sat in his lap, his daughters stood on either side of him. It was unusual to have more than the author pictured on the jacket, but for this one, he'd wanted the whole family. A testimony to the title.

"Thank you, Father." Steve replaced the book. He couldn't wait to show it to the girls. Sorting through the rest of the mail, he made his way down the hall to check on Iris. When he didn't receive an answer to his knock, he peeked inside her room. Iris's bed was made and empty. Sam's car hadn't been in the drive. Steve closed the door with a shrug. Iris must be feeling better. Some things a dad couldn't fix, and there were some things, as a guy, he'd never understand.

He climbed the stairs to his office, making a quick detour to Sam's room to leave her mail on her bed. A piece of pink paper with his name written on it protruded from beneath the stack of pillows. Curiosity got the better of him and he slid it out. Project SETH was underlined at the top, notes on dinners and trips followed in Iris's neat handwriting. Steve sank to the edge of Sam's bed. So many points of confusion came into sharp focus. His jaw dropped as he read through the list. The last entry was underlined and circled. *Talk to Callie today.*

"Oh, girls, what have you been up to?" He reviewed this morning's scene in the hall and realized his sympathy for Iris had been seriously misplaced. He'd been had.

He tucked the pink pad of paper back under the pillow, careful to leave it just as he'd found it, and picked up Sam's mail. He'd give it to her in person. When he turned to leave the room, his eyes fell on the picture of Lee Anne Sam kept on her bedside table. Steve picked it up and studied it intently. "Our daughters are scheming," he whispered. His fingers caressed the image preserved behind the glass. "Our daughters..." He closed his eyes on a sigh. "You did a good job with them." Steve stopped and tried to restore some order to his thoughts.

"I wish…well, I wish a lot of things. Most of all I wish you could have known how sorry I was…am. I loved you so much, darlin'. I'm sorry I didn't have the strength or wisdom to make better choices. I'm working hard to fix that now. This is going to sound weird, but I wish you could meet Terri. You would have liked each other. She's smart and organized, like you. She loves Iris and Sam." The pink pad caught his eye a second time. "Looks like those feelings are mutual." He replaced the picture, bracing himself against the regrets that always threatened to overwhelm him when he thought of his deceased wife. Instead of sadness he felt the peace of deciding to move forward.

Project SETH, huh? He'd never worried that his daughters would have a problem accepting Terri in the role of stepmother, but he never dreamed they'd go to such lengths to make it happen, much less be five steps ahead of him in the process. The more he thought of it, the more it made him smile. Sneaky, devious, and sly, but those weren't always negative words. Steve made up his mind to put a little more effort into granting their wishes.

"Father, I'm not just praying for myself now, but for my whole family. We need You to soften Terri's heart. She's become such an important part of each of our lives. Please show me how to reach her for all of us."

His thoughts went back to the last item on Iris's list. *Talk to Callie.* Steve grinned. "Out of the mouths of babes." He removed his phone from the case at his waist. Maybe some *guy* advice would help. He headed towards his office punching in Benton's phone number as he walked.

****

Steve sat across from Benton at one of the Sonic picnic tables. The carhop brought out two banana splits, collected their money, and skated away.

"You did *not* see me eat this so late in the day," Benton cautioned Steve. "Callie takes a dim view of me ruining my dinner."

"She won't hear it from me. I just appreciate you breaking away from work early."

"Not a problem. We're moving along pretty well. Another week should see us done and Terri will be back in her own house, snug and comfortable. Besides," Benton continued, "you made it sound important."

"This is probably one of the most important conversations I'll ever have, and your timeline makes it all the more urgent."

"I'm listening."

"I'm in love with Terri, and I want to marry her."

Benton grinned. "This is not news to most of us."

"She's an infuriating, stubborn, unpredictable, exasperating woman."

"And you love her because of those things."

"Well…" Steve dribbled chocolate syrup over his ice cream with a spoon. "Yeah."

"So, what's the problem?"

"She hates me."

Benton rubbed his forehead. "Son, you've got a lot to learn about women. I've known Terri for most of her life. I've never seen her so messed up over a man. It's my personal opinion that she's crazy about you."

Benton scooped up a couple of spoonfuls of ice cream before he continued. He pointed his spoon at Steve. "I'm not saying there aren't some issues to work out, but I don't think 'hate' is part of the equation. A blind man could see how you both feel. He could also see there's trouble in paradise. What did you do to make her mad?"

"Why do you assume it's me?"

"One of those lessons you have to learn—it's always the guy's fault. I learned a long time ago that if I get up every morning, raise my hands to heaven and tell God, 'I am man, I am wrong,' I'm covered for the day."

Steve laughed at Benton's sarcasm.

"So..." Benton prompted.

"Long or short version?"

"Short. My ice cream won't last through the long one, and I wouldn't be able to keep two of these a secret."

"I went to Kelsey's visitation session last Friday and called her father the idiot he is. I invited him to renew his relationship with Christ if he had any hopes of restoring his family. He's now gone missing, and Terri blames me for being too harsh on him."

"Were you?"

"Not in my 'been there, done that' opinion."

"Well, good for you then."

Steve took a deep breath of relief, grateful Benton had not dismissed the situation by telling him it hadn't been that bad. It had been, and continued to be, that bad. Steve chopped up the banana in his treat. "For years I visited missions and shelters whenever I could. My one goal was to prevent someone from making the same mistakes I made. I think...hope...I followed

God's direction in what I said to Kelsey's father." He shrugged. "So, what should I do to get Terri past it?"

"Pray." Benton's shrug mirrored Steve's own. "I'm a younger Christian than you are, but I've learned there are some things you just have to let God work out. You called it like you saw it. As much as I love Terri, I'm inclined to go with your opinion on this one. Probably not the answer you wanted, but it's the best I can do. Just don't give up on her. She's worth the effort."

Steve mulled Benton's advice. "What else?"

"What else, what?"

"You mentioned *issues* that needed to be worked out. What else? I know there's something I'm not seeing. Even before last Friday, Terri was spending half her time avoiding me. So, what else?"

"You want me to meddle, do you?"

"If that's what it takes to get everything on the table once and for all, yes."

Benton studied his friend across the table for a few seconds before he answered. "Callie wants you and Terri together as much as I do, but she'll skin me alive if she finds out I broke this confidence." He shook away his own hesitation. "But we men have to stick together. Terri wants kids."

"OK."

"OK? Just like that? OK? You have grown daughters and a grandchild, but you'd start over?"

"Well, yeah. It's one of the things I've asked God for. A chance to enjoy what I missed out on. I'm only thirty-nine. I figure I've got twenty or twenty-five more active years left. I could have a couple of kids in college before I cross the line into senility."

"Senility, huh?" Benton shoved his trash to the

center of the table. "Terri is of the opinion that you're satisfied with the status quo. She's afraid that if she gives in to her feelings for you, it will mean sacrificing her dream of a family of her own."

Steve ran his hand through his hair. "I never said anything like that to her. Why would she think that?"

"I'm just the messenger, Steve. The workings of a woman's brain have been a mystery since Eve. You're gonna have to figure out the hows and whys on your own. Good luck with that."

"You know," Steve mused out loud, "a lot of the things she's said and done over the last few weeks make sense now. She's always apologizing for Kelsey being in my hair and going out of her way to make sure they both spend as much time downstairs as possible." He pushed his empty dish to the center of the table with the rest of the trash. "Thanks, Benton. You've been a big help. I can see I've got my work cut out for me, but at least I have some direction now."

"There's more," Benton said.

"What?" Steve asked in alarm.

Benton grinned. "Relax, kid, not with Terri, but you need to have a serious discussion with Samantha and Iris about your plans before you take this too much further. They lived without you for a lot of years. They might not be ready to share your attention just yet. You need to make sure they don't have a problem with any of this."

It was Steve's turn to smile. "I don't think that'll be an issue."

"You need to be sure," Benton cautioned him.

"You need to talk to your wife when you get home tonight," Steve said. "Those girls are way ahead of the power curve on this one."

22

Have SETH update. Can't discuss it in the house. Needs major privacy. Meet me in Callie's Sunday school classroom right after church tonight.

Iris re-read the typed note she'd found folded on her pillow Wednesday afternoon and paced her room. What could Sam have found out since their lunch with Callie? And when? They'd been together most of the day. Sam had gone to the library to study for a while before church. Iris couldn't call her because she couldn't find her phone. Asking to use her dad's phone meant another lecture on responsibility. After the eggroll thing last night… *I don't think so.* There would be no chance to talk to her sister before church and no chance during service since the school-aged kids met in the gym while the college kids held class in the fellowship hall. Curiosity would kill her between now and the time church was over. She looked at the note again. The rest of the afternoon would be torture.

****

Iris raced out of the gym just as soon as youth service was dismissed. She hoped Sisko dismissed the older kids on time because Sam's note sounded important, and after stewing for several hours Iris was desperate to talk to her sister.

She rounded the corner to Callie's classroom. Sam

came from the other direction just as she reached for the doorknob. "Thank goodness," Iris hissed in the dim light of the deserted hallway. "Tell me," she demanded, leaning against the closed door.

Sam stopped and stared at her with a mystified expression. "Tell you what? You told me to meet you here."

"I did not."

"I got a text message at the library. It said to meet you here after church."

"From my phone?" Iris asked. "I haven't been able to find my phone all afternoon. I didn't send you any messages. I'm here because of your note."

"What note?"

"Samantha!" Iris whispered in annoyance, digging through her bag. She fished out the piece of paper and shoved it in Sam's face. "This note."

Sam read it silently, her eyebrows arching high on her forehead. She took out her phone and scrolled through her messages. She turned the small screen so Iris could see it. "Same message, word for word."

"Well, if you didn't write this, and I didn't send that then who…?" Iris's voice faded away, and both girls took a step away from the closed door, watching it like they would a coiled cobra.

Sudden sweat prickled Iris's forehead "Oh man." The two words more groaned than spoken.

"Who?" Sam wondered aloud.

"I don't know," Iris answered. She pushed Sam forward. "But you go first."

"Me?"

"You're the oldest."

"Yes, but this whole thing was *your* brilliant idea," Sam reminded her.

"I don't suppose we can just walk away?"

Sam shook her head. Both girls continued to stare at the door for a few silent heartbeats. With a heavy sigh, Sam locked her arm though her sister's and threw open the door.

Iris felt inside the doorway for the switch and flipped on the light. The breath caught in her throat as the light revealed their father seated behind Callie's desk.

He was kicked back in the chair, hands behind his head, feet propped on the corner of the desk. He rocked forward slowly, grinning at the sight of his daughters framed in the doorway. Steve picked up Iris's missing cell phone from the desk and sent it her way in a gentle underhanded toss. He motioned to two chairs arranged in front of him. "Ladies, come right in and have a seat. Tell me everything you know about project SETH."

****

Sean jerked his fingers away from the grinding teeth of the circular saw Thursday morning. His hands shook as he shut off the power and looked around to see if any of the rest of the crew had noticed his lack of attention and *almost* accident. Everyone seemed to be focused on their jobs. Everyone but him.

He sighed as he stacked the lumber he'd just finished cutting. Five days and he still had no answers. Five nights living on cold sandwiches and sleeping on a colder cement floor. Five mornings trying to wash and shave in the lukewarm water of the nearby convenience store. Five afternoons hiding in his beat-up truck, waiting for the rest of the crew to leave so that he could sneak back to the job site and make himself at home.

Home. Sean rolled the word over in his mind. He missed Ella and Kelsey with a fierceness that threatened to overwhelm him. But how could he go home to his wife when he had no plan to get their daughter back. Their house had stopped being a home the day he'd proved just how stupid he could be. Or had the damage been done months earlier?

"Anderson, we need some two-by-fours over here."

"On it, boss." Sean picked up a stack of neatly cut lumber and carried it inside. The noise of busy power tools, pounding hammers, and loud music pumping from three boom boxes did not drown out the annoying little voice whispering in his right ear these days. That little voice kept reminding him that this wasn't where he needed to be. That this wasn't the path to his future. This could be a stepping stone, nothing more. An acceptable means of supporting his family while he explored...what? The ministry? Sean almost laughed at that idea.

The red suited figure sitting on his left shoulder laughed the loudest and reminded Sean of the facts, just in case he forgot. *You got your girlfriend pregnant at sixteen. You barely have a high school diploma. You played with drugs and got burned. Your wife is hardly speaking to you. They yanked Kelsey right out of your arms. What do you have that God would still want to use?*

"Lunch." Every tool went quiet at the boss's shouted word. Men headed to their trucks in twos and threes in an effort to beat the crowds to the local fast food joints. A few more pulled out brown bags and books. Sean had been eating cold sandwiches three times a day for too many days. The idea of lunch held no appeal. He headed to his truck. *I'll just close my eyes for a few minutes.*

"Anderson."

Sean turned to find three men sitting at a makeshift table consisting of sawhorses and plywood. One was shuffling a deck of cards. "We need another player. You in?" He shook his head and kept walking. Once out to the truck he climbed in and leaned his head against the back window. He was exhausted. *I just need a plan.* His eyes drifted closed.

He jerked up in his seat, heart pounding, his breath coming in noisy gasps. His eyes and his nose both ran. Sean used his sleeve to dry his face. One thought ran through his mind. *Drive, just drive.* The truck roared to life and gravel spewed from under the tires as he raced from the construction site. *The dream.* Kelsey crying for her mommy. A stern-faced judge banging a gavel. *Unfit parents.* Ella on her knees in front of a tall black desk, hands raised, begging for the return of their daughter. The voice of the judge echoed in his head, creepy and distorted. *Unfit...unfit...unfit.*

He stopped at the single stoplight at Garfield's main intersection. Ahead lay the interstate, but he couldn't leave just yet. When the light changed, he turned left and drove to Tiny Tikes Day Care. Terri Hayes. Sean had looked up her name and address in the phone book, had driven by her house a time or two in an effort to get a look at Kelsey, to see if there was any chance to grab her and run.

It hadn't taken him long to realize that she and Kelsey weren't living there. Workers swarmed in and out the door, the black truck from his failed stakeout dominated the drive most days, and a large construction dumpster sat in the front yard. But even from the street he could see the backyards fenced as one. It didn't take a genius to add two and two. Terri Hayes owned the day care. His daughter was surely spending her days there.

Sean parked across the street, cut the motor, and waited. Kids crowded the playground equipment behind the fence. If he waited long enough he might get a glance of Kelsey. *Now's the perfect time to grab her.* He pushed that thought aside. Nothing like stalking the wrong couple to make a guy realized he wasn't cut out for a life of crime and running from the authorities.

He sat up a little straighter. *There she is.* Kelsey ran from the corner of the house, her blonde curls held back in pigtails above her ears. Ella called them puppy dog ears. His daughter dashed for an empty swing. She tripped, and Sean reached for the door handle of the truck. Her cries traveled across the street and echoed inside the cab of the pickup. Fifty yards away and he couldn't even comfort his own daughter. A strange woman picked Kelsey up and brushed her off. Her cries vanished as she received a quick hug and a boost into the swing. The woman stayed close and pushed his daughter while they both laughed.

Each note of laughter drove a dagger through his heart. Sean started the truck and drove. His family would be better off without him. If he was out of the picture, Ella might have a chance. He was the one who'd lost his temper. He was the one who'd brought drugs into their home. He was the stupid one. With him gone, there would be no reason not to let Kelsey come home. *Where am I going?*

"Don't know, don't care," he whispered aloud.

Terri

****

Terri watched the two little boys sitting in front of her desk late Thursday afternoon. The office chairs they occupied dwarfed their skinny six-year-old bodies. The boys slumped deeper into their seats while Terri looked on. She allowed their guilty silence to stretch out a bit, aware that it made an effective tool both for expressing her disapproval of the fight between the two best friends and as a cool-down method. Her pen tapped the papers on her desk in time to the music playing in the background. Davy and Ben belonged to the large group of kids Terri inherited each day after school. They were two of the oldest, two of the ones she'd had the longest.

"Boys, I'm ashamed of you."

"Yes, ma'am," they answered in unison. Their small feet swung above the floor, their eyes remained focused on frayed shoelaces.

"Either of you want to tell me what the fight was about?"

She waited for several moments and sighed when the only answer she received was continued silence. Terri walked around to the front of her desk and leaned back against it. "Both of you look up here, please." Maintaining her severe expression became a struggle as two pair of blue eyes, one surrounded by freckles, the other by sunburn, complied with her request. "Both of you boys have been enrolled here since you were babies," she reminded them. "Did you forget that you're two of my big boys?"

They both shook their heads solemnly.

"Did you forget the big boy rules?"

The boys shook their heads again.

"I didn't think so. Ben, what is big boy rule number one?"

"To always have fun," Ben answered.

"That's right. Davy, what's the second rule?"

"That the little kids are watching, and we have to be good *samples*," Davy provided.

"Examples," Terri corrected, "but you're right. I depend on you bigger guys to be good examples for the little ones. Do you think fighting on the playground is a good example?"

Davy answered for both of them. "No, Miss Terri."

"What do I make the little guys do when they fight?"

Davy and Ben looked at each other, horror etched in their expressions. Ben provided the whispered answer. "Hug."

"Yep," Terri said, trying hard not to laugh at the mortification she saw on their faces. "If you two are going to act like the little ones, I'm afraid I'll have to treat you like the little ones."

Davy held his hand out to Ben. Ben grabbed it eagerly. The boys seemed more than willing to end their argument like *men*. They shook hands and faced Terri with hopeful expressions.

"We're made up." Ben assured her.

"Are you sure?" Terri forced some doubt into her voice. "Because that looked like a pretty serious fight."

Both boys nodded enthusiastically as Terri straightened and held out her hands. "OK, if you're both sure." She walked them to the office door and bent down to pull them into a three-way hug. "I love you guys," she told them. "Now, go on back out. You've got about thirty minutes before your mothers get here."

They raced out the back door, and Terri felt a real smile on her face. They really were just like her own. The safety buzzer on the front door of the center sounded, drawing her attention to the front of the large common room. A young woman entered the center. A little girl clung to her shirttail. They stood in the entryway, looking around uncertainly. Terri hurried forward and held out her hand. "Hello, I'm Terri Hayes. Welcome to Tiny Tikes. What can we do for you?"

The other woman took Terri's hand with a smile. "Hi, I'm Melissa Rogers and this is my daughter Carrie. We stopped by to look at the facility and check on availability. We're moving to the area in a couple of weeks, and I'm going to need a good day care. This one comes highly recommended."

"That's what I like to hear."

"You're the owner?"

"Yes. I'll be happy to show you around." Terri bent down and smiled at Carrie. "How old are you, Carrie?"

"Five."

"Do you go to school?"

Carrie shook her head.

"She should have started kindergarten last month, but I held her up until we got moved. I didn't see the point in enrolling her twice."

Terri nodded her understanding. "Would you like to go out to the playground with the other kids while I visit with your mom?"

"Can I, Mommy?"

Melissa released her daughter's hand. "Go on."

Both of the women watched Carrie sprint out the back door.

"She's adorable," Terri told Melissa. "Is she your only child?"

"Yes. Her father and I are divorced. That's the main reason I jumped at the chance when this transfer was offered. Garfield seems like a nice quiet place to raise a child and a forty-five minute commute on the interstate isn't all that bad."

"I think you'll like it here," Terri assured her. "Let me show you around the center. The good part of this whole thing is you'll only need after school care, or we couldn't take her. We're in a holding pattern for all-day care right now with a long waiting list."

"Oh good," Melissa responded. "I've been told Tiny Tikes is the best in town."

"We like to think so," Terri said, starting her tour. Thirty minutes later they settled in chairs in Terri's office. "Well, what do you think?"

"I think everything I heard about Tiny Tikes is true, and I think Carrie will enjoy her afternoons here."

"I'm so glad you feel that way. If you'd like, we can get some of the initial paperwork out of the way while you're here."

"That would be perfect."

Terri shuffled through the papers and folders on her desk, knocking a stack of books and a picture of Steve and the girls to the floor in the process. "I hope you'll excuse the mess in here. My house flooded a couple of weeks ago. I had to transfer all my personal office stuff over here while things are being repaired next door. I'm having issues finding what I need sometimes."

"Don't worry about it." Melissa bent down to retrieve the fallen items. "I'm packing for my own move. It's never pretty."

Terri saw her visitor compare the framed picture to the one on the back of Steve's book. She put the items back on the corner of Terri's desk. "You have a beautiful family of your own. I've read your husband's books, they're very good."

"I'm not married," Terri said as she rummaged through papers. "The baby is my God-daughter, the older girls and their father are just good friends."

Melissa picked up the picture again and studied it more closely. "How good?"

"Hmm?" Terri asked absently, concentrating on the day care contract.

"Is he yours?"

Terri looked up. "Excuse me?"

Melissa held the frame up and tapped Steve's picture with a perfectly manicured, blood red fingernail. "Steve Evans. Are you involved with him?"

"No," Terri answered hastily. "Why?"

"You're kidding, right?"

When Terri merely raised her eyebrows, Melissa continued. "Single, good-looking, *successful* guy." Melissa replaced the picture and placed a hand on her chest. "Single, lonely, new woman in town. If he isn't yours, I just might ask for an introduction once I get settled."

"Hmm." Terri gave her visitor a little smile and a shrug. "He's pretty involved with a new project right now. Between that and his family, he doesn't have a lot of time to socialize."

Melissa tilted her head and grinned. "Is that a fact?"

Terri shrugged in response and bent back over the contract. Once the paperwork was complete, Terri escorted Melissa and Carrie back to the front door of the center. "Did you have fun with the kids?" she asked the youngster.

"Yes. Can I come back, Mommy?"

"Just as soon as we get settled into the new house."

Terri stood at the door and watched as they walked to their car. She hurried back to her office with the intention of dedicating a few minutes to organizing her desk. When she picked up Steve's book her hands began to shake. *Just who does that woman think she is? Going to breeze into town with her bleached blonde hair and snap up the most eligible bachelor in a hundred mile radius.* She shoved the book in the drawer and slammed it closed. *I mean, really, she can have him, but let's exercise some restraint. He could be an axe murderer for all she knows.* Her actions became more and more brisk with each item she put away. Finally, she picked up the picture of Steve and the girls and felt her heart pound in her chest. *Steve better think twice if he…*

If he what? "What am I doing?" she whispered into the empty room. *I'm jealous.* "Well, that's just…stupid." Terri lowered her head to her desk. "God, I'm jealous. I don't want to be. I've got no right to be. I've made up my mind that Steve isn't for me." *Haven't I?* "Oh, Father, I'm so confused. I'm angry at some woman I just met for expressing an interest in a man I don't want. I'm tossing things around on my desk. My heart is pounding. Why is my heart pounding if I don't care?"

She sank slowly into her chair. "I can't work this out on my own. I don't know what I want anymore or how to get it. I know I've asked for Your help about a million times in the last few weeks. Forgive me for asking for Your advice and then yanking my problems back into my own hands to worry with on my own. If there's a solution to this mess, please show me." Terri sat there for a few more minutes. Her heart rate gradually returned to normal, her mind a million miles away. Had God already answered that prayer?

For the first time in her life she had a way to get what she wanted. Gary wanted to build a life with her, make babies with her. Six months ago she wouldn't have hesitated to say yes to his proposal. Terri shrugged. Maybe the *nothing* she'd felt when he kissed her was simply left over irritation at Steve. *And maybe I'm grasping at straws.* Was there any way to know for sure if she didn't give him a chance? She picked up her cell phone and paged back until she found Gary's number. Her nails tapped an impatient beat on her desk as the phone rang. A muttered "Great" filled the office when her call went to his voice mail.

You've reached Gary Carr. Sorry I missed you. Please leave your name and number after the beep.

"Gary, it's Terri. Call me back when you have a few minutes."

Terri dropped the phone in her pocket with a crisp nod and finished cleaning her desk in a more controlled manner. With her office put to rights she needed something else to divert her nervous attention. She decided to take a walk next door to check on Benton's progress in her house. He didn't need her hanging over his shoulder every day, radiating impatience, but it had been a couple of days since her last visit.

The progress in her house stunned her. The walls had received new sheetrock days ago, but now they boasted fresh texture and paint. Her wood trim gleamed with a shiny coat of oak colored varnish. The odor of fresh lacquer thinner hung in the air and stung her nostrils. She trailed through the kitchen and down into the living room, her footsteps echoing on the bare cement floor. She found Benton in her study, screwing in the covers to the electrical outlets. "Wow."

Benton turned around with a smile. "Like what you see?"

"I'm amazed. I can't believe you got all this done in less than three weeks."

"I made you a promise, didn't I?"

"Yes, you did." Terri stopped as the silence around them registered. "Working by yourself today?"

"Yep. I have the other guys split between two other jobs with three or four more waiting for our attention."

"God's really blessed your business this last year."

"That's a fact," Benton agreed. "I'm not complaining, but I wish He'd bless me with a few more experienced hands. Mitch has been a Godsend. I need a couple more just like him."

"I'll keep my ears open for you." She looked around a final time. "How much longer, do you think?"

"Impatient to get back, are you?"

"Well, it's home…"

Benton looked around at his handy work. "We've still got some odds and ends to take care of, but I think we can meet that four week mark. Have you picked out your new carpet?"

"Not yet. It's been so hectic. When you give the word, I planned to take a day off and go look for carpet and furniture."

"Consider the word given. The carpet installers can have it by Wednesday, if that's what you want."

Terri frowned, puzzled by his remark. "Why wouldn't it be what I want?"

"I had an idea I wanted to run by you this weekend, but since you're here, if you have a few minutes, we can talk now."

"OK," Terri agreed hesitantly.

Benton made a motion that took in both houses. "Both properties are yours, free and clear, aren't they?"

Terri nodded. "Yes. I was able to buy both places with what Mom and Dad left for me. I had a small bank note on the original alterations for the day care, but I paid that off six months ago. That was one of the reasons I wanted to expand over there."

"How about expanding over here?"

"Excuse me?"

"You said it yourself. A second house would be perfect for what you want to do. Where better than right next door to the existing facility?"

"I need a place to live."

"Hear me out. I've been giving this some thought. You said you wanted space dedicated for infants. The living room and study are perfect for that. You could put a half dozen cribs in here for a sleep area, more if I did smaller built ins along two of the walls, and you could have the larger living room space for a play area."

Terri considered the possibilities while he continued.

"You also mentioned long term care. We could turn the two smaller bedrooms into boy and girl dorm rooms and then divide your larger room into two smaller sleep areas to give your overnight employees some privacy. Build an enclosed walkway between the two houses, install an intercom, and you'd be set for just about any scenario."

"That's not half bad, Benton."

"Now's the perfect time. You've still got some insurance money to play with. Why borrow the money to expand the building next door and just get part of what you want? Spend your money on a new home and have it all."

"I like it. Can I have the weekend to think about it?"

"Take your time. I can draw up a rough plan to show you by Sunday. I can even direct you to some suitable houses to consider buying if you decide to go that way."

"Thanks. I needed a project to focus on and this is as good a one as any."

"Problems?"

"Just life. I was praying for some direction earlier. God might just be trying to give me some."

23

Sean drove. He took Interstate 40 east towards the Arkansas state line. The radio in the old truck blared at almost full volume in an attempt to drown out the voices shouting in his ears and erase the images of the dream from his mind. Once he reached Ft. Smith he'd make a decision about the next direction, but for now, this was as far as his mind could plan.

Ft. Smith thirty miles.

He nodded as he passed the sign. *Good, almost two hundred miles between me and Garfield.* Not nearly far enough, but he needed a rest stop. Something to drink, a bathroom, and maybe a map to plan the next leg of his escape. The next exit advertised a large truck stop. Sean took the access road and pulled to a stop in front of the orange, red, and yellow façade of a Love's. He reached for the keys and his eyes fell on a faded photo duct taped to the old metal dash. Ella, newborn Kelsey wrapped in a blanket, the smile of contentment on his wife's face the brightest thing in the picture. For three years the snapshot had reminded him of why he worked so hard. Today it only reminded him of his failure. Ella's smile seemed a thing of the past, just like the feel of Kelsey's hand in his. His hand shook when he reached out to rip it from its place. He couldn't do it.

Leave it there. Sean slammed out of the truck. Once in the store he took care of business in the men's room and stood in front of a shelf of snacks trying to decide what sounded good to go with his soft drink. A little girl rounded the corner and ran headlong into his leg. She looked up, stumbled, and landed on her backside at his feet. Wide blue eyes studied him from six feet down and her little lip began to tremble. He stooped down and reached to help her up. "Don't cry, baby girl."

"Angie, there you are."

Sean looked up to see a harried young woman rounding the corner. She stopped as her eyes met Sean's.

"She tripped," Sean said. "I don't think she's hurt."

The young woman shook her head. "These racks of treats are just too much temptation. She jerked right away from me, and I couldn't catch her." She lifted the child from the floor, checked for obvious injuries, and faced Sean again. "Sorry."

"Not a problem." He turned back to the shelf.

"Bye."

Sean looked up at the whispered word. The little girl was waving to him over her mother's shoulder. Blue eyes crinkled in a sunny smile. He lifted his hand to return the motion and realized tears were streaming down his face. *What am I doing?*

****

Terri had just finished tucking Kelsey into bed on Thursday night when Iris came bounding down the stairs.

"Dad needs you to come upstairs really quick."

"What for?"

"Don't know. I'm just the messenger. He's on the phone in his office and he told me to come get you."

"Good grief." Terri started up the stairs. "Can you stay down here for a few minutes?"

"Sure thing." Iris flopped onto the sofa and grabbed the remote. "Take your time."

Terri gained the main floor and continued through the house and up the second flight of stairs. She was not a big fan of being *summoned*. If the man wanted to talk to her, he could come downstairs once he got off the phone. She rapped on the door to Steve's office, shoved it open, and stood in the doorway with her arms crossed and a piece of her mind on her lips.

"OK," Steve said into the phone. "I've got Terri here right now." He stepped back to his desk and picked up a note pad. "Give me the address. We'll be there as soon as we can."

Terri heard him promising away her evening and narrowed her eyes at him. She waited until he laid down the phone. "What are you—?"

"That was Ella," Steve interrupted her. "I didn't want Kelsey to overhear. Sean's home, and he wants to see us."

"Oh, thank God," Terri said, her annoyance forgotten. "Did she say where he'd been?"

Steve shook his head. "Just that he came home earlier this evening and wanted to see us. How soon can you be ready to leave?"

"Now. Just let me tell Iris what's going on."

Steve wagged his cell phone at her. "We'll let Sam know on our way out, and we can phone Iris from the car if we need to. Ella was crying. I think we should hurry."

"Upset crying or I'm-glad-he's-back crying?"

"Sweetheart, I'm a guy. Crying is crying. I don't differentiate."

Terri rolled her eyes and followed him down the stairs and out the front door. "Men!" she muttered under her breath.

****

Steve parked in front of the rundown apartment building and looked at Terri skeptically, taking in the absence of both boot and cane. "Their apartment is on the fourth floor, and Ella said the elevator hasn't worked since they've lived here. Can you make it up four flights?"

"Are you going to carry me if I can't?" Sarcasm dripped from her words.

"If I need to." Steve's answer matched sarcasm with sarcasm.

"Well, you don't," she assured him, motioning up the stairwell. "I walked up two flights just to get to your office earlier. I'll be fine."

Terri trailed behind him up four flights of dingy, badly lit stairs. At the top of the landing he stopped to look for the correct number. "Great," he said. "No numbers. We need apartment three. There are two doors on each side, want to make a guess?"

Before Steve could make a choice, Ella opened the back door on the left. "Thank goodness you came." She reached out for Steve's hand and pulled him into the apartment. "I'm so sorry to interrupt your evening." She nodded at the couch and a motionless Sean. "He won't say anything to me. He won't tell me where he's been for the last few days or what he did. All he said was he needed to talk to you."

Steve put his arm around Ella's shoulders and gave her a light squeeze. "Stop apologizing. This is what friends do." He passed Ella back to Terri and crossed to the sofa. When Sean refused to look up, Steve twitched up his pant legs and crouched down in front of him.

"Sean, I'm here to listen if you're ready to talk."

Sean shook his head, his eyes boring a hole in the floor between his feet. "I've wrecked our lives," he whispered.

"Kid, you're still breathing. God still loves you, and your woman is still by your side. I'd say dented, not wrecked."

The younger man sat with his head in his hands. "What am I going to do? I don't know what to do."

"You're going to fight," Steve answered. "We're going to help you."

"But what if…"

"The first thing you're going to have to do is get past the *ifs*, *ands*, and *buts*. You can't change yesterday, but you can redeem today, and you can fight for tomorrow. I'm not going to lie to you and tell you how easy it's going to be. It's going to be the toughest challenge you've ever faced." Terri remained silent as Steve sat cross-legged on the floor in front of Sean. "Look at me," he said.

Sean raised his head just enough to bring his eyes level with Steve's. Steve cocked his head to the side and studied eyes that were red from weeping but otherwise clear. He nodded, pleased at what he saw. "You bragged to me about being clean six days ago. Still hanging in there?"

Sean nodded. "It's tough man, but yeah."

"One hard question, Sean, and you've got to be

straight with me. Was it just marijuana?"

"Just?"

"Gotta know your enemy, son, before you can battle it."

Sean nodded again, "Just marijuana," he confirmed. "Marijuana and stupidity."

Steve let the remark pass. "Besides knowing the enemy, you have to know what you're fighting for. What are you fighting for, Sean?"

The young man's response was a hoarse whisper. "My family."

Steve nodded and patted the empty space next to Sean. "Come have a seat, Ella.

Ella sat and pried Sean's clenched hands apart. She took one of his hands in hers.

"Close your eyes," Steve instructed. Sean offered a puzzled stare. "Humor me. I want you to get a good picture of Kelsey in your mind. A happy picture of the three of you." He paused for a few seconds. "You got it?"

Sean nodded and raised Ella's hand to his forehead. "Yeah," he whispered. "Oh, Ellie, I'm so sorry."

"Sean, you've been struggling in the dark, weakened by an army that you can't fight alone. I want to share a Scripture with you. The Bible says in Second Samuel 2:29-31, *For thou art my lamp, O Lord: and the Lord will lighten my darkness. For by thee I have run though a troop: by my God have I leaped over a wall. As for God, his way is perfect; the Lord is tried: he is a buckler to all that trust in him.*"

Fresh tears rolled down the younger man's face, and Steve motioned for Terri to take a seat on Sean's other side.

"Sean, there are some things in life, no matter how good they are or how much we want them, we can't do by ourselves. This is one of those times. If you're sincere about wanting to fight this battle and win back your family, the first thing you have to do is be man enough to admit you're too weak to fight on your own. You're going to have to ask Christ to take control of your life and allow Him to be your strength. Are you ready to do that?"

"Yes."

"Then let's talk to God." Steve closed his eyes. "Father, we are so thankful that no matter how far we stray, You always welcome us home with open arms. Thank You for that and thank You for Sean and Ella."

****

Steve drove home in silence. Terri sat beside him, hands clasped in her lap, head bowed. He knew she was working through the last few days, and he didn't mind giving her the space she needed. They pulled to a stop in the drive, and Steve turned to slide out of the car.

Terri stopped him with a whisper. "Please wait."

Steve closed the door and sat back as the dome light faded away.

"I'm sorry," Terri began.

"Terri you don't have to—"

"Yes I do and you need to let me. I'm so sorry," she began again. "I was naïve, just like you said, and worse, I was judgmental, reactionary, and unreasonable." She swallowed. "I can deal with those things where they apply to me, but my attitude could have undermined everything I was trying to do for

Kelsey. And I know I haven't made this week a pleasant one for you." She shrugged. "Sorry seems pretty lame after the way I've growled at you all week."

"I survived," Steve assured her.

"That doesn't excuse my behavior. I know I hurt your feelings. Can you forgive me?"

"Sweetheart, there's nothing to forgive." He reached across the seat and took her hand in his. "We all operate out of our own experiences. I did what I had to do to get my point across to Sean. Given the same set of circumstances, I'd do it the same way again. You approach things from a loving, gentle relationship with God that you've enjoyed all your life. You see the good in people, and because of that, you bring out the best in people. As far as my hurt feelings go, we're just going to have to learn to trust each other." Steve kissed her fingers in an attempt to take the sting out of his words. "I'm sorry for my part in our disagreement."

Terri squeezed the hand the hand that held hers. "I apologize for my part, too."

"Two halves make a whole," he said. "I'd say that we were completely made up."

The memory of two little boys shaking hands in her office flashed through Terri's mind. "Do we hug now?"

"What?"

Terri shook her head. "Nothing. You just reminded me of how childish I've acted this week." She looked at him, her eyes shining in the dark. "I don't want to fight with you anymore."

Steve nodded in agreement. "Neither do I. If I were a rogue, I'd use this opportunity to tell you how much you need me. How much you need my worldly experience to balance out your innocence."

Terri smiled in the darkness and Steve knew that the worst was behind them. "But I'm not a rogue. I'm just the guy who loves you."

He raised the center console out of the way. "Come over here." He pulled her closer in the dark and tilted her face up to his. "I told you that the other day when you were angry with me. I meant it then, and I mean it now. I love you, Terri." He leaned close and brushed her lips with his. "One of these days I'm going to find the chance to tell you under better circumstances."

Terri studied him in the light reflected from the porch. She rested her head on his shoulder with a smile. "I did you a big favor today."

"How so?"

"I saved you from the clutches of a wicked woman with evil designs on your body and your fortune."

Steve laughed and snuggled her closer. "You did?"

"Yep. She was in my office drooling all over your picture. I could almost see horns through her bleached blonde hair."

"Blonde hair? Long or short?" He held her tighter when Terri sputtered and struggled to sit up. "Let me rephrase…Thanks?"

Terri relaxed in his arms. "You should thank me. She wasn't your type at all."

Steve closed his eyes and took the final plunge. "Who is my type, Terri?"

"Someone like me," she whispered, raising her face to watch his expression. "I heard what you said the other night. I was too angry to acknowledge it."

"And now?"

"I'm almost thirty years old, Steve. I haven't said this to a guy since I was in junior high and Kyle Barrett managed to steal a few kisses under the football bleachers. I love you." She grabbed the front of his shirt with both hands and pulled him down. Terri initiated the kiss, but Steve took it over, took it deeper. With a broken groan, she surrendered control of the kiss, and her heart, into his capable hands.

The porch light began to flash on and off and they broke apart like guilty teenagers. Steve gritted his teeth. "I'm going to kill them."

Terri laughed, fanning her hand in front of her face. "I'd almost be willing to help you if they weren't right. We need to go inside where it's safe."

She sat back in the seat. Steve saw the puzzled expression on her face. "There's something strange going on with those two," she said.

Steve dropped a kiss on her head before opening his car door. "You don't know the half of it." He extended his hand to help her out of the car.

They walked hand and hand to the front door. Steve fumbled on the dark porch with the key. "At least they could have left the light on," he complained, trying to stab the lock in the dark.

Terri stopped him. "They did us a favor," she whispered, moving closer to him. "I think the circumstances are better now."

Steve took the hint and pulled Terri back into his arms. "I love you, Terri Hayes."

"I love you right back, Steve Evans."

He ran his hands down her arms and entwined her fingers in his. Lips, hands, and hearts joined in a good-night kiss that nothing conspired to interrupt.

****

Steve made his nightly trip through the house, turning off lights, adjusting thermostats, and locking doors. He whistled a soft tune. His job was to make sure everyone in the house got tucked in safe for the night. God had given him so much to be thankful for. He didn't mind the time it took to protect it.

He peeked in on Bobbie, cracked open Iris's door for a whispered good night, and headed up the stairs. Light glowed from under Sam's door. He knocked and opened it to find her bent over a textbook.

"Night, Sam."

"See you in the morning," she answered.

He thought about going to his office for a while but turned toward his bedroom instead. The décor here was definitely masculine, dark heavy woods and deep colors in the drapes and comforter. The thought of eventually rearranging his space to accommodate a woman's taste made him smile in anticipation. His discarded shirt sailed in the direction of the hamper. *The sooner the better.*

"Thank you Father, for giving me a second chance, in more ways than one. I don't deserve it, but I don't intend to waste it. The girls and I all know what we want. There's no point in waiting to make it happen."

****

Terri felt as if she floated around the apartment. After sending Iris back upstairs she opened the door to Kelsey's room and stood by the little bed. She brushed the curls from the toddler's forehead and bent to place a good-night kiss on the plump cheek. "Things are going to be all right now, baby," she whispered. "It's going to break my heart to let you go. I'm so happy for you and your parents. I guess we all get a happy ending this time."

She continued on to her room, undressed in the dark, and crawled into bed. Her cell phone began to vibrate, dancing across the top of the nightstand. Terri picked it up and looked at the display. *Gary.* The called rolled over to her voice mail while she held the phone in a limp hand. Once it was silent, she checked her messages. Five missed calls, all from the same number. He could wait until tomorrow. The conversation they would have then would be much different than the one she'd originally planned.

Terri returned the phone to the table, hugged a pillow close, and closed her eyes. It was all so simple. Steve loved her and she loved him. She'd come so close to messing it up. Part of her heart still ached with doubt for the future, but she knew how to fix that.

"Father, forgive me. Forgive my stubbornness, my doubt, and my reluctance to accept the gift You've been trying to give me. The Scripture Steve quoted to Sean tonight took my breath away. Your way is perfect. All Your promises are true. If this is Your will for me, then I trust You to protect the promises You've made to me my whole life. Thank You, for reminding me of that tonight."

24

Terri tightened the bow in Kelsey's hair and brushed the cracker crumbs from her shirt. "Ready to go?"

"Yes! Mama, Daddy."

Terri stooped down to the toddler's level. "Sweetheart, do you want to play a game in the car?"

Blonde curls bounced as Kelsey nodded in excitement.

"If you can sit in the backseat and not say Mommy or Daddy the whole way, we'll stop at the park on the way home. Can you do that?"

"'K."

Benton came from the house next door. He selected a hammer from the toolbox in the back of his truck and stopped by Terri's car.

"Where are you ladies headed off to?"

"Kelsey's visitation." She laid a hand on Benton's sleeve. "Her father rededicated his life to Christ last night. Terri smiled at Kelsey through the back window. "We're going to be able to give her a happy ending, due largely to Steve's intervention. I hope they come to church on Sunday. I'd like the chance to introduce them to everyone."

"That's wonderful news, Terri."

She bit her lip. "You want to have a piece of her happy ending?"

"What did you have in mind?"

"You said yesterday you needed some experienced help. I know Kelsey's dad has had some issues, but I also know he helped his father run a construction crew before their business failed."

"Terri—"

"Benton, I'm not asking you to trust him with your life. But would you pray about it? I watched his life change last night, but they need help in so many other areas."

Benton tucked his chin down and stroked his beard. "I'll pray about it, Terri. Introduce me to him if they're at church Sunday, and we'll see how I feel after I meet him."

"That's all I'm asking. I've got some more good news if you think you can handle two in a row."

"I think my heart can take it."

"I've decided to take your advice about the house. I'm going to talk to Steve and the girls tonight about staying with them for a couple more weeks while I house shop."

"I thought you couldn't wait to get out of there."

"I never said that."

Benton took a step back and looked down at her.

"OK, you've obviously been talking to Callie." She grinned and opened her car door. "If I thought your old heart could stand three shocks in a row, I'd give you a piece of better-than-wonderful news."

"Hit me," Benton said. "I'm in the mood to live dangerously."

She threw her arms around Benton's neck. "Steve and I aren't fighting anymore. I think I'm in love."

"Took you long enough."

"Benton, I've never felt this way about anyone in my whole life. I agree it took me a while, but—"

"Sounds like Kelsey isn't the only one working on a happy ending."

"Hey, not so fast. I haven't even been in love for a whole day yet. I'd like a chance to savor this part of the experience before I consider happy endings." She climbed into her car, rolled down the window, and shut the door.

Benton leaned on the sill. "Can I share this with Callie? She'll strangle me if she finds out I knew and didn't tell her."

"I don't care if you climb up on my roof and share it with the world." She pulled from the curb with a brilliant smile and a happy wave.

"Mama, Daddy… Mama, Daddy… Mama, Daddy…"

Terri laughed and turned up the radio.

****

After three weeks Kelsey seemed to know the drill. She held Terri's hand quietly during the short walk from the parking lot to the center, but the minute they walked through the door she let go and raced to the playroom to see her parents. Terri let her go, heart already aching at the thought of losing this child.

Cindy moved beside Terri with a smile. "I told you so."

"Told me what?'

"I told you I had a good feeling about this case. I think we are about to see great things."

"I've already seen great things. Ella and Sean have both re-dedicated their lives to Christ since we were here last week."

"And that's just part of it," Cindy assured her.

"They've passed their first home inspection. They're both enrolled in the required parenting classes, and Dad just passed his second drug screen."

Terri looked down the hall, tears filling her eyes in a mixture of happy and sad. "That's wonderful. How long?"

Cindy put her arm around Terri's shoulder. "Love hurts sometimes, doesn't it?" She pulled Terri down to the bench. "First thing we'll do is loosen the visitation restrictions a bit. You won't have to keep them separated at church. In fact, I'm going to authorize overnight Saturday visits. Starting this weekend, they can have Kelsey at noon on Saturday and return her to you on Sunday afternoon. We'll give that a try for a couple of weeks and see how everything progresses. This will be your last interrupted Friday afternoon for a while."

Terri fished in her bag for a tissue and dabbed at her eyes. "I know this is how it's supposed to work, and I'm grateful for Kelsey's sake that God worked things out so quickly." Her eyes focused on the closed door to the playroom. "I knew it wasn't a permanent situation. I just didn't expect it to sting quite this bad."

Cindy patted her leg. "You've done a marvelous job with Kelsey under some difficult circumstances. I don't expect you'll be childless for long. Unfortunately we always have children looking for someone to love them."

****

Iris and Sam put dinner on the table Friday night while Steve and Terri got the little ones settled in their highchair and booster seat. Terri reached for her own chair and found Steve's hands there before hers. He pulled out her chair and, once she was seated, bent down, turned her face to his, and brushed her lips with a casual kiss.

"I saw that," Iris teased in a singsong voice.

"You're gonna see more," Steve responded, dipping down for a second helping of "sugar."

"How was your day?" he asked, smoothing a hand across her hair.

Terri's cheeks heated with embarrassment at the open affection. "Busy," she answered, trying to ignore the warmth in her face. "I have lots of good news to share as soon as everyone gets settled."

Conversation lulled in favor of passing food and filling plates. Sam used her fork to mash up some vegetables for Bobbie while Steve sliced the roast that had been simmering in the slow cooker most of the afternoon.

"You want a piece of this, Kelsey?"

The toddler nodded.

"Just a small piece," Terri cautioned. "She's not much of a meat eater."

"Don't keep us in suspense," Sam encouraged. "What's your news?"

"Well," Terri said, "The first part is actually Kelsey's news. Cindy told me today that things are going so well, starting tomorrow she'll be spending most of every weekend with her parents. The goal is to get her back with them completely in a month or so."

Samantha reached across the table to squeeze Terri's hand in a show of support.

Terri shook her head. "It's OK. I've already had my moment. This is how the system is supposed to work. I'll need to get used to it if I plan to continue with the program."

"What else?" Iris asked in an obvious effort to change the subject.

Terri took a drink of her tea, suddenly nervous about giving a voice to her plans for the first time. "Do you think you guys can put up with us for a few more weeks?"

Steve sat back, an odd expression on his face. "What's up? I thought Benton was just about done at your place."

"He is, but he's convinced me not to move back into the house." Terri grinned at the three speechless expressions around the table. She held up a hand to demonstrate how nervous she was and laughed when it trembled slightly. "I'm expanding my business into the other house... and I'm scared to death," she finished softly, taking a deep breath to steady her nerves. "I need a place to stay while I am house hunting."

When silence greeted her request, Terri looked sidelong at the others seated around the table. She bit her lip. "If it's a problem..."

Steve picked up his fork. "Terri, we've all loved having you here. Take as much time as you need."

"Thanks, guys. Benton says he knows of several properties I might be interested in. In the meantime, I'll let Cindy know I need to put any future foster parenting responsibilities on hold until I can get back into a place of my own."

****

Steve ate his dinner on autopilot with his daughters and Terri chattering around him. He nodded and grunted in the appropriate places while they discussed new furniture and decorating ideas. They debated the pros and cons of buying a house in town versus the country. Proximity to the mall seemed to settle that question for the three females. Thank God he had a few more weeks to keep Terri close and work on nurturing their newly acknowledged relationship. But he took note of Terri's unwitting reminder. The issue of children still remained unsettled between them.

****

According to the display on her phone, Gary had called five times today in response to her message yesterday. She dreaded calling him back; the conversation would be so much different than the one she'd planned twenty-four hours ago. Terri punched in the numbers and closed her eyes. It wouldn't be fair to leave him hanging any longer than she had. The call connected and barely rang a half a time.

"Terri, I was about to get on a plane."

"Sorry, it's just been one of those days. Kelsey kept me hopping."

"No worries. I was just a little concerned when I couldn't reach you. So…"

Terri worked to calm her churning stomach. *Jesus, give me the right words.* "Gary, I enjoyed our visit the other night. I'm flattered by the things you said, but no." Silence greeted her response. "I like you a lot, but I've prayed about it, and I just don't see our lives going in the same direction. I'm sorry."

"No worries," Gary repeated. "I had my chance six months ago, and I blew it."

"Gary—"

"I guess I'll keep looking for God's direction in my life. I'll let you know if He lets me come home to Oklahoma. So long, doll face."

The phone clicked as he broke the connection. Terri lowered it and stared at it for several seconds. "Bye," she whispered.

****

Iris got a dose of her own medicine Saturday morning as someone pounded on her bedroom door long before she was ready to get up.

"Go away." Iris turned over and drew an extra pillow over her head. She peeked out from beneath it when she heard her door open. The pillow fell back into place as Sam stepped into the room. "What do you want?"

"It's Saturday morning. Get up."

Iris raised the pillow again so she could glare out at her older sister. "We've done the zoo. We've done the lake. We don't have any SETH plans for today. Get lost and leave me alone."

Sam's smile was gleeful as she yanked the pillow away. "Dad said to get up. He told me to remind you that he'd cooperated with our schemes for the last few weeks. Today he needs our help."

Iris replaced the pillow with the comforter. "To do what?"

"He didn't say, but he did mention three of your favorite words."

Iris lowered the blanket to nose level, brows arched in question.

"IHOP, shopping, mall. You've got thirty minutes

to get dressed."

****

Terri climbed the stairs alone on Saturday night. It felt odd not to have Kelsey holding her hand the whole way. Kelsey had gone with her parents earlier in the afternoon. Even though Terri understood the miracle God was working in that family, she still worried. Steve's dinner invitation came as a welcome diversion. She wandered through the kitchen and finally found Steve and his daughters in the living room. Everyone had on their Sunday best, even Bobbie. Surprise stopped her in the doorway. "Oh, is everyone going?"

Steve turned at her question. "That's up to you."

Terri continued into the room, took a seat on the sofa next to Sam, and pulled Bobbie into her lap. "I'm good with a group night out," she answered, placing a kiss on Bobbie's chubby cheek.

"Not what I meant," Steve said as Iris took a seat on Terri's other side.

Iris leaned her head against Terri's shoulder. "Terri, do you love me?"

Terri was caught off guard by the question. She shifted around on the sofa so that she could look at Iris's face. "Of course I do," she answered, bewildered at the question.

"Do you love me?" Samantha asked quietly.

Terri turned to her other side. "Sam, what's up with you girls lately?"

"Do you?" Sam persisted.

Terri put an arm around Sam's shoulders. "You know I do."

Sam smiled and handed Terri a folded piece of

paper. Terri shifted the baby and unfolded the note.

Do you love me, too? Bobbie.

Terri slumped back in the sofa and buried her head in the baby's neck with a sigh. "Yes baby, I love you, too." She raised her eyes to look at Steve. "What's up with you guys?"

Steve shook his head with a smile. "You'll understand in a bit." He crouched down in front of her and stared into her eyes. "Do you love me, Terri?"

"Yes," she whispered. "Each and every one of you, with my whole heart."

Sam took the baby out of Terri's arms as Steve fished in his shirt pocket. He took Terri's hand in his empty one and continued to stare at her intently.

Terri squirmed under his gaze. "What?"

In answer to her question, he held out his other hand so that Terri could see the ring that rested in it. Heat engulfed Terri's whole body while her heart pounded against her rib cage. She forced her eyes from the ring to Steve's face.

"Terri, will you marry us?" he asked simply. "We shopped for this ring today as a family. We're asking you as a group, cause it's not just me that you're marrying. If you take me, you get the whole package. I can't promise you sanity or privacy, but I can promise you we'll all love you every day of our lives. The four of us make a pretty good team, but there's a big empty space in our hearts with your name on it. Having you here for the last few weeks has shown us what we need to make our family whole. We can't wait to see the miracle God makes of this family if you'll say yes.

"I love you," Steve continued. "You're what I've been praying for. Marry me." He took a deep breath. "Have babies with me."

His words washed over Terri, and she closed her eyes. "You want more babies? When we were watching Dave and Lisa at Sam's party you said…"

Steve closed his own eyes. "Is that…?" he stopped. "Sweetheart, I was amused at them and worried about the outcome of the day. Three children under the age of three is challenge enough to make anyone hesitate, but I'll tackle it if that's what God has planned for us. Building a family with you, taking advantage of the second chance I feel like God is giving me—I can't wait. I've already picked out a name for our first son."

"First? How many do you want?"

"As many as God gives us. I want to be Psalms 127 happy."

At Terri's puzzled look, Steve quoted the passage for her. "Children are an heritage of the Lord: and the fruit of the womb is His reward. As arrows are in the hand of a mighty man; so are children of the youth. Happy is the man that hath his quiver full of them…"

Steve squeezed her hand. "Will you make me happy?"

Terri looked at Sam and Iris in turn. "This has your blessing?"

"More than we could ever tell you," Sam assured her.

Terri took a deep breath, held out her hand, and allowed Steve to slip the ring on her finger. She put her arms around her soon-to-be stepdaughters and leaned forward to allow Steve to kiss her.

"I accept, all of you," she said through her tears. Steve pulled her to her feet so that he could seal their engagement with a proper kiss."

"Are you going to tell me?" she asked.

"Tell you what?"

"The name you've picked out for our first son."

Steve smiled down at his bride to be and turned to grin at his daughters. He leaned down and whispered into Terri's ear.

"I like it. Is that a family name?"

"In more ways than one," Steve assured her with a smile. He tightened his hold on her and looked into her eyes. "I love you, Terri Hayes."

Terri didn't respond with words. She winked at the girls on the sofa and pulled their father down to her level. This time, she took her time kissing him.

25

October thirty-first. A day for spooks and goblins. A day for white satin dresses and yellow rose petals. Terri stood in Callie's Sunday school classroom looking into a full-length mirror Samantha had hauled in from somewhere. She struggled to keep the tears out of her eyes as Samantha secured a gauzy cloud of white netting to her freshly styled hair. Today her dream became a reality and she looked...she shook her head at her reflection and pressed her hands to her nervous stomach...she looked like she'd always imagined she would.

Iris handed her a tissue. "Don't cry. You'll mess up your makeup."

Terri nodded and blotted her eyes with care.

Sam fluffed the veil. "Perfect."

A knock sounded at the door and Callie, Karla, and Pam crowded into the small room. Their chorused "Aww" gave Terri the last boost of reassurance she needed.

"Good?"

Karla moved forward to envelope the bride in a hug. "Better than good. Stunning."

Terri accepted hugs and similar sentiments from the other two women. She sniffed and linked hands with her *almost* stepdaughters and her three best friends. "I've been warned not to cry, but I have to say thanks. There's no way I could have put this together in such a short time without your help."

Callie winked at her. "We've planned this day for years."

Pam nodded. "Anything that gets our husbands into tuxes works for me."

Terri smiled. "Glad I could help."

Callie released her friend's hands and reached up to check the condition of her own blonde hair. "The reception hall is decorated. Kelsey and Bobbie are standing by." She nodded to Iris and Samantha. "Mitch and Harrison are waiting to escort these lovely young ladies down the aisle, and Benton is a nervous wreck. He just knows he's going to get tangled up in your dress or something and ruin your big day." She smiled. "I think everything's ready except you."

Terri took a deep breath. The man she'd waited her whole life to find was just down the hall, anxious to see her, excited to build a life with her. Oh, it was going to be such an adventure. Her stomach settled. "Let's do it."

The three older women took time for a final hug before leaving to find their seats in the crowded auditorium of Valley View church.

Samantha handed Terri a bouquet of yellow and white roses. "Here you go, Mom."

Terri bit her lip but couldn't stop the fresh tears that sprang to her eyes. "Mom?"

Samantha and Iris nodded. "If you'll let us," Iris whispered.

Terri gathered them close. "I love you guys."

The door cracked open a second time. "Everyone decent in here?" Benton asked.

Samantha let him in.

Iris whistled. "You clean up nice."

Benton fiddled with his tie. "The role of father of the bride is a serious responsibility." He took Terri's hands. "Thank you for giving me this honor. I know your mom and dad are smiling in heaven today."

Terri grabbed another tissue. "You guys are determined to make me face my groom with red eyes." She leaned forward to kiss her surrogate father on the cheek. "Let's go."

She watched while waiting just to the side of the auditorium entrance. Kelsey went down the aisle first, hand in hand with Callie and Benton's two-year-old grandson, Trent. Together they pulled Bobbie in a wagon decorated with bows and streaming ribbons.

Mitch escorted Iris to the front. Harrison escorted Samantha then took his place as best man. Terri heard the music change and took a deep breath. Benton squeezed her hand and started forward.

Terri's eyes locked with her groom's, and her heart soared. Steve smiled at her as she took her first step down the white runway sprinkled with rose petals and silver glitter. If she was *stunning* then Steve was gorgeous.

Benton stopped before Pastor Gordon.

"Who gives this woman in marriage?"

Benton cleared his throat. "Callie and I." He kissed Terri's cheek and placed her hand in Steve's.

Terri raised her eyes to Steve's and prepared to face the future God had planned for her before she was born.

Epilogue

Twelve months later.

"Aunt Telwy!"

Terri smiled, allowing the door to the day care center to close behind her. She lifted the tray of cookies she carried out of the danger zone and braced herself for the enthusiastic onslaught headed her way.

Kelsey stopped just short of a tackle and reached up to rub the rounded mound of Terri's pregnant belly. "Kick me," Kelsey commanded, and was immediately rewarded with a soft thump against her outstretched palm. "Good boy," the four-year-old giggled.

"Girl," Terri insisted.

"Boy," Kelsey countered.

Terri smiled down at the little girl wearing a shiny Cinderella costume for today's Halloween party. "You aren't giving that up, are you?"

Kelsey shook her head and took Terri's free hand. Together they walked back to the kitchen area of the center. Sean and Ella were at the small table finishing a late lunch. Sean jumped to his feet and hurried over to take the oversized tray.

"Give me that."

The tray was gratefully surrendered. Terri sank into the nearest chair and propped her swollen ankles up in the seat of a second. She took a deep breath and stretched to relieve the ever-present kink in her back, frowning when it refused to give.

Sean caught her expression. "Everything OK?" he asked warily.

"I'm fine, Sean. Relax. I've got at least four weeks to go."

Sean ran a hand through his hair. "Having you both pregnant at the same time is driving everyone crazy," he said. "You two are just going to have to learn to take things a little easier."

Ella pushed away from the table, exposing her own swollen middle. She rubbed her six month belly affectionately. "Ashleigh and I are just fine," she told her husband as she pulled Kelsey to her side.

Kelsey leaned over to speak to her mother's tummy. "I love you, sissy," she called loudly.

"You're as bad as Steve," Terri told Sean. "He's following me around the house like a mother hen. You'd think this was his first baby, not his third." She shook her head. "I keep telling him I feel fine. He keeps ignoring me. He was full of excuses this morning. It's our anniversary. The doctor's appointment would tire me out. I'd need my rest for tomorrow."

"I still can't believe you guys are going to be on television tomorrow morning," Ella said. "It's so exciting."

"Intimidating would be a better word," Terri said. "There will be a whole production crew in my house at six in the morning. I'm just glad they didn't have a problem coming here to do the interview. I feel pretty good, but I don't think a trip to New York City is anywhere in my immediate future." She put her feet on the ground and levered herself out of the chair. "I guess we all better get back to work. Tell Benton I said thanks for getting you over here so quickly. That drippy faucet was driving everyone bananas."

Sean picked up his toolbox. "Not a problem. I replaced the faucet assembly for you. The warranty paperwork is on the cabinet. I'll let the boss know to send you a hefty bill." He leaned over to kiss his wife and daughter good-bye. "Don't work too hard," he whispered.

"Not a chance," Ella answered. "Steve's coming by to take pictures during the party. We'll be lucky if he doesn't tie both of us to our chairs for the duration."

"Good for him," Sean said. "I better run. Sisko needs me at the gym early this afternoon to help prepare for the fall festival tonight. I have to get the inflatables inflated, and the hot dogs hot. I hate to brag." His chest bowed out smugly. "But I'm not sure how he managed to get everything done before he had me to delegate to."

Terri laughed as Sean headed out the back door. She looked at Ella. "Is he always that humble?"

"He's been pretty insufferable ever since Sisko agreed to mentor him," Ella answered. "Dave's trying to dull his glow with grunt work. It's not working." The younger woman changed the subject. "So, did you change your mind?"

"About the ultra sound?" Terri shook her head. "Nope. The technician asked us, again, if we wanted to know what we were having. We both told her no." Terri nodded to Kelsey. "This one is unwavering in her opinion that it's a boy."

"Oh, that's just because she thinks she can have a sister and a brother at the same time," Ella said. "In case you haven't figured it out, she's staking claim to both babies."

Terri reached out and pulled Kelsey into a hug.

"Come here, squirt. This one can be yours too, whatever it is. Babies can't get too much love."

"You're a stronger woman than I am," Ella admitted. "I couldn't stand not knowing."

"Nothing wrong with that. But we're all good with being surprised. Everyone except Iris. She's going to drive us all crazy before the baby gets here."

****

Iris narrowed her eyes as Benton's chuckle echoed through the phone.

"No."

"But...I know Callie knows. She manages the clinic. I'll bake you cookies—"

"Look sweetheart, you can bake me all the chocolate chip cookies you want, but I can't tell you what I don't know. Callie hasn't told me. I haven't asked. You're just going to have to wait this out like the rest of us. Trust me, you'll survive."

"Don't do this to me, Grandpa." Iris knew she was whining like a baby. She didn't care. "I made a bet with Sam that I could wheedle the information out of you. If you don't come through, I'll have to clean the kitchen for a week."

"Sorry, kiddo, but I think you've been had. Sam and I had this conversation a couple of weeks ago. She knew I didn't know."

Iris sputtered. "That...that..."

"I've got another call coming in. I gotta go. Bye."

Iris stared at the dead phone in her hand. Samantha would pay for this one. Just as soon as tonight's party was over and the television crew cleared out of their house in the morning, she would pay...

****

The makeup technician—Madge according to the badge she wore around her neck—handed Terri a large mirror and offered words of reassurance. "Take a look. I know it's probably a little heavier than you're used to, but the lights will bleed most of it away."

Terri laughed at her reflection. "A little heavier?" She grinned back at Madge through the mirror. "I didn't wear this much makeup when I was a toddler playing dress up."

Madge patted Terri's shoulder. "Trust me, it'll be fine." She offered Terri a hand to help her out of the chair and motioned for Sam to take her place.

Leaving Madge to ooh and ahh over Samantha's perfect complexion, Terri picked her way cautiously back to the living room. Cords and cables snaked across the floor in every direction. It was a minefield for someone who'd lost her sense of balance and couldn't see her feet.

Iris snickered when she got a look at Terri's heavy stage makeup.

"Keep laughing, girlfriend." She jerked a thumb in Madge's direction. "You're next." Terri found a seat on the couch where she hoped she'd be out of the way and smoothed her new purple shirt over her stomach. The muscles under her hands tightened a second before the pain blossomed. Terri sucked in a quick breath and struggled to maintain a pleasant expression. *Oh, baby, not now. This is Daddy's big day*. She worked to breathe normally while the pain faded. Probably just a twinge, but she noted the time on the mantel clock. She jumped when she felt a hand on her shoulder.

"Stage fright?"

Terri turned to look over her shoulder. Steve was already made up, dressed in the suit he'd purchased for their wedding, dark hair freshly trimmed and just brushing his collar. "Hey, handsome. How come your makeup looks so much more natural than mine?"

Steve tugged at his lapels. "I'm the star, remember? I have to look good."

Terri narrowed her eyes. "Ha ha. We'll see how much of a star you are when…"

"You're both looking fresh and ready to go." Summer Adams, the news journalist conducting the interview, came around the corner and motioned for Steve to join Terri on the sofa. "The girls are almost done. Do either of you have any questions for me before we get started?"

When they both shook their heads, Summer passed each of them a sheet of paper. "Read over these questions for me. We probably won't have time to ask them all, but we want you to be prepared for things we might talk about." She focused her attention on Steve. "You're comfortable talking about your life before you started writing?"

"Absolutely," Steve answered. "It's the reason I write."

"Great. We won't go too deep," she assured him, "but we will need to establish some general background information." Summer paused as the girls joined them and fished out papers for both of them as well. "All right, we go live in fifteen minutes." She looked at Iris and laughed at the nervous way she clutched her paper. "Relax." She offered a friendly smile. "You're all going to do fine. You need to try to forget about the cameras. Pretend you're entertaining a friend in your living room. Once we get started, you'll be surprised at how fast it goes."

A second pain twisted through Terri's belly. She glanced at the clock. Fifteen minutes apart. *Jesus, help me get through the next couple of hours.*

****

Summer held up a copy of Steve's book for the camera. "That's our show for this morning folks. Steve's new book will be on the shelves in time for Christmas." Everyone else held their place until a disembodied voice came from behind one of the lights. "We're done."

Steve flinched when Terri grabbed his hand and doubled over with a low groan. "Terri?"

His wife put up a hand to stop him while the one she held received enough pressure to crush a soda can. She pulled in a gulping breath. "We need to go to the hospital. *Now!*"

Steve knelt in front of the sofa and waited until Terri was able to meet his eyes. "How long and how far apart?"

"All morning," Terri answered. "Three to five minutes apart." She grabbed his hand again. "And getting closer."

Steve looked around at the equipment and strangers that cluttered their home and felt the first grip of panic. "Terri…girls…"

"Just go," Sam told them. "We'll stay here until everything's cleared away. We'll drop Bobbie off at Tiny Tikes and head over to the hospital just as soon as we can."

Iris held up her phone. "I'll call Callie and the others for you."

Summer grinned as Steve helped Terri to her feet, searching his pockets for his keys. "Can we add a special announcement to your interview?"

Steve answered her with a grin of his own. "Tell the world, Summer. We're having a baby!"

****

The sound of a baby crying brought everyone in the waiting room to their feet.

"It's a boy, isn't it?" Iris asked as she looked at Callie. "It just has to be a boy."

Callie shook her head. "Five more minutes."

Iris made an impatient gesture and resumed her pacing.

"This is almost the hardest part," Mitch said. "Knowing that the baby is here but still not knowing."

Karla shushed him. "Don't be a tease."

The door to the hall swooshed open to admit Pam and Harrison. "Are we late?" Pam asked. "We came just as soon as the judge dismissed our client's case."

"Right on time," Benton told them. "We—"

The double doors to the delivery room whispered open, discharging a nurse dressed in green surgical scrubs, her eyes crinkled in a smile above the paper mask still tied behind her head.

Iris fired questions at her in rapid succession. "How's Terri? Where's Dad? Is the baby here? What is it?"

The nurse pulled away the mask. "Just fine. With Terri. Yes. I've been sworn to secrecy." She answered Iris's questions in the order they had been received.

Iris groaned in frustration. "What?"

The nurse grinned and pointed to Iris and Sam. "You two can go on back. Your father is waiting to introduce you to a perfect little baby." She looked at the rest of the group. "I'll answer your questions just as soon as the girls are out of earshot."

****

Terri looked into the face of her own personal miracle. Ten fingers and ten toes had been accounted for and the sleeping baby now rested in the crook of her arm. She looked up at Steve with unashamed tears. "We did good."

A noise in the doorway drew her attention. Iris and Sam entered the dimly lit room. Their smiles were almost reverent as they approached the bed.

Terri nodded at Steve. Giving him permission to answer the question Iris had been asking for almost nine months.

"Samantha, Iris. Meet Seth."

Don't miss CALLIE,
Book One in the Women of Valley View series
AVAILABLE NOW

Three dire circumstances. Three desperate prayers.
One miracle to save them all.

Callie Stillman is drawn to the evasive girl who's befriended her granddaughter, but the last time Callie tried to help a child, her efforts backfired. Memories of the tiny coffin still haunt her.

Samantha and Iris Evans should be worried about homework, not whether they can pool enough cash to survive another week of caring for an infant while evading the authorities.

Steve Evans wants a second chance at fatherhood, but his children are missing. And no one seems to want to help the former addict who deserted his family.

For Steve to regain the relationship he abandoned, for his girls to receive the care they deserve, Callie must surrender her fear and rely on God to work the miracle they all need.

Thank you for purchasing this Harbourlight title. For other inspirational stories, please visit our on-line bookstore at www.pelicanbookgroup.com.

For questions or more information, contact us at titleadmin@pelicanbookgroup.com.

Harbourlight Books
The Beacon in Christian Fiction™
an imprint of Pelican Ventures Book Group
www.pelicanbookgroup.com

May God's glory shine through
this inspirational work of fiction.

AMDG